THE 6TH DREAM

SAMUEL J FISHER

"THE 6TH DREAM"

ISBN-13: 978-1463571948

ISBN-10: 1463571941

Special thanks to my family for all their patience, and sacrifices made during the writing of this work, to my wife Ria, and my sons Samuel and Christian. I would like to send out a thank you to the wonderful staff at Starbucks on Lundy's Lane in Niagara Falls, Ontario, Canada, and all of their support. To Wikipedia, the free online encyclopedia anyone can edit, Wikipedia founded by Jimmy Donal Wales 2001.

Table of Contents

PROLOGUE

I look at the clock on the wall, and at the monitor in front of me displaying vital signs. I look down on the patient lying on the table under my watchful care. I glance at the surgeon and the nurses all around. I glance over at the glass partition where there is a group of medical students watching the procedure with keen interest. I wonder if any of them can read my thoughts.

I listen intently to all around me. Hearing calls for sponges, suctioning, sutures, and clamps, more lights, less light. They all echo routinely in my head.

I look again at the students, and they are all watching with great intensity. Some are taking notes, others furiously tapping keys on their laptops and some even speaking into recording devices. I am surprised that not one in this class had left to vomit upon seeing the first cut. There is usually at least one. I wonder what their dreams are like given the pressure and competition of medical school.

The patient is under and I wonder if he is aware of the wonderful dreams he is experiencing right now. I always feel jealous and cheated at these times. The man is having a triple by-pass, and everything is going smooth. Vitals are fine.

The surgeons and nurses are working quickly. There is blood everywhere. There is always blood. The procedure is long and exhausting. It is my job to keep the patient sedated, and stable. Still no student has vomited even with the man's chest cavity opened and all exposed. I wonder why? Maybe they do not dream, for you must feel to truly dream.

My mind tries to discern what this man may be experiencing right now. What world has unlocked and come alive in him. Where is he right now? Is he caught in the past, the present or maybe his unconscious projections of what the future may hold? I wish there was some way I could know, and compare them to the content of my own dreams.

I suppose you have guessed by now that I am an anesthesiologist. Day in and day out I put people to sleep. I imagine they dream, but they are unaware of them. It is that fact that makes me feel jealous and cheated. Not the fact that they dream, but the fact they are not or cannot enjoy them. What a terrible waste that is.

Five more hours and I will be finally at home. Surgery complete, paperwork and all reports filed. I will prepare myself a quick dinner, and then I will be free to sleep and get back to my own dreams. I now have ten scheduled days off. I will take a much needed vacation, but I will not leave my home unless I need to. My vacation is alive in my head and in my dreams. Which one will manifest I do not know, that is not something I can control. Maybe it will be new, maybe it will be a replay or a continuation of an old one. I hope for a continuation those are the dreams I love.

This is my tale... these are my dreams, and this is the way I live my life!

FRIDAY 11TH OF JUNE 2011

I lie down in my bed to wait and will for sleep to come. Shutting my eyes and then opening them to other worlds with the greatest of possibilities, to be what I never could be here. It will not be long now for I have taken something to help me to relax. It is a great little pill and I can feel its warmth emanating through me. At the first sign of the warm feeling I begin to count backwards from ten. Ten, nine, eight, seven, six, five, four, three...

I am fishing by a stream. It is early morning and it is very cool, I can see my breath. It is so cold my fingers do not work as well as I would wish. I fumble with the rod and reel, and the tying of knots. I am alone. I cast and cast but I have yet to catch anything here, I never seem to. There are hundreds of fish swimming back and forth or coasting in the currents. None bite or nibble, they pay absolutely no attention to any of my offerings...

There is a kite and kayak beside me and the wind is picking up. I am then in the kayak racing downstream. I have abandoned the fishing equipment, or was it ever there I cannot recall, but I have brought the kite with me. The sun is warming this earth. I can feel its heat on my face, a direct contrast to the ice cold water splashing over me. Massive amounts of fish are jumping over the kayak. They are saying hello, mocking my inability to catch any of them. Did I really try? There are thousands and I vow I will catch one of them before my time is through...

Now I am hiking through some bush. The kite is slung over my back like a shield. I am eating a cinnamon roll that I picked up from the bushes here, for they grow on them. I put a cup that I am carrying, but cannot remember where it came from, into a puddle that has formed from a dripping tree. The puddle is full of some sort of latte. The foam is perfect and the temperature extremely hot. I taste Macha powder, a form of green tea...

A dog is approaching from my left. A male and he is large and beautiful. He is almost totally black except for a white star in the center of his massive chest. The animal is extremely happy to see me. Jumping and barking all around. The dog finds a tennis ball and wants me to play. I pick up the ball and I throw it as far as I am able to. He comes back with it and places it at my feet as I walk. I am happy to see him, but then he disappears. I continue walking alone now, no more cinnamon buns, and no more lattes, my cup has disappeared...

I am then in an open field and the wind is fierce but the sky is blue and the sun is shining. I am holding onto a piece of wood attached to some twine. I have let all of the twine out and the kite is flying high over my head. I have to squint to see the speck in the distance. There are a couple of hawks up there with my kite...

I am now flying on the kite and it is huge. The hawks are flying with me and we are speaking. They tell me what they have seen soaring above mankind. They tell me of their conquests and their battles. It seems this pair has been flying over this earth for an eternity. I tell them how I see the world and how full of shit it all is. They laugh as they bid me farewell, and safe travels...

I wake up and look over to the clock beside me. It is only 4:30 am. I have to urinate. I hate to get out of bed for this. I go to the bathroom and pee. I wash my hands and splash warm water of my face. I stare into the mirror and recall the dreams I just had. I call them jumbles. Back in my bedroom I take another pill this one stronger than the first. I lie down, I feel the fire coursing through and I begin the count again. Ten, nine, eight, seven, six, five...

I am walking down a quiet cobblestone street. There is a beautiful woman walking with me, and she is holding my hand. I pull it back quickly.

"I am not diseased... what is with that look of complete disgust", she says.

Where am I, and who in the hell is this. I try to act composed and hide my confusion as best as I am able to.

"We are supposed to be a couple... now take my hand... you have been so distant lately like you have been elsewhere in your mind and not here with me", she said, obviously agitated and pissed off.

Slowly my mind wraps around things. The woman's name is Jessica and we are in Paris. We are here at the command of those we are contracted to. The mission is simple. We are to recover a USB drive in exchange for eight numbers. There are two of us because we know four numbers each, and are not to divulge our numbers to the other under any circumstances. We are to repeat our numbers separately to the holder of the USB drive once the information on it is authenticated. The drive will be inserted into the laptop I am carrying, and the information sent into the wireless abyss. Once we get confirmation we deliver our part. It will be a nice, clean, simple exchange of information. We are waiting for a text stating where the exchange will take place. All we know is that it is supposed to be in this area of Paris.

"Sorry... I just let my mind wander away for a bit... I am all here... I always am you know me", I said confidently.

"Glad to see you are here... we need to stay focused... we have been walking this area for two hours now", Jessica said, maybe a bit nervous.

"You know the game... they probably have eyes on us making sure we are alone", I answered.

"Have you spotted them yet", Jessica asked.

"Of course… and so have you", I said.

"I count ten", Jessica said with conviction.

"Twelve", I corrected her, a hint of sarcasm in my voice.

"Let's compare then", Jessica said still quite confident.

"Why not… it looks as if they are not convinced about us yet… we will make the rounds one more time and then settle down in that café over there", I said pointing across the street.

"That sounds good… I could use a cup of coffee or tea", Jessica said, a bit calmer now.

We walked the route we were given in our instructions. We pointed out their spotters to each other. I was right, there were twelve of them. I have worked with Jessica before on many occasions, and she would have to buy the beverages. That was the penalty for being wrong. We arrived back at the café. We settled into a quiet area of the sidewalk terrace, and ordered coffee. It was very humid out tonight on this summer's night in Paris, but the hot beverage was refreshing just the same. We made small talk acting like any other couple on a first date. We spoke of fictitious jobs, family and friends. A routine dialogue we had developed and had much practice with in the past.

"It has been too long", Jessica says, now anxious.

"Just thinking the same thing Luv", I replied, looking around us.

"What do you want to do", Jessica asks.

"Abort for now and wait for further contact later", I said.

"You want to just walk away… but they are watching us", Jessica says, surprise is in her voice.

"I know that is what makes me want to walk... they must know by now that we are clean... there should not be any problem", I said.

"A third party maybe", Jessica asks.

"Very possible... and if they have not made us as the contact we should walk now", I said; now I was a bit anxious.

"Contact our control and advise that we are booking out", Jessica said.

"Texting message as we speak", I said.

"From your pocket", Jessica asks, slightly impressed.

"Yes... it is a practiced gift... now let's move... we will take route Charlie... we will have a safe escort waiting for us", I said.

"Is a cleaner team moving in", Jessica asks.

I took the device out of my pocket, and I read the rest of the text response and I replied, "Yes... we have thirty seconds to get the hell out of here".

"That is generous of them", Jessica said, quickening her pace to match mine.

"Very... I only asked for ten", I said laughing.

We got up from the table and locked arms and walked away from the café headed south towards extraction point Charlie. We did not look behind us, but with practiced ears we both heard the muffled sounds of suppressed gunfire. All of hell was breaking loose behind us.

A text message rang through, and it simply read, "Well played confirmed payment as agreed". I showed Jessica and she was as confused as I was. This was supposed to be a simple exchange. That is what we were contracted for, but now I believe that we had just set up our "contacts" to be murdered.

"Change of plans Luv", I said sternly.

"What do you mean", she asked, a little confused.

"I am not getting into any vehicle with these people... not after what just happened... we are on our own... are you with me... do you trust me", I said, maybe a bit too sharply.

"Of course... and yes you are right... come this way... follow me... I have friends that can help us", Jessica said, now serious.

I followed and we turned back north and then west avoiding the pick-up point. We had effectively disappeared. Another text rang through, and this one read, "Well played again... I will be in touch... I have a lot of work available for the two of you". I showed this one to Jessica as well.

"Partners are we", she asked, raising an eye.

"For now... just for now", I said...

BEEP, BEEP, BEEP, BEEP, BEEP, BEEP, BEEP, BEEP, BEEP, BEP, BEEP, BEEP, BEEP, BEEP, BEEP, BEEP, BEEP, BEEP, BEEP, BEEP...

I wake up groggily and still under the effects of the pill I took. I looked over at the alarm clock and tried to focus on the time but I could not seem to quite make out the numbers. I hit the button on top silencing the alarm. It must be 615 am and I had forgotten to turn off the alarm after my past week at work. Stupid dumbass shithead I thought to myself. Then I tried to focus and remember the dream I just had. I tried to commit to memory the events in Paris with the beautiful Jessica so that I may continue the dream later.

I attempt to go back to Jessica but it is to no avail. I feel too rested even after waking twice. I slept lightly and had images and glimpses of dreams but nothing concrete...

I was back at the stream, and this time the dog was sitting with me. The dog had brought me a tray of sweets and an espresso. I enjoyed them as he laid his head on my lap. I shared what I could from the tray and he ate ravenously...

I was flying through the air, my arms outstretched acting like wings. I was speaking to the birds flying around me. We all then started a game of tag, and the cardinals were winning. I tried as hard as I might but could not catch those little buggers...

I was swimming in the ocean around coral reefs. I was swimming with sharks, rays, octopus, whales and all sorts of different marine life, but they all kept their distance. I did not have any diving equipment but I was breathing under water. I was looking for something, and then on the bottom of the ocean floor I saw...

SATURDAY 12TH OF JUNE 2011

Then I wake again and this time for good. I go to the washroom and relieve myself. It must be an after effect of the pills for I had nothing to drink. I will watch this next time I take any of them, for they are of my own invention. I wash my hands and face. I contemplate a shower, but I think I will make some breakfast first. I must sleep longer tonight, maybe I will experiment with the other concoction of chemicals I had made. The syringes are ready sitting in the fridge. I think of Jessica while I cook, and what had happened and the people that were killed because we had set them up. The USB ruse and the payment and hint of future contracts linger in my mind. I know it is not real, but it is where I want to be. I finish breakfast and jump into the shower. I must get this started so that it may end. Jessica and I are running through the streets of Paris looking for safe refuge and I must get back to her.

I go to the front step of my home, and I pick up the paper on the ground. The headlines read, "MORE DEVASTATION FOR JAPAN", "UNREST CONTINUES UNDER CALLS FOR MIDDLE EAST REFORMS", "GAS PRICES REACH RECORD HIGH", "FOOD PRICES SOAR BEYOND AFFORDABILITY", "13 MURDERED ON STREETS OF NEW YORK", "MAN SENTENCED FOR KILLING CHILDREN", "EARTH QUAKE ROCKS MEXICO". I take the paper and throw it in the recycle bin. Nothing redeemable to read, not a single word, death and devastation is everywhere. I want to go back to sleep, but there are things I need to do. I have errands to run, and then maybe I will take a nap. Even a short jumbled dream is preferable to what I read and see in the news, and the looks on the faces I see on people walking the streets.

I hate the routine errands. I hate getting gas for the car, banking, groceries, toiletries and all that other shit. Everyone I meet is miserable. Shopping carts almost empty even the staples are outrageous. Eating healthy is killing people's spirits, and emptying their pockets. I need to go home and go back to sleep. Everyone should sleep and dream of better things. The teller at the bank hits on me, but only after she sees my bank balance. I am fortunate that I have an excellent income. She attempts to make small talk, attempts to be flirtatious, but I just nod and smile trying not to encourage anything further. She is attractive, and very sexy, but not a part of my dreams. I could use a good night of sex though, but that would interfere with my plans to dream. Maybe I will go to a massage parlor later today, and pay someone to relieve that type of stress. I have tried to cultivate friends with those types of benefits, but they just ended up complicated and my dreams were horrible. A massage parlor it is then.

I arrive back at home and I shower. A little hotter and a little longer, the masseuse used quite a bit of oil today. The release of stress was good though, and the massage was excellent. I just may return to her again.

It is now time for a quick bite to eat and then some sleep. It is 6 pm, and by the time I prepare my dinner, and consume it with a glass of wine or two it will be time for sleep. The syringes in the fridge are calling my name. I thought about foregoing dinner but decided to go ahead with it. I need my strength tonight if I am going to run through the streets of Paris with Jessica.

I steamed some of the asparagus, roasted some parisienne potatoes, glazed some carrots with brown sugar and grilled myself some beef tenderloin and a lobster tail. These are the fruits of my shopping adventure today. I feel guilty though seeing some of the carts and the look of dismay on the people picking items up and then putting them down after seeing the price. There was a lot of Kraft Dinner, bags of potatoes and rice being bought today. These are the items that are a little bit cheaper, when you stretch them out over the course of a week or longer.

I ate my dinner alone and in silence. I pour myself a second glass of Rosemount Shiraz. I will be careful not to inject myself for at least three hours to dissipate some of the alcohol in my blood stream. I flipped through some channels on the television, checked my e-mail, and all the other routine things that come with being at home. It is now 11 pm, and I relieve myself in the washroom for hopefully the last time. I turn off the alarm completely. I go to the fridge and retrieve one syringe with what I hope is a magical potion for sleep, lengthy sleep. No side effects. Jessica is waiting and I need to get to her.

I lie down and inject myself like a junkie. I remember pushing on the plunger of the needle with my thumb. I remember taking the needle out and applying pressure to the small wound with some cotton. I remember placing the spent needle on the small night stand to my left. I remember feeling the numbness spread through me, and that is all...

I wake up on some dirty side street and I look around. This is no side street it is an alley. I am in an extremely worn sleeping bag, and I feel a numbing cold down to the core of my being. I hold up my hands and they are gross, dirty, scarred, and old looking. My nails and knuckles are bleeding. I smell of body odor, shit, and urine. I feel my face and there must be three years of beard growth, and it is all wet and matted, greasy. My lips are cracked and bleeding. I feel through my hair and it is the same. It feels like it has not been washed or cut in ten years. There are others sleeping here just as disgusting as I was. Maybe some were worse it is hard to tell. I am thirsty I crave water. I am hungry.

One of the others here gets up and stretches. I think it may have been female at one time, but time and the elements have taken its toll. It is full of sores, scrapes and scars. It sucks in air through its nose and spits out the vilest putrid gunk from its mouth. I try not to vomit. I try not to be sick. It farts, and it is sickly and most likely wet, and then I vomit.

Then another shoves me from behind. This is male, but again it is hard to tell.

"Come on man let's get to the shelter for breakfast", it says, voice cracking as it gets louder.

"What the fuck... get off of me... leave me alone", I say looking around me with wild anger and maybe a touch of fright in my eyes.

"Jesus Bobby don't you know me... its Freddie... Jesus it is been like this the last few weeks you sleep like a dead man and forget who we all are by morning", Freddie said concerned.

I look around again and I feel so confused but then it all comes creeping back to me. My name is Bobby and I have been on the streets since coming home from the Vietnam War. It is 1975 and this is New York. Freddie and I were there together.

We lived but died at the same time. Now here we were, heroes in our minds, begging for handouts.

"Come on Bobby we need to get to the shelter it is the first of April... you know what happens on the first... it is clothes day... we may just find something clean this time... come on get going", Freddie says with excitement.

"Sorry man... Jesus Freddie I know you... and I know what day it is now... I am right behind you", I said.

"Good to see you together... I don't know what I would do if you one morning you did not come back to reality", Freddie says.

"I want a shave and a haircut today... you think that is possible", I ask.

"Well only if Ava is there today", Freddie said winking.

"I want a shower to", I said quickly.

"You... shave... shower... haircut... what's up Bobby... what you figuring on", Freddie asks like he knows something.

"I want a job... maybe get off this street", I say.

"Yeah right man become Mister Donald Fucking Trump", Freddie says laughing.

Then I start thinking to myself. Why not?

"It is time we do something Freddie... I don't want to die like this... or end up like them", I said pointing to the filth around me.

"Ok Ok man I'm with ya... just like in the bush I got your back", Freddie says.

"I know... now let's go... if Ava is there she will help... she will know what to do... she has been bugging us about it forever", I said.

"You still dreaming", Freddie asks with concern.

"Every night... you", I ask, slightly concerned as well.

"Fucking right... that dam hill", Freddie says shivering.

"Yeah me to... we lost everyone there", I said, looking to the ground and then up into the sky.

"You saved my life", Freddie said.

"Yeah... just to bring you back here to this", I said waving my arms.

"You saved my life man", Freddie said.

"Naw... all I did was push you in that hole... dive in with you and pull what was left of Stevie over us... I can still smell him... still hear the screams... you know", I said.

"Yeah... I know... every night", Freddie says.

"Let's go Freddie... let's go see Ava", I said.

I took a dirty rag out of what was left of my pants pocket and wiped some tears from my eyes. That dammed hill, Stevie, Chris, Frank, Jimmie, Ross, all dead. That dammed hill. I want off the streets. Freddie and I just like in the bush. We got off that hill. I know we did, I just know we did...

It is pouring now and the sun is bright, as bright as I have ever seen. Where is all of this rain coming from? I look up and there is not a cloud in the sky. I am in a boat, and the air smells like the sea. The taste, the air has left in my mouth, is that of a fresh scallop. I am not really alone, but there are no other people around. The sails are high. Where am I going? I do not really care. The dog is with me the big black one from all of the nights before. He appeared out of the sky landing with the kite also from all of the nights before. I jump from the boat and land on sand. Where did all the water go, it is receding the farther away I look. I seem to be on an island of sorts, and all that rain has turned to snow. The dog and the kite stay on the boat and it floats away. The water has returned for them. I am not worried for I know they will be back. I find a water fall and jump into the pool it empties into. There is snow everywhere but the air and the water is warm. Then it turns cold and the water flash freezes around me. I am trapped, I cannot move. I scream but all that comes from my mouth are a bunch of small ice cubes...

I am now in a café, a Starbucks that I am very familiar with. I order a Green Tea Latte, extra hot, and a cinnamon bun. I sit at a table and it turns to dust around me and the scene of the café disappears giving way to a mountain range. I sit with the cinnamon bun and the latte surrounded by snow capped cliffs. The big black dog comes from behind me and steals the bun from my hand and I laugh. The sound of my laughter echoes through the valley below, and I laugh some more. I have never laughed so hard, my stomach hurts and tears are pouring down my face...

I am back in the frozen water on the small island. I still cannot move. My nose itches and it is driving me insane. Then I feel myself being pulled down below the ice. Then a cave forms around me and I can move around, I shout and the sound echoes, no ice cubes...

I stink again. I am walking with Freddie and we are almost at the shelter. People avoid us with looks of complete horror and disgust. Children point saying things to the adults with them. I fought for this country, and this is how we are treated. I am ashamed for all. Ava will help us off of the streets, she has to.

"I really am looking forward to a shave and shower", I said.

"I just want a hot meal", Freddie replies licking his lips and wiping his chin.

"If we clean up do you think anyone will hire us", I ask.

"No problem buddy... we will get this", Freddie says.

"It could take months to get back into presentable shape", I said.

"Yeah... probably... where do you want to get a job", Freddie asked.

"A restaurant... plenty of food in a restaurant", I said.

"Where we gonna live", Freddie asked.

"At the shelter... at first... even if we have to sleep on the ground or share a bed... we can shave and shower everyday and as long as we are working there will be clean clothes for us", I said.

We arrived at the shelter, and Ava was there. She looked happy to see us. I asked for a shower and she smiled. Ava had been around the shelter for years now. Her father had taken to the streets quite a few years ago, and he was never seen from again. She has devoted her life to rehabilitating and reintegrating people from the streets back to the world. I hoped she would take us for her next project. We or I was ready.

I told Ava of my plans and she squealed with delight. She got us some towels and washcloths, some soap and shampoo. I got the water as hot as I could take it and I scrubbed with more vigor than I ever had in the past, even more than after a stint in the jungle and we were rotated to where hot water was available. I stepped out of the shower and there was a clean robe on the small table by the door, Ava. I put the robe on and stepped out and found that Freddie had found the same. Besides the cracked lips and skin on our cheeks, and a few sores that should heal, I thought we looked dammed good. Well, good in a sense if you consider where we have just come from, and the neglect of hygiene on our parts.

Ava knocked and asked if she could come in. She entered the shower area with razors and barbers tools in hand. She had brought in a folding chair and motioned for me to sit down. She took some clippers and worked it through my thick beard bringing it down to stubble flush with my face. She then ran the clippers through my hair and shaved it right to the scalp. Ava then lathered up my face and took a straight razor and gave me the best shave of my life. She then did the same to my scalp. I went over to the sink and ran water over my face and bald head. I looked into the small mirror and smiled to myself. We had gotten off of that hill. Ava repeated the process on Freddie. She handed us some very clean clothes and stepped out for us to change. I found them to be a pretty good fit. Freddie had not fared so well, but he just rolled up his sleeves and bottom of the jeans and made the best of it. We then stepped out and got a hot meal, Ava saved us a fair portion. We were off that hill, maybe not all the way but relief was coming, relief was coming...

I can feel cold steel in the palms of my hands, and I can hear screams of pain all around me. There are fires everywhere. Thunder, lightning, and rain are punishing my body and my soul for some forgotten or unknown sins. The rain feels like tiny shards of glass and they are tearing my flesh. The rain is tearing everyone apart, and that is the reason for the screams...

I look around and I am in a hospital bed. There are hundreds of us in this room. Our blood seeping through the bandages we are wrapped in. Hundreds moaning and calling for help. The room is cold, I am cold. Life is leaving running away...

I am in a jungle, or maybe a rainforest. I do not know for sure. Is there a difference? I am naked but I cannot see my limbs, my hands or my feet. I see faces in the shadows and hear my name being called…

I am lying face down now on a flat bed. No not a bed, a table. I look to my left and my right and I notice I am at the massage parlor. A soft velvety voice is whispering into my ear telling me to flip over onto my back. I comply and fight to keep the white towel in place around my midsection. I feel hands on my feet kneading the soles. I close my eyes and feel those hands moving further up my calves to my thighs and then to…

I am talking to Ava now. I am telling her that Freddie and I are looking for work. Ava pulls a clipboard down from the bulletin board and flips some pages. A restaurant not far from here is looking for a dishwasher, an industrial building a little farther a night cleaner.

"Is there anything for the two of us", I ask with great excitement.

"Not together they are all single postings", Ava responds.

"If we get jobs… will we be able to stay here while things work out and we get a place", I ask with the same enthusiasm.

"I will make room here… if you both get the jobs… you have to keep them… and I will require weekly reports", Ave said like a Mother talking to her misbehaving child.

"We know the rules… so how about it… can you get us the jobs", I ask.

"Which would you prefer", Ave asks.

"It does not matter… as long as we are working and getting paid", Freddie said.

"Good… that is what I want to hear", Ava said…

I am back on the massage table. The young girl is smiling her hand working under the towel. She goes to lift the towel off and...

I am back in the cave and I am no longer alone...

I am walking into a Starbucks and my latte and cinnamon bun are waiting on the counter. I thank no one for I am alone and I sit on the floor. All the tables and chairs are gone. I see a computer but there are no keys on the key board...

"Freddie I will place you at the restaurant and Bobby at the building... is that agreeable", Ava asks.

"Yes... that is fine... when will we start", Freddie asks a little hesitantly.

"I will make the phone calls... I will be right back", Ava said.

"See Freddie everything is going to be fine", I said confidently.

"We will see... do you think our dreams of being back there will go away", Freddie asks.

"No I do not... I think those we will have to carry and bear for all of our sins", I said...

Back on the mountain peak everything is calm and serene. Peace settles into my soul. The dog is sitting at my left side. There is a pair of eagles on my right. There is also a horse nearby. I can hear him but I cannot see him. I get up and start to walk around. The dog follows close and the eagles take off and circle overhead. I hear splashing and giggling coming from my left. I walk that way and find a clearing with a small clear pool. Two women are playing and swimming in the nude. They see me and beckon me over, but it is not a place I can go. I try to move closer but my feet and legs are not complying. I move away from the pool and then they work fine. They take me further away for I cannot move in their direction at all. When I stop moving away my feet and legs do not work to move closer. I cannot see them or hear them anymore. The horse appears and I settle into the saddle on his back. A Winchester Rifle is lying across my lap. The horse moves off, the dog follows and the eagles keep watch overhead...

The fires still burn and all are still screaming. The lightning and thunder are even more ferocious than before. A man runs up to me, he has a gun in his hand. He runs up to me screaming, skin is peeling away from his face, his arms, and all over his body, from the force of the rains. He points the gun at me and pulls the trigger, the roar is deafening as fires spews from the barrel. He misses and he bursts into laughter, a sick laughter. He then collapses into a bloody heap at my feet. I kick him but he does not move. I pick up the gun, tearing it from his grip. I then walk away. My skin is now peeling just like his was. I stumble and fall over the bodies in my path. The screams I hear are now more powerful then the thunder for they belong to me...

I wake up slowly. I can make out cloudy shapes and nothing more. The effects of my concoction are wearing off. I pick up the clock. At least I think it is a clock. I try to concentrate on it. I see colors. Yes I definitely see the color red. I believe that numbers are forming. The clock reads 1430. I have been asleep for 14 hours. I lie back down and try to remember parts of what I had dreamt. I stayed there for more than an hour. It all starts to come back to me. The dog, the eagles, the horse, the massage table, Freddie, Ava, all of it came back to the forefront of my mind. No Jessica though, I had hoped to see Jessica. The concoction worked perfectly. I feel rested and ready to finish this day.

I went to the washroom and relieved myself, washed my hands and my face. I went to the kitchen and made some food and sat to eat. I will not turn on the TV, the internet, or read the paper today. I will get some yard work done. The grass needs cutting, and some of the bushes trimmed. I will wash down the drive and sweep out the garage. I will weed in the garden and harvest some vegetables. That should make me tired enough to settle down to sleep tonight, and wear off the 14 hours of sleep.

I step into the garage and press the button to open the overhead door. It is a beautiful late summer day and I forget about the dreams for a little while. This is the one of the things a dream cannot reproduce. The other things are the intimate touch of a woman, the taste of food and wine, and the true feeling of being alive. I stare into the sun and let its warmth soak into my skin. I pull out the lawnmower and begin the routine pattern. Thirty minutes later and I am done. I put the mower away and start clipping some of the bushes. Satisfied with the result I move to the back and begin cultivating the garden pulling weeds as I find them. I then return to the garage and retrieve a basket for the fruits of my labor. A salad will be on the menu tonight. Tomatoes, cucumbers and onions, that is all, dressed with some olive oil and balsamic vinegar. I will grill some beef tenderloin and slice in on top on the salad. It will be excellent.

After three hours in the yard, I need a shower. It is 730 pm, I will have everything prepared and finished by 9. I will settle down with a couple of glasses of wine, inject myself and sleep again as I did last night. A whole new round of dreams awaits me.

The shower feels great, and the lingering memory of the dreams came rushing back to me. I love remembering the dreams. The more detail I can remember the greater chances of continuing the thought inspired by the dreams, if not the very dream itself.

After drying off I dress in my sleep clothes. I go down to the kitchen and pour myself a glass of wine. I move to my den, settle into my chair behind my desk. I look around the room, and at the items I have accumulated over the years. I look at the suits of armor in their glass cases. I have six of them, three medieval knights and three samurai. They look across the room at each other. What would that fight have been like? I often wonder about this. Along the walls behind their cases is their armory. I have collected 136 swords and 23 other forms of weaponry from their time periods. I imagine that the men that may have worn that armor, and had carried those weapons, to be extremely fierce warriors. These are not imitations. All of the items in this room have been proven and authenticated as original works. There are few places with a greater collection of this type of artwork.

I close my eyes and allow epic battles to play like movies in my mind. I imagine I am the hero, charging into the fray, hearing the clash of steel and the screams of men. My sword is bright red with the blood of my enemies. I imagine I am a Crusader defending pilgrims of the Holy Land, Christian and Muslim alike. I imagine I am a Samurai defending a young woman's honor from thieves and rapists. I treat my sword like I treat a woman, standing in absolute awe of her symmetrical beauty. I imagine I take every task at hand to its highest level in pursuit of its perfection. I imagine sitting on top of my horse riding through my God's, my Kings or my Emperor's lands keeping an air of peace.

Sitting here in my comfortable worn familiar chair sipping my wine I think to myself. I think that I that I may have been born at the wrong time period. Then I think further, that I may have been there and my imagining is fuelled by remnants of past memories. I look at the clock on the left corner of the desk. I have been sitting here for almost two hours absorbed in these thoughts. The places dreams can take you that real life may not be able to.

I take the last sip and walk back to the kitchen. Here I pick up another syringe from the fridge and I go upstairs. I repeat the process from the night before and before I know it…

I am running the back alleys of... where? I try to concentrate on my surroundings and I realize I am not alone. Jessica is running in front of me leading the way. We stop at a green door and she knocks tree times. I male pokes his head out, smiles and allows us entry. We are rushed up stairs, and we tell our new friends our tale. It is all over the news, a New York style Gangland killing they are calling it. The police are looking for a male and a female that had been spotted fleeing the scene as persons of interest. They described us perfectly. Jessica introduced me to the male and two females in the room. The male, Marc did all of the talking.

"Jessica we will get you two a change of clothes... you will both need to dye your hair... Valerie and Tanya will help you... and your friend will have to shave", Marc said sternly.

"Agreed... Sean you first", Jessica said.

I was then led away further into the building by Valerie and Tanya. They were very quick and practiced at this. They had my hair cut and dyed and gave me the closest shave of my life before I could have time to think and flirt with them. They were cute, and with all the excitement I just realized how dammed horny I was. I was ushered out of the room before I could protest and Jessica ushered in. They were just as quick with her. When Jessica joined me in the room I was brought to I hardly recognized her. Our pictures were taken and in a few hours new passports were handed to us. Our cell phones had been disposed of along with our old clothes and all we had carried in with us. We were taken to the airport and flown to Portugal.

"Why all of this Jess... we could have worked more for them", I said.

"No... when I told Marc what had happened and explained more while you were being transformed he recognized the signature of the people we had just worked for... they would have killed us as soon as they could", Jessica said with a slight hint of fear in her voice.

"What do you mean their signature", I asked.

"Marc is very well connected all over Europe and he has seen these people work before under the same premise that we were working under... when they are done they kill the operatives they employ", Jessica said.

"What now", I asked.

"We wait for Marc to tell us it is safe... he will be enquiring as to how hot a commodity we are", Jessica said.

"Commodity... do you mean there may be a bounty out on us", I asked raising my eyes and arms to the heavens.

"Yes... and then Marc will produce two bodies spreading our DNA through the hair they collected and we will be effectively dead... at least the aliases we were using will be dead", Jessica said.

"That will not work... I cannot stay a blond forever", I said joking.

"We will both have to keep our changes... until this group is eliminated that is", Jessica said.

"Eliminated", I asked.

"The people Marc works for... are looking for them... retribution for some past actions", Jessica said.

"Past actions", I said.

"Yes... they set up and killed Marc's brother and sister the same way they were going to do to us", Jessica said...

Freddie is talking to me about his week at work, but I am not really paying attention. I am exhausted, the building I have been assigned to is huge and the work required immense. The accommodations that Ava had found for us is not the Ritz but much better than our tent in Nam. I nod and smile, but Freddie knows I am not listening. He pretends not to notice and carries on with his tale. I think of Ava much more than I should, and she checks on us more than she has to. There is a change in how she looks at me. At least I hope there is. After a few months of hard honest work, proper exercise, proper meals, a roof and a regular shower, I am slowly becoming the man I once was. I look at my reflection. I am lean, good looking, with life in my eyes. I think of my parents and of contacting them. I have not done so since the first week of coming back.

"So what do you think...? Bobbie... what do you think", Freddie asked.

Freddie then slaps me on the back.

"Hey... what the fuck", I said.

"I have been talking to you for over a half hour now... I have been asking you... so what do you think about all of it", Freddie said.

"Whatever you think is necessary", I said.

"So you think we should rob a bank... run for president... and cut off our fingers", Freddie asked.

"What... dam Freddie... you know I wasn't listening... quit fucking around", I said.

"Where were you", Freddie asked.

"I don't know... nowhere special... just daydreaming... just after we got back from hell... remember I took Julie out before she told me she had been fucking all of my old friends while I was away", I said.

"Oh yeah... I remember that night... I also remember having to bail you out of jail too... you kicked the shit out of two of the guys... I remember", Freddie said.

"It was three... but then it could have been four or six... I was too pissed to remember", I said.

"When are you going to ask her", Freddie asked.

"Tomorrow... when we check in at the center", I said...

Jessica and I lounged on a small beach below a cliff area of Algarve. Like a couple in love on their honeymoon. Just like the couple in the passports that Marc had procured for us. Upon returning to the hotel there were a couple of messages and a cell phone from Marc. I went to the bar and Jessica went up to the room. I guess she went to read the messages and make a phone call. About an hour later Jessica joined me and ordered a bottle of Shiraz.

"Well what did our benefactor have to say", I asked.

"Everything is fixed and we can return to our normal lives", she responded.

"How can it be fixed already", I asked.

"It just is", she said briskly.

"What is with the tone", I asked.

"All of Marc's help has come with a price... and he is asking us to pay up", she said.

"Pay up... how... with what", I asked raising my voice.

"Marc has a small job for us", she said.

"A job... what job", I asked still raising my voice.

"It is out of our comfort zone... way out... but I think we can do it", she said.

"What kind of job is it", I asked.

"We have to kill someone", she said, no hesitation or soft delivery.

"No... no way... I do not do that... steal info and deliver it that is what I do", I said, yelling it in my head but all Jessica heard was an emphatic normal tone.

"We have no choice", she said.

"There is always a choice... not me... killing is not me", I said with as much conviction as a whisper can carry.

"This time there really is no choice", she said.

"And if I don't", I said.

"Then we will not be breathing by tomorrow", she said.

"Tomorrow... when are we supposed to do this job", I asked.

"In one hour... there is a package with all we need at the desk", she said.

"What do you want to do Jessica", I asked.

"I want to live... I like this life with you... these past three weeks have been amazing... I could stay here forever with you... and I am pretty sure you feel the same", she said.

"Could you kill Jessica... have you killed before", I asked.

"For this I would kill... this freedom... and I could ask for forgiveness later... from you... from God... whatever it took", she said.

"We are running out of time then", I said...

I was in the Himalayas. I could tell this by the Sherpa's all around me, guiding me up the mountain. I was looking for spiritual guidance. I had yet to find any thus far. Here in Tibet it was different, there was holiness here, a reverence for life and mankind. I was sure to find God here, or some evidence of His existence. I wanted answers to the question of Heaven and Hell.

I feel at peace, and the further into Tibet I roam the more at peace I seem to be. I imagine the hand of God reaching out to me...

I then fall, and it feels like thousands of meters...

I am swimming now, faster I cry to myself, faster. There is something behind me I can feel it...

I float through the air past the people I have known. I am collecting balloon strings as I go, and the more I collect the farther into the air I am carried. Up past the flight paths of birds and through the levels of misty cloud they carry me. The air pressure up here hurts and the balloons begin to pop. Pop, Pop, Pop, Pop, Pop, Pop, Pop, Pop, Pop, Pop, Pop, Pop, Pop, Pop, Pop, Pop...

I continue to fall...

I land in my bed, but there are no walls around me. Shadows turn to monsters. They are clawing at my flesh as I slowly disappear into them...

I am still in my bed, sweating profusely. The shadows are no longer monsters. They have been transformed into beautiful women. They are clawing at me, fondling and massaging me, licking and sucking me deep into their mouths and other hidden places. I give in to them. I can feel their hair as I grab it, their shapes taking solid forms under the touch of my hands...

I am now taken to a cliff with the same black dog at my side from all of my dreams before dating back to my childhood. He watches over me ever so vigilantly like a protective parent. The dog lies down and places his head in my lap and I absently pet and scratch behind his ears...

Freddie is yelling at me to wake up. His voice is ever so distant but becomes more prominent and louder as I swim up from the many heavy layers of sleep.

"Bobby... oh man... you have to get to work... BOBBY YOU GOTTA WAKE UP... WAKE UP", Freddie yells.

"Ok Ok... what time is it", I respond groggily.

"Its ten pm man... you have to be at work in thirty minutes", Freddie says.

"Shit", I said, spitting out the word.

No time for a real shower just a quick dance under the water, and a fresh coat of deodorant. No lunch again either. I will have to rely on the vending machine for some food. I hope it is not all expired this time, a chocolate bar and a soft drink only go so far. Trying to get out the door to sprint to work Freddie stops me.

"Bobby... Do not forget these things", Freddie says.

Freddie hands me a brown bag and a thermos.

"Just a couple sandwiches and some coffee", Freddie says.

"Thanks man", I said.

Freddie was an awesome guy, the kind you really would like to go to war with. I was so tired I slept like a dead man.

The lunch date with Ava took a lot out of me and I stayed later than I should. I meant to sleep before but I was way too excited, like a kid at Christmas. I told her I was off tonight, or she would have ended the date early, or maybe would have declined the offer all together. Out the door I went...

It's freezing out. I am walking, no coat, and no shoes. The rain that is pelting my body turns to icy snow. The wind picks up and I can barely see in front of my face. I try to continue walking, but I stumble and actually seem to be pushed backwards to where I had just come from. I do not want to go there and I am terrified, absolutely terrified...

Sand in my toes, my lips cracked. I see nothing but sand, nothing. The horizon shimmers with heat and I see things. I see men on horseback turning to dragons. I see the staff I carry in my hands turn into a sword. I see trees and lakes that are not there. I see water at my feet, but when I attempt to drink I come up with nothing but a mouthful of sand. I see apples, oranges, and steaks cooking over a fire. I see an operating room, lights blazing in the distance, doctors working furiously to close their incisions. I see children playing in a pool beckoning me to join them. I see nothing but sand, nothing...

I can see Jessica's athletic body through the clouded shower door. I want to join her, but I cannot. I am not here for sex or love. I am here for the money. I stare at the package on the bed and the pictures of the man we are supposed to kill. I do not know if I can do it. I am undecided. Why did Jessica leave the bathroom door open? Is she beckoning or just tempting me to come in? What did she mean earlier when she said she could "stay here forever with me"? The man in the picture is staying at this hotel and was scheduled to visit the pool in twenty-five minutes. We were to kill him there.

Jessica steps out of the shower and reaches for her towel. Our eyes meet and I cannot help but stare. She is beautiful, so beautiful. She dries herself and looks at me seductively. I started to burn the contents of the package in the metal trash can by the desk. Once the contents had been turned completely to ash I speak up.

"We have to be down by the pool in fifteen", I say.

"I will be ready in five... unless there is something you need or want me to do", she replies seductively.

"No... I will let you get ready", I said.

"Are you sure", she asks, or maybe better to describe it as a sort of purr.

"No I am not", I said, my voice weakening with my resolve.

And I left the room. I had never killed before not even to save my own life. My specialty is in industrial espionage. I retrieve secrets for those who commission me. I do not know if I can do this. I paced the hallways for a few more minutes and re-entered the room. Jessica was dressed wiping down every surface she could find in an attempt to muddle the evidence of us being in the room. We had no time to clean our existence for those who command had not left us enough room for that. Jessica said nothing. I gathered our bags and brought them down to the rental car, and checked out at the front desk. I asked if it was alright if we had one last coffee by the pool before heading off. The request was of course granted.

Jessica met me by the pool, and we chose a vantage point that offered us the best movement on the target according to the information received. Jessica carried a vial with her, a clear liquid inside. That liquid had to get into the targets drink, or on his skin, neither of us knew how yet. The liquid became deadly when mixed with alcohol. It could be ingested or absorbed and the result would be the same, massive cardiac arrest. We spotted the target. He had entered the pool area at the exact time the information said he would. He sat at the exact table the information specified.

Then an idea hit me, I ordered a triple scotch. When my drink came I took the vial from Jessica and poured it in.

"What now", she asked.

"A little clumsiness on my part", I said, winking but not convinced that this was right.

I picked up the glass, and tripped in the direction of the targets table. The liquid in my glass splashed all over the targets face, and eyes. He screamed in protest and outrage as I result of the stinging pain of the alcohol in his eyes. I offered my apologies, but he called me every name in the book in about six different languages. I offered a towel from the rack by the pool, but he whipped it out of my hands onto the ground. Employees of the hotel tried to assist but he pushed them all away and stormed off...

SUNDAY 13TH OF JUNE 2011

I see specks of light, and can hear the phone ringing. I am being pulled to consciousness, and I cannot stop it. I see more light as the sun shines through my blinds. My room is taking shape before me, and I realize I am no longer in a dream but very much a part of the living world. My phone is ringing and I try to concentrate on the display but I do not recognize the number. It says I have eight messages. Six of which were from the hospital and two wrong numbers. I sat up and looked at the time and the date. I had slept for twenty-three hours. This dose of my concoction really worked. I went downstairs and realized I was thirsty and famished. I drank four glasses of water, and made myself some sandwiches. I sat quietly eating them remembering what I had dreamed. It was good to see Freddie and Jessica again. They were two of my favorite people in two of my favorite dreams. I called the hospital back and confirmed my surgery consultations and schedule for my return.

The other calls were invites for parties and nights out. I never accepted but my colleagues were persistent.

I shower and dress. It was late at night. My errands would have to wait for the morning. I doubted I would sleep much and dared not take another injection this soon. I decided to go out, catch a late movie and then head to a bar for a few drinks. My plan would be to try to pick up a woman, but I knew I would probably end up back at the massage parlor just before it closed.

I looked at the newspaper but could find no movie I was really interested in. I locked my house and headed for a popular bar not too far away. When I got there I ordered a double scotch, a twenty-one year old Glenfiddich. It was my drink of choice. I chose a small dark table in the corner. It was early for the bar to be busy, a good time to visit and settle in.

A band was still setting up. I have heard this group before, they played some decent Jazz. Groups of people were filtering in and out. They were probably grabbing a quick drink before going elsewhere. A few single women came in and out, but did not order anything. They were hookers just checking on the clientele, they would be back later to pick up any leftover single guys who had had a few too many. Another hour or so and this place would be full, and I will just sit back and watch life go by slowly sipping my scotch.

I was on my third double and this place was full. Sweaty bodies from end to end. The music was really good, at least what you could hear above the roaring conversations of the crowd. I sat at my table and I watched and listened. I few women in groups at the bar smiled in my direction. One attractive Asian actually came over and sat for a little while and we had a decent conversation. She was really cool. I told her of my job and she explained hers. Her name was Le Si Shen and she worked in recruitment for a headhunter firm. I did not tell her of my fascination with dreams. I did not mention the fact that I used some pharmaceutical tools of my trade so that I may escape this life for the one that I wanted. We talked for an hour but her friends were getting restless for they had other plans. Le excused herself with grace, but we exchanged numbers and made a tentative date for coffee at 2 tomorrow afternoon.

MONDAY 14TH OF JUNE 2011

I am really horny, but that is the scotch talking with the thoughts of Le. I will abstain from the massage parlor and see where this chance meeting will take me. Tonight there would be no sleep, no dreams. After my last 23 hour stint, I think it would be wise to wait until tomorrow evening.

I sat sipping the remains of my drink and thought of Jessica, Freddie and Ava. I thought of the other dreams as well. I thought of flying kites, eagles and the dog that keeps me company. I thought of the worlds filled with pain, sorrow and neglect. I ignored the watchful eyes of the hookers as they picked the single men up from the bar like flies. I got up from the safe confines of my table and walked out the door into the warm summer night.

I decided to take a walk. There was a park nearby, not a safe place at night but I decided to take my chances. I found a bench and sat down. A Police Officer strolled by walking his assigned beat. Couples went by holding hands, and the girls giggled as the men they were with grabbed a handful of ass as they walked by me. Groups of young men and women walked by, probably up to no good but behaving as the Police Officer was near. I could hear them cursing and swearing and talking of going down to the lake instead and see what they could find there.

I got up from the park bench and slowly made my way home. I entered my house, and sighed at the emptiness that greeted me. I loved my dream world and would trade this life for that in a second. I did regret the fact though that I am alone here. Dreams are great but they are better when shared with someone. Freddie, Jessica and Ava understood this. I made myself a late dinner, a very late dinner, and sat alone. I flipped on the television and surfed channels until I found a movie that was a decent time waster. The news channels I flipped briefly to, I found were all so full of crap. It seems that absolutely nothing good was happening in the world. I tired from the movie and took a cup of green tea to my den. This room really was a reflection of me.

I just sat there in the quiet confines of my sanctuary and sipped the tea I had made. I could detect the faint odor of well oiled and polished metal, and that of well worn leather in the air. I decided to open one of the cabinets that held my collection of Katana swords. I took one down from the rack that was due for polishing and started to work. By the time I was finished I had two dozen complete. The sun was up and had been for awhile. I decided to make a late breakfast. I made myself an omelet. I cleaned the house a bit, some dusting, some vacuuming. I showered and got ready for my “date”.

I checked my messages and I deemed nothing to be of importance. It was fast closing in on 2 and I left my house. I decided to walk because the coffee house Le and I had agreed on was fairly close by. I walked in at 1:55 and saw Le sitting a table. I waved and smiled at her and she returned the gesture. She got up and met me before the counter and she surprised me with a light hug and peck on the cheek. We approached the counter and ordered, and I insisted on paying. We sat back down at the table she had just vacated. I looked around and noticed two females sitting not too far away and I recognized them from last night. Le and come with friends as back up. I was not offended at all. I respected her decision making and the quality of the friends she had chosen. I chose not to mention this to her and pretended I did not notice.

We began with the normal small talk. Events in the news and the weather as of late were our main topics. I found that she was just as disenchanted with the world as I was. She enjoyed the hot weather, but fall was her favorite. She hated the winters and the wetness of spring. We spoke of likes and dislikes. We spoke of hobbies. I told her of my obsession with swords and armor of all types. She listened attentively. I told her of my love of food and my prowess at cooking. We spoke of places we had been and some of the vacations we had taken. She admitted she did not get out much lately and was consumed by the travel requirements of her work. She inquired about the hospital and the exciting job I had. She mentioned doctors that she had placed there when the hospital was looking to fill a specific need. I told her I had worked with many of them. I asked her what her name meant and she told me Le means “happy” and Si “think… or like to think”. Le then tapped her cup three times. It was a signal to her friends, for they left right after. I mentioned this and we laughed over it. Things were going so well we decided to turn our coffee date into dinner. We decided on a quiet Italian bistro down the street. The food there was amazing. We walked to the bistro and she hooked her arm into mine. This was comfortable, strangely comfortable. I did not quite know what to make of it.

The hostess sat us at a quiet table. Well, they were all quiet now for it was early for dinner. Le asked if she could order. She explained that she liked to do this on all first dates to see if she had a proper handle on the person she was with. I consented. Le ordered two appetizers. One was shrimps and scallops in a garlic and white wine sauce. The other was stuffed Portobello mushroom caps. She then ordered the entrees. For me she ordered beef tenderloin, rare, over garlic mashed potatoes, with a red wine wild mushroom and blue cheese reduction, and asparagus tips. For her a whole chicken breast with peppercorn sauce over wild rice and glazed carrots. The meal was perfect. I asked how she knew what to order and she explained by the way I passionately spoke of food earlier. When she saw that menu item she immediately thought of me. We decided to skip dessert. Her car was nearby and I walked her to it. We tried to make plans for tomorrow but could only agree on a very late dinner. We decided on the same bistro, we would meet at 9 pm. This would give me time to dream. We kissed each other and parted ways. She offered me a ride but I said I needed to walk after all I ate. She smiled and waved. It had been a good night.

The walk was good it allowed me to clear my head. Upon entering the house I experienced that same empty feeling. For I wondered for a brief moment what things would be like around here with a woman, maybe some kids, a dog. These things I could not have for they would surely impose and affect my dreams. I would not be able to hide that from them.

I wasted no time. I locked the doors and headed straight for the fridge and the waiting syringe. Two more doses after this. I would forego the shower and headed straight upstairs. I quickly undressed and administered the shot. Warmth spread with calmness throughout my body and...

I am washing my hands and face in a pool of a river at the base and in the shadow of a large mountain. The pink blossoms on the trees around me are breathtaking. The wind causes some of the blossoms to leave the protection of the trees and they flutter and land all around me. I look at the reflection in the water, and I think it is me. I am wearing a Black Do (the chest plate of a Samurai warrior) and Black Hakama (pants), my Kabuto (helmet), my Kote (sleeve armor), my Tekko (hand guards), are close by my side. My katana is near laying on top on them. My Wakisahashi still at my waist, for I am never without this. The people refer to me as Hisoka, which means secretive. I hear a horse come up beside me and take a deep drink from the pool. He is as dark as any night could possibly be. He carries my Yumi (longbow), and my supplies, for I have been on a long journey. I have named him Torao which means Tiger.

I remember it all now, my mind a bit foggy and weary from the long trip is now beginning to clear. The effects of the crystal clear cold water. I have decided to camp here on the bank of this river and in the company of the blossoms. I imagined building a home here when all is done, and my time of service over. I will ask this of my Daimyo when this task is complete. This is a good place. There is protection from the mountains, running water and fertile ground, a good place.

My Daimyo, my Lord, whom I have sworn to serve, is dying. He has charged me to find his heir who was taken to these mountains years ago to protect and hide him from those who would kill him. He would be almost fully grown now. His training would have begun long ago and would be able to continue to rule his father's lands. The war is now over both sides suffering great casualties in the last ten years. I will find his son before he passes to the other side, and deliver him safely. There are still those left that I still call my enemy that would not have committed Seppuku and have turned Ronin to avenge their own master's death. For my reward I will ask for freedom from my vow of service, and this valley. For now I will set up camp, and sleep...

I am running as fast as I can. A car is barreling down on me. I turn and dive but there is nowhere to go, nowhere to hide. Curbs and buildings disappear the closer I get. I see more in the distance but...

I am crying in a corner. I hear voices but no faces. Everything turns black and blends into the shadows, even me...

I am in an open doorway of a small plane. I have a parachute strapped to my back. I wait for the signal from the jump master. The light goes green and he gives me the thumbs up. The feeling I am experiencing right now as I fall through the air is exhilarating and liberating. I look around, I flip over and the plane becomes more distant as the earth rushes to meet me. The instrument around my wrist beeps and is flashing. It is time to pull the cord and...

I am knee deep in a pit of mud and cannot free myself. The more I struggle the more I sink. Up to my waist, up to my chest, my neck...

Sitting on the bank of a small stream covered in mud from head to toe, the dog at my side. He is covered in mud as well. He jumps into the stream and comes out as clean as can be. He takes my hand and motions me to do the same. I jump in and...

I am now flying through the air on the backs of eagles. I am seeing the world as they see it, soaring into the sun, diving towards the earth. I have been accepted by the masters of the sky, and given an opportunity that all in this world would like just once. I have become a predator...

I return to the table by the pool to sit once again with Jessica. Hotel employees are flying around us, and I apologize as they pass. They nod their heads and try to smile. Jessica and I calmly get up and leave the area. The phone provided with the package of information on the intended target rings. Jessica answers. I can only hear her half of the conversation.

"Yes it has been delivered". "No I do not know the outcome". "Yes of course we will confirm", she said. The conversation then ends.

"We have to find out if we succeeded", Jessica says.

"How long will that take", I asked.

"I do not know... maybe we can go to the front desk and get our room for another night", she said.

"Do you think that is wise... what if they trace this back to us", I said.

"The guilty leave... the innocent stays", she said.

I thought about it for a minute. Maybe we could stay for a drink or two, and see how this plays out. I tell this to Jessica.

"How long before that stuff works", I asked.

"It is a slow absorption process... by the time it works it is no longer detectable and does not live long in the open air", she said.

"So it could take a couple of days", I said.

"Yes... in theory it could... but you did get the liquid in his eyes so the reaction could be immediate", she said.

"Your call", I said.

"I say we check back in... another night or two with me and that wall you built in front of you may come crashing down", she said touching my upper thigh.

"Keeping the bathroom door open while you shower is certainly not strengthening my resolve", I said sheepishly.

"So there is a weakness in your armor", she said.

"Yes... there is a weakness in my armor", I said quite matter-of-factly.

We then went to the front desk and asked for our room back. It had not been reserved as yet and the hotel was happy to have us stay. Our luggage was brought back up and we returned to the pool area for another drink...

I am back in the Himalayas trekking behind the Sherpa. Peace and tranquility rule here. Peace rules here in the quiet solitude and the majesty of this place. I am headed for a monastery higher up where I will stay for as long as I am welcome…

I am having coffee in a park. I am just sitting alone at the base of a great red maple tree. It is fall and the colors are magnificent. As the breeze picks up the helicopters fall and fly around me. My cup is almost empty and a spigot appears in the trunk. I place my cup under it and out pours some more. The aroma is magnificent. The dog comes and sits beside me, and a horse appears out of nowhere. Four eagles land on the ground in a square pattern around me. The eagles are looking out as if they are standing sentry. There is something bothering the horse for he is uneasy, stamping the ground and huffing and puffing. A low rumble is beginning in the deep chest cavity of the dog, and he is pulling his lips back barring his teeth. The eagles take flight in the same direction that a dust cloud in forming in the distance…

I am cooking in a strange kitchen. I plan to roast some red fingerling potatoes with pearl onions and whole cloves of garlic. I add some olive oil, oregano, salt, pepper, and freshly grated Parmesan cheese, to the freshly washed and cut potatoes. I open the cupboards and am trying to find a small roasting pan, and my quest is fruitful. I open the fridge and find some beautiful shrimp. They are huge and have already been cleaned and deveined. On the counter there is a fresh French baguette, and some whole cloves of garlic. I do not know who I am cooking for, but I hear voices in the other rooms around me…

I see shadows moving closer to me. They are as black as any night could be imagined. There is a spot light on me and it moves as I do. I have nowhere to run. I …

Freddie comes up behind me and slaps me on the back.

"How was your date with Ava", he asked.

"I don't know… let's not talk about it", I said.

"Come on", Freddie said.

"No... that is out of bounds for now", I said.

"Must have been some heavy shit", Freddie said.

"Not really... so... how is work going", I asked.

"Changing the subject... fair enough", Freddie replied.

"Fuck Freddie I am not changing the subject... I just do not want to talk about it yet... I'll... let you know... OK", I said.

"Yeah sure Bobby... sure... whatever you say... and work sucks I do not know how much more I can take... my boss is such a dick", Freddie said.

"Mine too... I think they all are", I said.

"Probably... but I need to find something else or go back to the streets man", Freddie said.

"No... No way... Neither of us is going back... hell no... we killed for this country and died a hundred times over... we ain't living on the streets", I yelled...

I am young, maybe eight or nine. I am lying on my back staring up into the clouds, seeing shapes and pictures in them as they pass by. There are four eagles screaming above, swooping and diving and it all seems familiar. There is a black dog with me and he is just a puppy. That is another familiarity that I cannot place. He runs and jumps all around. He licks my hands and tries to chew gently on my arm. He wants to play, but I just want to look into the clouds and dream...

There is a knock at our door. Freddie does not move. I groan as I get up and move across the floor and answer it. I open the door and Ava is standing there, and she is smiling.

"Hi", I said.

"Hi", she answers back.

I step aside and motion for her to enter.

"Hi Freddie... how is your job going", she asked

"Oh... don't ask... and Freddie", I said.

I did not finish my thought. I was going to tell Freddie not to answer, but it was too late.

"I hate the job and the guy in charge is a complete DICK", he spat out.

"They all are... Welcome to the workforce", she said laughing.

I laughed and Freddie got up from his chair and said he was going out for some air. He said his good-byes and told me not to wait up for him. Ava and I stared at each other. I broke the silence and asked her if she would like a cup of tea. She consented. It was not much of an apartment but Freddie and I had worked hard to improve it. We put on fresh paint, shampooed the floors, and kept it magnificently clean. A portion of each paycheck went into small improvements, plants, furniture and such. Ava noticed and commented on the differences.

"You guys have been busy", she said.

"Busy... What do you mean Ava", I asked.

"The apartment... it looks brand new... what a difference", she said.

"In Nam you learned to be as clean and neat as possible or you could die or become sick with all types of nasty things", I said.

"I see... is that all", she said.

"No Ava it is not... I wanted to show you how I am", I said.

"I was hoping to hear that", she said.

Ave moved closer to me, really close. She put her right hand on my chest and moved her hand in circles. She came even closer until our bodies were touching as one...

The floor falls out from under me and I am falling again. I land in an arena. I have full hockey gear on. I am playing in a game. There are thousands of people in the stands. I am wearing red, white and blue with a C H for the crest. I am the star for all the fans are chanting my name. I pick up the puck from a perfect pass and take in past center, around the defense and am alone on goal. I raise my stick in a high arc. I aim for the top right corner. The goalie does not see the puck...

I am searching rooms, I am frantic and panicked. I cannot find something. I go through closets, drawers, boxes and envelopes. It is not here. They are coming several vehicles have pulled up to the building I am in. Men get out and they are heavily armed. I still cannot find it, and I was told it was here. They are in, there is nowhere to hide. One levels a shotgun at me. I stare into the barrels and the man smiles and says, "Good bye"...

I am back in the Himalayas and we have camped for the night. It is absolutely freezing, wind and snow all around. I have been told it is two more days to the monastery. I have come to escape the life I have left behind, and to escape the sins of man. I hover over a fire and a boiling pot of water that was once snow. It will be pasta tonight and some hot tea that the Sherpa's are never without and seems to warm you through the night. It is magical. Two more days and I will be safe within the walled confines of the monastery and my new life...

My head has been shaved and I stand with thousands more just like me. We are all naked waking in a line. Fire falls from the sky and masters hover over us and are ever so generous with the whip...

Ava touches my shoulder beside me in bed. I turn over to face her and our lips meet once more. I know she has to go. Freddie cannot stay out forever. I told Ava I was worried about him, and she said she would look into placing the both of elsewhere. We held each other for a little while and then got up and showered together. Dried and dressed we sat in the living area pretending to watch TV when Freddie knocks loudly and walks in.

"How was your walk", I asked him.

"It is a beautiful night... you two should enjoy some of it", he replied.

"I think we just might... it is getting late and I need to see Ava home", I said.

"You do not have to do any such thing", Ava said.

"Of course I do", I said.

"My car is just around the corner", Ava said.

"Then I will see you to your car", I said.

"Do you work tomorrow", she asked.

"No I am not in for another two days unless they call me", I said.

"And you Freddie", she asked.

"I go back day after tomorrow for three then another two off", Freddie answered.

"Then the three of us will have lunch tomorrow... my treat... and I will see if I can straighten out what we have discussed", she said.

"And what have the two of you been plotting", Freddie asked.

"Come to lunch tomorrow and find out", Ava said...

I am back in line, being whipped and prodded. To what end, I have no clue. There are no words here except for those of our masters yelling at us to keep moving forward. Fire continues to fall all around us, its source unknown. A low rumble can be heard in the distance. Its origin seems to be from the front of the line, where ever that might be. I have been walking for what has to be days and have yet to see any end. I dare not look behind...

I am back trekking up the mountain, and my pack keeps getting heavier with every step. It is almost time to settle in for the night for the light of the day is disappearing fast. I set up my tent with the assistance of the others, without their help I would not survive this. I set up my cook stove, and start the heat. I plunge my hand out the tent door and scoop up some snow to melt and boil.

The pasta tastes like it always does, but the tea is warming and comforting. I try to read by the lamplight but the wind is too loud for concentration. I put some plugs in my ears and it dulls the noise somewhat. I decide to settle in and try to sleep. My sleeping bag is doubled, and is full of body warmers that will last through the night. My head goes down on what passes for a pillow. I am at peace with myself though, finally at peace.

I thought to myself, if I did not or could not wake up in the morning, all would be fine. I could easily freeze up here, and be found thousands of years later, frozen in time. I would be studied, along with my notes, recordings, and art samples and supplies that I have brought with me. I asked myself the question, what would humans a thousand years from now think of me? I do not know...

I am in shackles and what appears to be a courtroom. The judge stares down at me, and there is not a hint of mercy in his eyes. In fact as I look around there is no mercy in any of the eyes staring in my direction. They are all as black and devoid of life as could be possible. The man slams the gavel and the sound is deafening. Sentence has been passed...

Still in the never ending line of naked and shaved men and women. The rumble in the distance has become louder now. Am I getting closer to the end? I still cannot tell. The fires rain down even harder now and the whips fall more sharply and with greater purpose and accuracy...

Rough hands pull me from where I stood listening to the bastard judge pass sentence reading from a list of charges I do not recognize yelling guilty after each one. The rough hands pull me right out of the courtroom while the judge is still yelling after me. I am shoved up a set of wooded stairs. At the top, on a platform, a single rope hangs from a heavy beam ten feet above. I am to be hanged. I try to fight but there are too many. Up the stairs I go. The noose secured around my neck. I am offered a black hood and I shake my head in decline. One asks if I have any last words, but...

Jessica steps out of the shower and does not attempt to cover up. She walks over to me dripping wet and my armor is gone rusted away and tossed aside. I pull her roughly to me and kiss her deeply. She tears away the towel I was wearing and we fall into bed together.

We wake up the next morning and make our way to the pool side café for a bit of breakfast

“How did you sleep” she asked.

“Like a rock”, I said.

“You snore”, she said.

“After a night of sex like that... yes I guess I would... the hotel seems awfully quiet does it not”, I asked.

“Yes... it should not be this way”, she said.

A waiter eventually came around and in a feeble attempt at politeness took our order.

"What has happened... is there something wrong", I asked.

"You have not heard", he asked.

"No tell us", I said.

"A guest died last night... a massive coronary I am told", he said.

"That is unfortunate news... how very sad... was he old... did he have family staying here at the hotel with him, I asked.

"No he was not that old... maybe you recall him... you spilled a drink on him yesterday", he said.

I acted as somber as I could. I told the waiter I was sorry, and how unfortunate that was the only and last interaction I had with the man. The waiter nodded and smiled and left.

"Well... what now", I said.

"I will report this right now", Jessica said.

She took out the cell phone and typed in the text and sent it away. A few moments later it was confirmed and a package would be delivered to the front desk later this afternoon. We would then be free to continue on with our former lives, and that there was a load of work available. We accepted and would be informed of our next assignment.

"I guess we are stuck together for a little while", I said.

"After your performance last night I do not mind at all", she said, eyes brightening at the thought.

"What now", I asked.

"We wait for the package and then check out of here for good", she said.

"Where do you want to go", I asked.

"Where ever our next assignment takes us", she responds.

Our breakfast arrived, but we only picked at it even though the two of us were famished. It seemed the proper way to act given the circumstances. I finished the coffee though because it was excellent. Jessica did the same. We waited in the lobby with our baggage packed. We packed after one more session, but this time in the shower. The package arrived and I opened it. Our passports were there along with credit cards and a large amount of cash. There was a laptop, and upon powering up a message came across. Jessica and I listened to the instructions...

I was back at the bank of a fast flowing river. I have always loved the sound of rushing water. The black dog came out of the bush and sat beside me. I scratched his ears and I could swear I saw him smile. A picnic basket appeared beside me. I opened it up and found some fruits, cheeses and a bottle of wine with two glasses. Out of the water a beautiful long black haired Asian female emerged wearing a white gown. She emerged as dry as could be. The dog disappeared and she took his place beside me. I opened the bottle and poured some wine as she took out the rest of the contents of the basket and laid them out before us. She went to speak, but I did not understand her for she was talking in her native tongue...

I can smell apples and cinnamon. I am alone on a dingy city street, but all I can smell is apples and cinnamon. I follow the scent and it leads me to a bright red door. I open the door and enter the building. There are shelves and shelves of apple pies. I pick one up and it is still warm but there is no one around. Not a soul. I pick up the same pie once more and think, should I? I give in to the temptation and satisfy my salivating mouth...

At sunrise by the river pool I fill my pot and take it to my waiting fire. I am preparing to make tea. Tea is a hot indulgence on an otherwise cold trail. My horse Torao has found some greens to feed on. The wind is still present and is coaxing more of the blossoms to leave the branches that hold them. I set the water to boil and take out my Katana and go about the ritual of cleaning and sharpening. That is the way I start every day. The water is ready, and the tea is gratifying. I then set about inspecting and cleaning all of my armor, another ritual of the morning when time allowed.

Torao comes to me and nudges me. His belly is full and he is telling me it is time to get going. I pat his great neck and whisper in his ear that I know. I begin to break part of camp. I will just take the things I feel I need. The rest will remain here for this will be my camp when I return from the mountain. There is a small village, a secret hidden village in a valley protected by the very mountain I stand before. That is where the young man resides in which I have been charged to bring back safely. I know the route there for it is I along with a few great Samurai that had brought him there. I was very young then and not yet considered Samurai. I was accompanying my father learning the way, learning Bushido.

Samurai is a way of life that you were born to. Bushido, or the way of the warrior, was our only code. Samurai means to serve. Serve I have. Samurai is an honored lineage, you could not join.

"Come Torao... let us finish this journey and retire to this place which I believe is Holy", I said.

I led Torao away, giving him freedom from the burden of carrying me. I will ride when I am tired and save this brute of an animal's strength. It is a long dangerous journey back, and I know that before I return I will need Torao and my sword to serve yet again. Torao and I enter a cave which leads to a path to the village. The entrance to the cave is a mere crevice, enough for an animal, and then a man, but not both together. The exit of the cave is the same. Upon exiting we are greeted by an ever more wondrous sight then from the valley we just came. The blossoms here are incredible and they seemed to dance in front of us, heralding our presence. Soon we were met on the path by a very old lone armed man.

My eyes teamed with tears upon the sight of him. I had not meant to, and I told myself over and over not to, but the sight of my father after all of these years was too much to bear. The man challenged me.

"Identify yourself or find you impaled at the end of my blade", he said sternly, a tone I remember as a child.

"Father don't you recognize your own son... it is I Hisoka", I replied quickly.

"Hisoka... I have not heard that name in many years", he said.

"Father it is I", I said with conviction.

"If you are Hisoka what brings you here", he said.

"It is time to return... our enemies defeated... and have turned to run", I said.

"The wars are over", he asked a bit suspicious.

"Mostly... a few of those against us have turned Ronin... the others have committed Seppuku... It is time to return... our master is gravely ill and has summoned his son to take the mantle of Daimyo", I said.

"We will leave forthwith", he said.

"Father... you do not recognize me... do you", I said.

"I wish I could my son… but sight left me years ago… and with it any emotion I may have entertained at one time", he said.

My Father is a very rigid hard man. Bushido the only law he knows, and the only emotion had ever shown was in his theatrical teachings of the way of the warrior. I wiped the tears from my eyes.

"Come follow me… even blind I know this valley better than any… but once we leave the cave to the other side I will be as blind as can be", he said.

"I will be at your side Father as you were at mine during your instruction of me", I said.

"I would expect no less from any son of mine", he said.

And with that he was away down the trail. Soon we were in the village. Men were training and the women tending to their own duty. I could see my father's influence here, it was everywhere I looked. Groups of men were sparring with wooden Katana. Others were practicing Kyujutsu, the skill of the bow. I begged my father's leave to join them.

"It is good to hear and sense you Hisoka… my son", he said.

"It is good to see you… my Lord", I replied

We shook hands and embraced for the first time. Maybe it was the first time ever. I joined the group of men with Torao, my Yumi, and a few of my arrows. One man pointed to the circuit I was to ride hitting the proposed targets from horseback. Torao knew this game and needed no prodding from me. He was a war horse and always ready for battle, to him this was no different. We approached the first target on a turn, it was to my right. I swung my Yumi and pulled back the string. I dug my heels into Torao's belly and trusted he would carry me hands free. I let the first arrow fly and…

TUESDAY 15TH OF JUNE 2011

Pinpoints of light danced in front of my eyes. I could not ignore them. I blinked once, twice and on a third time my eyes stayed open. I propped myself up on my elbows and looked around. I was in my bed and had awakened. I looked at the time and it was early, too early to be awake. Twelve hours had gone by. I turned to my left side and stayed motionless thinking about the dreams that had passed. A lot has happened in my other lives and it excited me.

Now that I am awake there is a lot to do. Errands and messages to listen to and return reply if necessary. I rolled out of bed and dressed in some house clothes. I retrieved my mail and flipped on my computer to check my e- mail and such. I had quite a few messages on my answering machine, and more on the computer. I returned the ones from the hospital, and told them yes I could come back one day earlier. The hospital was trying very hard to accommodate a heavy surgery schedule. I listened to a message from Le twice, she was looking forward to our late dinner, and so was I. Dreams are great but they do not replace real human interaction. If one day they do, then I will be the first to sign up as their guinea pig. I tried to return her call, but did not catch her, only her answering service. I left a message confirming the time and place and the sentiment that I was looking forward to seeing her again.

I went up to my room after making a cup of tea, and I tidied up. I got rid of the syringes, dusted, vacuumed and changed the sheets, pillows, the works, just in case. I cleaned the whole house. It took me three hours and I was proud of the result.

I showered and ran some errands, picking up some necessary supplies for the house, and some dry cleaning that should have been picked up long ago. They knew me there and were used to my erratic schedule.

I then went to a nearby Starbucks. I ran into a few of my colleagues. They made the usual small talk inquiring where I had been and I told them just using my time to get my house in order. They nodded their understanding. My next vacation was in three months and I told them I would be going away for eight weeks, touring Europe. I wanted to see the places of some of my dreams. I ordered a latte, and I sat with them as invited. We talked shop for another thirty minutes. They got up to leave and I remained. I watched people come and go. I wondered about their dreams, I always did when I looked into their faces. I looked down at my watch, and it was just a few more hours until my "date". I had just enough time to shower and change.

I started to walk home for I rarely drove. A light rain had begun, and in this warmth it was refreshing. It was 7 pm when I walked into my house. That same feeling of utter loneliness began creeping up the back of my neck. There was so much missing from this life, and it was slowly slipping away. It did not have to be this way, and could still possibly change, but then what of my dreams.

Could I possibly get someone in my life that understands my need and desire to dream, and care about the people in those worlds that need my mind to live? I thought of all of this while I stripped off my clothes and stepped into the shower. I kept thinking of this for it does weigh heavy on my mind. I dried off and chose what I was going to wear. I tidied everything up, and left the entire house as neat as the best hotel room. I decided I would drive tonight, for it was warm out. I also drove in case we decided to go elsewhere.

I stepped into my garage and thought Mustang or Jeep. I chose the Mustang. It was more conducive to a date for not everyone likes to step into a Jeep. I drive a 2012 Mustang Shelby GT 500 Super Snake, red, powerful and rare. It was the opposite of my reclusiveness. The Jeep is a 2008 Wrangler Unlimited Rubicon, detonator yellow, again the color does not reflect my personality, not the one I show the real world anyway. The jeep is great in the winter and gets me to my cottage no matter the weather or condition of the road that leads to it. The appointed hour had arrived and I leave my lonely home.

I entered the bistro early as planned. I wanted to be there first. I chose a quiet table in the corner away from everybody. The waiter came around and asked if I would like to order, and I told him not just yet for I was expecting company. The waiter nodded and smiled and said he would return after my company arrived.

Ten minutes later Le walked in. I got up and met her a few steps from the door, and walked her over to the table. I pulled her chair out and motioned for her to sit, but she came up close to me instead and kissed me hard on the lips. Our tongues danced and teased around for a few seconds, and then she broke away and sat down. Le started the conversation and it was not labored but gracefully easy. Le spoke of her day and I let her talk. I smiled and asked questions and interjected a little about my own day. She wanted to know more. I then began a quite animated tale of some of the dreams I had had. She sat there with wide eyes as I told my tales. I only paused long enough to allow the waiter to take our order. Well, Le ordered yet again, it was something she really enjoyed to do.

"That was quite a story... I barely remember my dreams", she said.

"I have always been able to recall my dreams with the utmost clarity... ever since I could talk", I responded.

"Are your dreams always that complicated", she asked a bit skeptical.

"Every night", I said, in a serious tone

We continued our talk on the subject of dreams. We then talked of our childhood, our jobs, friends, places we would like to go to. I told her of my planned trip to Europe in the next few months and I learned this was something she always wanted to do. I would have invited her but it is too early for that, and I think she recognized the hesitation. Our food came and went, it must have been excellent, but I do not recall what it was but both of our plates went back empty. I was so engaged by our conversation that I do not remember any bite. I told her this and she laughed.

"No seriously... what did I just eat", I said, almost laughing.

"Come on... quit fooling around", she said.

"I am not joking... I really cannot remember what I just ate", I said.

"You were that much into your talk of dreams", she asked.

"No not just that ... but everything we just spoke of... I was that into telling all to you", I said.

She stared at me trying to gage my honesty. I stared back at her and she could tell I was not lying.

"You are serious", she said.

"Yes... now can you please tell me what I just ate", I said.

"Well we started the meal with antipasto... dried cheeses and meats olives peppers... you know antipasto", she said.

"OK... I know what antipasto is", I said.

"Then we had crab and broccoli stuffed Portobello mushrooms... then we had stuffed lobsters... and I just ordered dessert", she said.

"Well... was that so hard", I said.

"You seriously do not remember any of that... and you are an anesthesiologist", she said.

I think she was playing with me, but not quite sure how to take that jest.

"I remember now that you told me", I said.

"You were that absorbed in our conversation", she stated.

"I was that absorbed into you", I explained.

We stared at each other for quite some time. We held hands across the table, toying with each other's fingers. We both knew this date was not going to end up here. I guess my dreams will have to wait. Dessert came and this time I paid close attention to it. The dessert she chose was fresh strawberries and cubes of a light pound cake, accompanied by whipped cream, and small pots of melted milk and dark chocolate for dipping. We ate quickly, and both suggested going for a drive and then a walk.

"Could I follow you to your place and leave my car there before we go for that drive and walk", she asked.

"Yes of course", I said.

With that she followed me outside. Her car was parked right outside, mine further down the street. I pointed it out.

"That is your car... that is what we are going to drive in", she asked.

"Yes... what is wrong with it", I asked.

“Nothing… I was admiring it as I drove by… I just”, she began.

“You just what”, I asked.

“I just did not picture you with that car… I thought more along the lines of a BMW Audi or Mercedes”, she said.

“There is a lot you would not picture me in”, I said.

“Like what”, she asked.

“We will leave that talk for later… we will save it for our walk… now get in your car and keep up if you can”, I said.

With that I ran down the street, and sped away from the curb. She kept up turn for turn, and I smiled. We then pulled into the drive.

“Nice place” she said.

“Something else you were not expecting”, I asked.

“It is beautiful”, she said.

“The inside is better”, I said.

“I will see it later”, she said.

She said the last with a seductive smile on her lips. Le got into the car and I closed the door for her and we backed out and sped away.

“Where to”, I asked.

“Somewhere we can walk around water”, she said.

“You like the water”, I asked.

“Absolutely love it… so… what else will I be surprised about”, she asked.

"Quite a lot of things", I said.

"Like what... give me an example", she said.

"I like to play with swords", I said.

"Swords... what do you mean like knights and pirates and stuff", she asked.

"Something like that", I said.

"Do you actually fight with swords", she asked.

"I have been practicing the art of the sword since I was a little boy", I said.

"That is really kind of sexy... what other little secrets do you have", she asked.

"All in good time", I said.

We had arrived at our destination, a very quiet and private path by the water. I got out of the car and opened the door for her and she accepted my hand with a slight nod. We held hands as we walked and talked. She pressed for more information on me, and I artfully dodged most of the questions. We each spoke briefly on our childhoods, mostly humorous anecdotes and such. We walked down the path with the water to our right. It was a fast running stream about ten yards across with a gravel bottom. The water was as clear as glass during the day, and it fed a small lake further down. I planned to walk partway down the lake and then retrace our steps to the car.

We said less and less the further we went, because we were both listening to the water flow by. I thought of sleep and dreaming. I thought of Jessica, Freddie and Ava and my horse Torao. I thought of the bow and the sword. Le could tell I was deep in thought. She spoke.

"Where are you right now", she asked.

“What do you mean”, I responded.

“Where were you just now”, she asked.

“Every now and then I allow my mind to wander”, I said.

“And where did you wander to”, she asked.

“Well listening to the water I was just imagining myself in full Samurai Armor on the back of a great black horse charging into battle with my katana sword held high over my head”, I said.

“And you do this often”, she asked.

“Yes quite frequently... I love to imagine and day dream just like a little kid”, I said.

“I think I like that... the picture you just imprinted on my mind is extremely sexy”, she said.

Le then stopped walking and kissed me deeper than before, and I responded in kind.

“Let’s get back to the car and to your house... I would like to see these swords you frequently play with”, she said.

“You do not want to first continue to the lake and then turn around”, I asked.

“Only if you want to”, she said.

She then let her hand drift down below my waist, and rubbed my balls and inner thigh.

“Well do you want to”, she asked.

“Want to what”, I said.

“Walk to the lake”, she said.

"Well now that you mention it... it is getting late... and I would love for you to see my sword", I said.

"Let's go then", she said. Le then took off down the path running and yelling, "Race you to the car".

I chased after her and fifteen minutes later we were at my front door and I was fumbling for the keys, because Le was fumbling with my pants.

We entered the house and she was amazed when she looked around. I live in a very large house. Le let go of my belt buttons and zipper... I told her to feel free and have a look around.

"I only rent an apartment... with all of the moving and time spent away on my job... this is amazing and beautiful... the art... the furniture", she said.

"Come I will give you the tour", I said.

Le followed me to all of the rooms and we ended up in my den after a brief stop in the kitchen for some wine. She stood with her mouth open as I walked to my desk and sat down. She slowly walked down the center aisle taking it all in. She was staring intently at the suits of armor, and inspecting the display cases of the swords.

"Can you take one out for me", she asked.

"Of course... which one would you like to see", I asked.

"Could you give me a quick lesson", she asked.

"OK... then I will choose this one", I said.

I unlocked the case and took down a Paul Chen Oriole Katana. I told Le to follow me to my studio in the basement where I practice.

Once in the basement I told Le to put on one of the Kevlar suits I wore. She clumsily got into it and I improvised the straps to make it fit better. I set up some new bamboo poles and showed her how to strike. The bamboo sheared clean, not a splinter.

“It is very sharp as you can see”, I said.

“Yes I can see”, she said.

“Your turn... just as I showed you”, I said.

Le mimicked my stance and brought the Katana up over her head and swung downward at the angle I showed her. She cut the bamboo clean.

“See as I told you let the instrument do the work... you are just its guide... each sword has its own soul”, I said.

“Do you really believe that”, she asked.

“Yes... I do”, I said.

“Would you like to learn more or is that enough for the first time”, I asked.

“I think that is good for now... may we go back to your den... there is so much more I would like to look at”, she said.

“Yes by all means... it is by far my favorite room”, I said.

In the den I took the Paul Chen and placed it in a carrying case, and then put it aside. Le kept marveling at the collection. She asked questions now and again, she asked to see various items up close. I answered and obliged all of her inquiries and requests. After a few long moments of silence she stood in the middle of the room and asked me to come to her. I came around the desk and she met me halfway.

We kissed and she began unbuttoning my shirt, undoing my belt. Le then took off her own shirt and stood in pants and bra. We embraced again and I undid the bra and took the straps off of her shoulder and let it fall to the floor. I went to take her to the bedroom but she stopped me.

"I want to fuck in here", she said.

"Alright", I answered.

We continued removing each other's clothes, and ended up writhing on the floor. When we had finished we walked to the bedroom and did it all over again. We then both slept and I...

I was riding Torao out of the valley I wished to be my home. I was leading a long procession of armed men through the onslaught of blossoms driven by the winds. By my guess it would be ten days before we are deep into my Daimyo's lands and the protection they afforded. I had spoken briefly with my new Lord and realized he was not his father. That was a great disappointment. My own father rode at my side. We rode, talked and camped. Two days later we were attacked by a band of bandits. It was a brief battle for they were no match for the group of Samurai I lead.

Their first attempt was very poorly thought out and executed. Their volley of arrows kept falling short or completely missing their marks, and we laughed at them. This made them angry and foolish for by the time they realized we were Samurai it was too late to turn back their futile charge. These men must have been farmers with no training who had probably stolen their arms from the battlefields of the fallen. We cut down and ended their aggression in a matter of minutes. There was no honor in their deaths or for us in killing them, but they gave us no choice. My father may have gone blind, but he was still lightning fast with his Katana, and his instincts sharp. He accounted for three of their deaths, this man could see just fine, an amazing example of the other senses compensating for what is not there.

The men talked of it later. I told them there would be more attacks and not to take any of them lightly for there were many Samurai of our enemy that refused to commit Seppuku, and would love revenge and redemption and attempt to take back their honor. I knew this to be impossible for their honor waited them at the end of their own Wakisahashi or Tanto, and on the battlefields that we had driven them from.

We left the bodies and rode on. There really was no honour to be found in this. All of our swords had found blood, and all had been since wiped clean. My father was the first to speak.

"How is it that peasants and farmers attack", he asked.

"I do not know what drives men to these decisions", I replied honestly.

"I have been in a protected valley for too long... is that the way of things now", he asked in a bitter tone.

"It has been this way for a long time now... everyone has a sword or a knife", I replied...

There was a tap and a slight pulling nudge on my shoulder. Le whispered into my ear.

"I have had a good nap... and I can feel you are ready for more", she said.

Her hand was fondling the hardness below my waist. This reminded me why I lived alone. My dreams are too important to me. It was the dream that made me hard not Le, not this time, but I could not tell her that. Could I? No. I turned and kissed her deeply and we fucked again.

WEDNESDAY 16TH OF JUNE 2011

We did not get back to sleep but laid there together, her head across my chest as I stroked her long hair, and watched the sun come up. I took a quick shower, dressed and told Le I would make some coffee. I asked if she was hungry and she replied an emphatic "yes". I told her I would whip up some breakfast then, and down the stairs I went. As I was making coffee I heard Le enter my bathroom and turn on the shower.

Thirty minutes later with breakfast on the table, Le came down the stairs and entered the kitchen. She was wearing an old shirt of mine and a pair of my sweat pants.

"I hope you do not mind the clothes", she said.

"No not at all", I said.

"What did you make", she asked.

"I hope you like a good omelet", I asked.

"That depends on what kind", she said.

"How about... mushrooms... roasted peppers... onions... and parmesan reggiano cheese", I asked.

"I have never tried that combination... but it sounds wonderful", she said.

"Sit down and take a bite and then tell me how I did", I said.

Le took several bites. In fact she said little between bites. After she was finished she could not say enough about how good it was.

"Is life around here like this all of the time", she asked.

"What do you mean", I replied.

"The sex... the breakfast... this wonderful coffee", she said.

"Only on my days off", I said.

"I look forward to more days off then", she said, smiling.

After breakfast we went for a walk to a nearby park and wooded area. We sat on a bench and watched the world go by. Kids were playing, people were out with their dogs, and it was noisy, chaotic, and calming all at the same time.

"Have you ever thought of retirement", Le asked.

"Yes actually I have given it quite a bit of thought", I said.

"Me too", she said.

"Strange of you to ask", I said.

"I know but it is something I have given a great deal of time thinking about and wanted your opinion", she said.

"My opinion", I asked.

"Yes... you are a professional and have your act together... I have seen your house... your cars... the way you fuck and make breakfast", she said.

"What is it you want my opinion on", I asked.

"Retirement... the whole concept... when is a good time to go... how much money is enough... what to do with the time after... all of it", she said.

"Well... everything builds on one another", I said.

"What do you mean", she asked.

"I am going to retire when I walk into work and say this is my last day… I do not want to do this anymore… money is tricky… I do not know what will happen in the future… and what to do with the time depends on the money… you can volunteer… take up hobbies…. travel", I said.

"Stage one and two is taken care of… all I need to figure is stage three", she said.

"Go on", I said.

"I walked into work the other day and I had that very thought… I do not want this anymore… money I have… my problem is dealing with the time", she said.

"You are going to retire", I said, sort of as a half-question half-statement.

"Yes… I am… I know this is kind of weird and awkward… but will you come with me", she said.

"You are asking me to retire with you", I said.

"Yes… I am", she said, hesitantly.

"After one night this is kind of sudden", I said.

"One night… three dates… three whole dates… come on we are not complete strangers…all I ask is for you to think about it… take a chance with me… walk into work tomorrow and think about it", she said.

I had a great night, and this thing with Le feels awfully comfortable, except of course when she woke me up in the middle of a dream. I do not know. I do not know what to think. I sat there staring at the children, and all the people. The silence was tense. She woke me in the middle of a dream, but I wasn't pissed. I really wasn't. All my life I got pissed, loud noises, a loud car going by, horns honking, my parents telling me it was time, alarm clocks, but not this time.

"Yes Le... I will think about it... to tell you the truth retirement had been a large weight on my mind for quite some time... I will think about it... in fact that is why I have taken two months off as a leave in three months... to test the notion of retirement", I said.

"Really", Le asked.

"Truly", I said.

"What are your plans", Le asked.

"To travel around Europe... would you like to join me", I asked.

"Yes... I guess I could hang in at work for three more months", she said.

"That gives us three months to get to know each other", I said.

"What... three dates and one night is not enough for you", Le said laughing.

We decided to go for a drive, and maybe do some shopping. Le promised no more heavy conversations or questions, unless one popped into her head. I vowed to tell Le never to wake me again, and to tell her how important my dreams were to me. Not even for sex, emergencies only. Once my eyes were closed a glass door enveloped me with the warning in bright red letters across it, "Break Glass In Case Of Emergency". I hoped she would understand. That conversation would be interesting I'm sure.

We talked like we had known each other for years and years. The conversation was absolutely effortless. We drove for hours making the occasional stop, grabbing some food and other little things. It was a good day.

I drove Le back to my house and her waiting car. She was going to go home and grab a few things and then come back to spend the night. Tomorrow if the weather held we planned a hike and a picnic.

She drove away and I went inside and I realized I was definitely missing something in my life. I do not know if this was it, because it was too early to tell. I cleaned up the kitchen from breakfast this morning and went up and took a shower. I then went to my den, sat at my desk and waited for her return. I had been alone for so long, and this went against all of my original plans, but I was really looking forward to her return. The phone rang and it was the Hospital asking me to come in tomorrow. I consented and asked for the days schedule to be sent to me. I went to the computer and printed it out and left it on my desk to look over later. Leaning back in my chair with my feet up on the desk, I must have fallen asleep because...

I was back in the Himalayas trying to shield myself from the cold fierce wind. The monastery was now in sight, or at least the lights were. We would camp one last time before we arrived. It was a hard hike up and I thought these monks, these men and women, must be tough bastards to do this regularly.

We made camp and I scurried into my tent and enjoyed the warmth it afforded. Well, not really warmth but at least shelter against the wind. I started my dinner, pasta and meatballs, well what passed for meat balls in a mess of freeze dried noodles and some ketchup like sauce in a bag.

I felt very much alone. There was not much conversation with the Sherpa. They seemed to only speak when it was necessary. During camp though I could hear their voices carried by the wind, excited tones, laughing. I hope not at me for making this crazy pilgrimage.

I came here for two things, first to find peace. That is, if that was truly possible. Second I wanted to attempt to restore ancient works of art. This monastery has magnificent murals that needed a great deal of care and attention, if they are to be saved and preserved...

DING! DING! DING!

I woke with a start. The doorbell startled me awake. Le was here already.

DING! DING! DING!

I gathered my wits and went down the stairs. I opened the door and Le greeted me with a deep long kiss. She was carrying a small travel bag, a bottle of wine and a grocery bag.

"You look tired", she said.

"Yes a little... I fell asleep in the den", I replied.

"If you need to rest on your last night off I understand", she said.

"No... no not at all... the short nap did me good I just need a few minutes to adjust", I said.

"Well... go and rest some more... you prepared breakfast I will make dinner... I brought something special", she said.

"Let me help", I offered.

"No... I do not want it... now go to your sanctuary... I will fetch you when it is done", she said.

"Let me sit and watch you for awhile... we can talk while I adjust", I said.

"OK... but only for a little while... what is on your mind", Le asked.

"Well... I have never had to do this before... I mean I have never discussed this with anyone before", I said.

"Discussed what", Le said.

"Something you should know about me before we go any further", I said.

"Like you were married before and have like six kids", she said in a huff, hands on her hips ready for a fight.

"No... nothing like that... more about an obsession of mine", I said.

"What other than the swords", she said.

"Yes... a much deeper obsession than the swords", I said.

"Go on... but take your time... we do not have to do this now", she said.

"Yes I do", I said.

Le was taking things out of her bag. I could not wait to see what she was going to turn out. I grabbed the bottle of wine.

"May I", I asked.

"Be my guest", She said.

I opened the bottle and poured two glasses. The wine was a Merlot from Rosemount estates in Australia, and one of my favorites.

"This might be a long tale", I said.

"We have a lot of time... almost two hours of prep and cooking time", She said.

"Alright then... I will start", I said.

I then went into a long single dialogue and explained all I could. I talked for an hour straight and hardly stopped for breath. Le said nothing, asked no questions, and made no smart remarks. She prepared a dinner that most would die for, and did not miss a beat all the while. She listened to every word, every syllable. I told her all, the dreams, and the lives intertwined into them. I told her how it started as a child, and how it has enriched my life. I told her everything. When I was finished I retired to the den and allowed her to finish preparing the feast and absorb all I have said. It was the first honest conversation of this type I have ever had.

I sat at my desk and stared at all that I have collected here. All the time and money spent. I thought of all I told Le. I replayed it all in my mind and concentrated on all the expressions that I could recall. It did not seem to faze her at all. Maybe my love of dreams was not so “out there” like I thought.

It was not long before Le knocked on the door. She smiled, I smiled. She announced that dinner was ready, and I got up and followed her down to the dining room. The least used room in the house. Well in fact it had never been used. Cleaned religiously but never used.

Le made seasoned double fried chicken, sugared carrots, steamed asparagus, fresh cut French fries and an apple crumb for dessert. We ate everything, killed the bottle of wine and retired to the living room. We flipped on the television, and could find nothing to watch. We decided to go to the den. Le wanted more history lessons and the stories behind what I had collected. That was the dominated dinner conversation. Le did not mention any of what I told her during dinner prep, and that worried me. The questions would come soon. I knew that, it was now a matter of when and where.

Le came in and inspected the armor thoroughly. She asked a few questions and I answered them all. Le then asked to see the swords one at a time. After the thirtieth the questions came flowing out.

"These dreams are they more important than what you have here", she asked.

"Do you mean more important than this room... this house... my career... future plans... us... what", I asked.

"More important than this room... that is a good place to start", she asked.

"This room is a reflection of who I am and the dreams that have shaped that... each of these swords and the armor is a reflection of me... precise.... symmetrical...they are all an end result of the pursuit of perfection over a lifetime... but they are physical possessions and in the grand scheme of things that is all they are physical possessions", I replied quite honestly.

"More important than this house... your cars... your career... what you have built here", she asked.

"Again this house is a physical possession... same as the cars... they can all be replaced... my career on the other hand is a manifestation of my dreams... an outlet... putting people to sleep to perhaps dream as perhaps I... seemed the natural choice", I said.

"How about us", she asked.

"Well... lately when I have come home or woke in the morning I feel like I was missing something... I never felt alone before... but lately I have felt very lonely... my dreams always compensated for that made up for my lack of friends and companions relationships... but I realize now that they cannot make up for physical touch or a real conversation... but I do not want to give them up and let those characters that I have cultivated... cried with... bled with... and loved... I know they are dreams but they are a great escape for me allowing me to take the chances I would never have the opportunity to take... to be a spy... a Samurai... a great artist... an explorer... a soldier... an assassin... they make me a better person", I said.

"I see", she replied.

Le then continued with the swords until she had held them all. She wanted to know about their history, and I told her what I knew.

"Join me in the shower", she asked.

"Are you OK with everything", I asked.

"Absolutely", she said.

She then came around the desk and straddled my lap, and kissed me. Le then got up and took my hand and led me to the bathroom. We undressed each other and played in the water. After Le joined me in bed and we had great sex, better than the first time.

"Sweet dreams", she said.

We then both drifted off to sleep, my arm around her and her head resting against my chest...

Torao senses danger close by. I can tell as he shakes his head in defiance to my commands prodding him forward. He lowers his front quarters telling me to stop the procession and tread more carefully. I order the column to halt. My Father is at my side and he comments that there is something strange in the air up ahead. He can detect the odor of men carried by the wind. Then a dust cloud appears a sure sign of men riding hard and fast. I order the men to fan out in a double line. I wanted to make it seem like we were a larger force. I doubt that would matter, for the cloud that approaches is immense.

"Maybe we should attempt to avoid what is approaching", I said.

"Do you think they have seen us", my father asked.

"No... no yet... that are not close enough for that", I replied.

I then order the men to split into four groups. First a protection detail for our Lord, which was to retrace our steps and avoid confrontation at any cost. Second a group to remain here with me and judge intent of what approaches. The third and forth were to deploy ahead on our flanks to assist when needed. My father went with the protection detail for that was his original charge from his Lord. I stood my ground, Torao and I. We would wait and see what fate brought us on the wind, and atop horseback...

I am approaching the gates of the monastery. What an arduous journey this has been. I look in awe at the buildings. What a feat of architecture and persistence to build this on the side of a mountain at this elevation. These Tibetans are an extremely peaceful people. It is a good thing for the world. If they were to be aggressive and warlike, like their neighbors, they could have conquered the world.

It is their peace and reverence for all forms of life that has brought me here. This land is filled with the kind of peace that I have sought my whole life and tried to portray in my paintings, and in those I have come here to restore. As I pass through the gates in between two rows of bowing monks my memories of the past are erased, they disappear, banished never to resurface...

I cannot move it is as if I am in some sort of box. Walls are pressing tight against my shoulders, at my feet, and the top of my head. I can feel the ceiling with the tip of my nose, the floor with the back of my head, my elbows, and calves and against my ass. Yet everything is clear I can see everything around me. I think I am being suspended, but I cannot see any wires, or how this could be possible. I try to scream...

The sun is shining bright. I am lounging on a towel on a beach. It looks to be a vast ocean in my magnificent view. In my left hand a very cold Stella Artois. I am all alone. At least I think I am...

I am now in a cave and I have disturbed a horde of bats, and they are angry, flying into me, biting and scratching at every possible chance. I try to cover my face and as much of my body as is possible. I am curled up in a little ball on the floor of this cave. The smell is putrid...

I am caught in a huge spider's web. I cannot move. The material used binds me tight and the more I struggle the worse it gets. I can see the hairy ugly bastard approaching, and imagine myself being sucked dry...

Ava is lying beside me, and I have this strange guilty feeling that I cannot sense the source of. I start my new job in the morning. Maybe that is a part of it. I do not know. The night classes I am taking will eventually get me a college degree. It is part of a government initiative to reintegrate soldiers who have returned home from war. I guess being in that room with others who had survived what Freddie and I have, sharing memories, stories and what not. Bringing back to life if even only temporarily in my mind, and on the tip of my tongue, those that I watched die, maybe that is a source of my guilt.

Ava and I spend as much time together as possible. We do things that I thought the war had stolen from me. Things like picnics, parties, carnivals, theater, to name a few.

Freddie is happier at his new job. He is assisting in a kitchen of a small restaurant. Freddie is also taking classes, but he has enrolled in culinary school and hopes to be one day referred to as chef. Both he and I owe a lot to Ava, all the work she has put into rehabilitating us miscreants of the street.

I do not know if I love her. I am not sure if I am capable of that emotion yet. I turned it off for so many years I do not know if I will ever be capable. Ava and I have discussed this and she understands. What we have is comfortable, sexual, and everything I need right now.

I do like to watch her sleep though, especially after sex. Her eyelids flutter and her face contorts as she dreams. She farts in her sleep, and at times snores uncontrollably. I have never mentioned the farts to her, but have complained about the snoring. She laughs it off and I wonder how she would react to the other. I will save that for a future conversation. Maybe when we are old and grey, holding our grandchildren in our arms. That way she will not hit me.

I sneak out of bed, shave and take a shower. We are at her place. I do spend quite a bit of time here. Freddie needs his space. There are a couple of women he is screwing on the side, nothing serious. Freddie could never be serious like that.

I left Ava a note. I know she wanted to see me off on my first day, but she was snoring and farting, and did not have the heart to disturb that...

I am back fishing, this time on a quiet pond. I am sitting on a granite rock face, enjoying the quiet solitude and the sunshine. The black dog is with me, and it is good to see him. Fish are jumping all over the place, but I still cannot catch one...

BEEP... BEEP... BEEP... BEEP... BEEP... BEEP... BEEP... BEEP... BEEP...

THURSDAY 17TH OF JUNE 2011

I look over at the clock, and it is time to get up for work. Le awakes with me, and this is nice. I swing out of bed and head for the kitchen to start a pot of coffee. Le comes down and says she will make breakfast, while I shower and get ready to return to work. I stop by the den first and look at my schedule for the day. Three by-pass surgeries await my touch. I also have three consults on two future procedures. It was to be a very busy day over all.

Le had a cup of coffee waiting for me on my desk, after I stepped out of the shower. I sat down and took a few sips, and thought about retirement and my upcoming travels. I thought about my dreams and the stories unfolding in them. I swing my chair around and stare out the big window behind me...

I am sitting in a meadow and my big black dog is with me. He places his head across my lap, and I scratch his nose, his ears. This is peaceful...

"Paging Doctor Logan... dam... you know I do not know your last name", Le said from the door. I am pulled to reality, by her voice.

"Come to think of it... I do not recall ever telling you", I said in return.

"Well... excuse your ignorance", she said.

"I am Logan Charles", I replied.

"Pleased to meet you Mr. Charles", she said. We both laughed.

"I cannot believe we left that out of our conversations... of retirement and spending a couple of months in Europe", Le said.

"I guess it did not matter enough", I said.

"Well Mr. Charles... breakfast is served and is getting cold", Le said.

"Then let's have at it Miss Shen... it is going to be a busy day", I said.

Shortly after breakfast I am in my Jeep going to work. I have plenty of time. I left Le at the house, gave her a key and the code to the alarm, and instructions on how to lock up. It is weird thinking about someone alone in my house. I am not worried, but it is not something I have ever done before.

In the doors I go. Two lefts and a right, up the elevator to the third floor, one more left and into my office. Turn on the lights, the computer. Open the files on the day's events. Turn on the recorder and my monologue starts setting up the background for the cases. This part is all very boring, mechanical, and necessary. A quick look at my watch, it is time to go to work.

It is time for scrubbing and donning gowns sterile for surgery. In the room all checks, and the patient is wheeled in. A few words of assurance and the injections start. The patient is not awake for long, all vitals check out. I wonder if she is dreaming.

She looked to be athletic at one time, so maybe she is running with wild horses, or diving in the deep ocean. Maybe she is reliving her wedding or her honey moon, or other special day in her life. Possibly she is a little girl again at a birthday party with lots of balloons. Maybe singing or dancing on a grand stage with thousands of eyes upon her. Maybe she has experienced none of these, or maybe all. I do not know.

This routine is performed two other times today. The dreams I think they are having change though. One man I thought would be on horseback riding the frontier, or maybe looking for gold. The other one, possibly a pompous chef in a prestigious restaurant, yes that is it. He is being fawned over by strangers who would not know good food, just that the price was so outrageous therefore it must be good.

I think more about what Le said though, and less about the dreams. She wanted me to think about retirement. Today was a good day, no complications, very little stress. My consults went well and all involved are on the same page. It is strange but for the first time I felt like walking away. How am I going to feel on a bad day? I wonder what Le is doing. Is she still in the house? Should I call her? No, she will think I do not trust her. I sit at me desk in my office and continue the monologue finishing the details on the day. My assistant will transfer the notes into written reports.

I then did something completely out of character. I suddenly packed all of my personal things. I did not keep many here, and recorded my resignation. I took the device and my things and dropped the recorder on my assistants desk and left. I never looked back, and I smiled all the way to my Jeep.

I decided not to tell Le what I just did. I wanted to see what the next few months would bring. I felt elated, I felt free and that I had done the right thing. This is the right thing.

I went to the park and took a long walk. I was in no real hurry to get home. I doubted Le would still be there. I have yet to call her, or receive a call from her for that matter. I thought she may have left a text or something. I watched people walk by, and I walked by them. It became darker sooner than I expected, but then I looked at my watch it was nearing 9 pm. Where did the time go today? I headed back to the car, the park was thinning out, and everyone was leaving.

I pulled into the drive, and Le's car was gone. I shut off the alarm and walked in. Everything is how I left it. I went to the kitchen and poured myself a glass of wine, cut up some cheeses, grabbed some olives and such and took it all to my den. I checked the phone and there were no messages. Odd I thought. I had thought there would be at least one from my assistant. Maybe she did not get far enough into the transcribing of my notes to get the message. What a surprise for her in the morning.

I sat there and sipped my wine, and had a couple bites of cheese. I picked up my cell phone and thought of calling or texting Le but thought better of it. There were no notes, I had thought for a moment I might find at least one. I sat there and stared at my swords, and the other things I had collected here. I need a shower.

I finished the wine, the cheese and the olives. I went to the bedroom and on the pillow there was a note. It read simply, "Sweet dreams... see you in the morning... Le". Morning I thought. How early would she be? I laughed to myself, she wanted me to sleep and dream.

I went to the shower, and found yet another note. "I will let myself in and start your breakfast... Le". Then I thought should I take the injection tonight? There is no telling how long I may sleep, and I did not tell her that part. She may think I am a crazy junkie, and run away. I think I would. No, no heavy drugs tonight, just a simple pill.

I showered the day away. Hospitals are such dirty places. I put on some sleep shorts and went back to the kitchen for another glass of wine. I thought of making something to eat, but found I was not really hungry for anything. I went back to the den. I always end up there, always. I turned on my computer and television. With the computer I checked my mail and secured the house. I checked out the news on the television, and there was absolutely nothing worthwhile. Some gorilla video on YouTube was garnering a lot of attention. It is strange what people think is amusing and important enough for a news spot. I give up, society really is shit. Absolutely shit.

I leaned back in my chair and tried to find a movie, and there was nothing. I turned everything off and sat in silence. Silence is good.

An hour went by and I was ready to dream. I went to bed, took a pill and waited...

My room is sparse, but at least it is warm and I am alone. I have been served a meal of tsampa, (roasted barley flour), thukpa (a noodle dish), and soja (butter tea). My bowl of thukpa has what I would guess to be mutton. It is better than it sounds, and a welcome change to the freeze dried meals I had on the trip here. It is peaceful here. In the morning I have been told I will be taken on a tour of the pieces I am to restore or oversee the restoration of. I am told I will have some help from a few very talented monks and art techniques passed down to them by ones before.

I take time after the meal to unpack, and make this room as close to home as possible. The Sherpa's have brought all of my gear that they had been packing. I was smart enough to bring an air mattress with me, and a small air pump. The cot in the corner with the ropes would never do. I have my toiletries and cook supplies. I set up a kitchen and bath as best as I could. Now I have no room for much else, just a small seating area in which to eat. My art and restoration supplies will be stored elsewhere, and will be at my hand when called for...

I can smell cinnamon. The smell is strong enough to wake me up. I am confused and disoriented. I do not know where I am. I do not recognize anything in this room. The smell of cinnamon is so strong. I get up and look out the small window. I look out onto a quiet street, by the look of the cars it is the mid to late seventies. I back away from the window and leave the room. There are three doors in the hall. One opens to another bedroom, one an office area and one a bathroom. I enter the bathroom and look in the mirror. I am Bobby, but I do not recognize this place. Where is Freddie, where is Ava? I find a stairway and go down. The stairs lead to a foyer to what I would guess is the front entrance of the building. The smell of cinnamon in the air is ever stronger now, and I follow the scent. I pass a living area, a dining area, and enter a kitchen. Ava looks up from the paper she is reading and says, "Well good morning".

"Good morning", I reply back. Now I am really confused and Ava senses it.

"What is it Sean... you have had the same confused look on your face each morning since we moved in here after the wedding", she said.

Jesus, I think to myself. Wedding, dam, am I married. How and when did this happen. Then it all comes back to me. Freddie was an absolute ass, but everyone loved him. Yes, I am married. I have a great new job after graduating from the GI program. I remember it all now.

"Sorry... just still sleepy... the cinnamon woke me up...Where is Freddie", I asked.

"I am sure he will smell the baking and will be here very soon... are we still on for the beach", she asked.

"You bet", I said, still a bit confused but going with the flow.

I guess we were going to the beach, news to me, but I will keep that to myself. My memory has been weird lately, disconnected, jumbled and confusing.

"After everything cools and Freddie and Jane get here... we are off", she said.

"Sounds good... I will grab a quick shower... Ok", I said.

"Knock yourself out... we have plenty of time", she said.

Who the hell is Jane I thought going back up the stairs. What is wrong with me? Maybe I should see a doctor or something. My head is just not right. The water feels good, and parts of my memory returns. Jane, a friend of Ava's cousin. Freddie met her at the wedding...

A cold dampness envelopes as the sky darkens around me. I am in a kayak, and am struggling to make land. Waves splash over me, and I can barley breath. The wind is stronger than I am. I can hear a dog barking and I try and paddle in the direction of the sound. The barking gets stronger and stronger.

I see it, land. I make it, and fall out onto wet sand. I can feel something dragging me the rest of the way to safety. It is my dog, the big black beautiful dog. He drags me to some steps. I get up and realize they lead to a small cabin. I crawl inside, and he follows. There is a fire on, and it is warm. I sit by the fire sipping on some hot tea, and dry off...

I hit Torao in the rear quarters, and he knows it is time to leave the fighting. He will return to me when I call and it is safe. My katana is bright red with the blood of those who have stood in defiance before me. The band of Ronin Samurai that attacked us is strong and well led. The tide of the battle is in their favor, and numbers are on their side. I am thinking that these are not Ronin after all. This attack is too well coordinated and seems to have been planned. I am thinking that the battles that we won for our Daimyo may have been staged to flush out his son, and it was not safe enough for his return as thought. I gave orders to get him back to the mountain valley where the pass could be forever protected. We were to stand here and make sure none of our enemies passed.

My father joined the fighting from the rearguard, as did a few others. I looked to my left and saw he fought like a tiger. I saw a blind warrior that could see through the blade of his sword. It was a sight I will not ever forget. That is the way he died, and I could not help him. We rallied and fought around his body, for I will not have them take anything from him, his sword or his armor. We rallied and fought like possessed demons.

As I knelt, bleeding from a number of small wounds, with the final three of our band. We paid homage to those who fought here and won this day for us. We gathered swords and armor to be passed on to their families, if we were ever to return. I took my father's body back to the safety of the hidden mountain valley, and showed him where I wished to make my final home. I think he will like his final resting place with the blossoms swirling around. I know he will...

I am on a tropical island, lazing around on a beach lounger. I look around and the resort is busy, Jessica is beside me smiling.

“Another successful job done”, she said.

“Fucking right... the money is great”, I said.

“Is that all that is great”, she smiled.

“No... this is great”, I said.

“What’s next”, she asked.

“I believe Argentina”, I said.

“Yes... that is right... the ring”, she said.

Our next assignment was to steal a family ring, an heirloom. The possessor controls the wealth and family secrets. The one who has it now has no idea what it really is. Twenty-five million to whoever can claim it. Jessica and I would keep forty percent. A fairly decent “finder’s fee”...

FRIDAY 18TH OF JUNE 2011

I wake up because someone is watching me. Le is sitting in the chair in the corner by the window in the room. She is looking out in the gardens.

“Good morning”, I said.

“Good morning... I did not think you were ever getting up”, she replied.

Le comes over to me and kisses me on the forehead. I can’t help it but I look down her shirt and all I see is boob. What a morning.

"Are you hungry", she asked.

"No... not yet... but after I shower we will see", I said.

With that I swung my feet over the edge of the bed and stood, arching and cracking my back, and knees.

"That's attractive", she said. I laughed.

"I am going to take a shower", I said.

"Sleep well", she asked.

"Yes... very", I replied.

"Good... breakfast will be served outside... come out when you are ready", she said.

We had breakfast and I pretended to go to work. I want to take the next couple of days and think this through. Conversation was good, and what was really a good sign, there was no sex. I believe then there is more to this than just that. I had a lot to think about.

I grabbed a change of clothes and out the door I went. I am now completely comfortable with having Le in the house. I decided to take the jeep, top down.

My cottage was about a five hour drive. I decided to go. I would tell Le that I was called away for a consultation, and would be away for a few days.

I stopped at the hospital first, and was met by shouting, surprise, and all sorts of different reactions. The news of my resignation has spread far and fast. Hands were shook. Recommendations for a replacement were made. I signed some papers, called Le and left. Cottage bound.

Top down, the warmth of the sun, music, light traffic all the way. Time flew and before I knew it, I was there.

I went through the routine of turning on the electrical, and the water. The cottage is completely green and off the grid. The place is completely solar powered, and I pull the water from the lake. It is filtered through a twelve stage process, and comes from an underground spring that feeds the lake. The septic is vacuumed to a natural lime bed deep in an underground cave. (What I can only describe as a cave) I then feed natural chemicals down the system to the bed that helps to further break it down, and destroys any bacteria that may form. It is all encased in granite. At least that is what the scans show. It is my piece of heaven on earth. I own it all, 3892 acres and two entire lakes, a pond and a great portion of a river system.

With all of that done, I got out my kayak, some gear and paddled to the other side of the lake. I set up a camp on the granite outcropping, made some coffee and stayed there until just before sundown. While there I saw two bears, and a moose. The bears crossed my beach by the cottage, something I would have to keep my eye on, for I did not recognize them. The moose stood in the shallow reeds to the east, feeding on the aquatic plants there. The loons were out and they called to me all afternoon. They were happy to see me I guess. I paddled back across, wary of the possibility of bears. No incident though, they are here often, but I do not feed them or leave anything out that might interest them. They have left me alone thus far, aware but ignoring my presence. I understand that they were here before me. I had purchased their backyard. This was their land, and I was just a tenant.

My dreams should be good tonight. I will call Le later, before I set down to bed.

I prepared a quick meal, nothing special, and ate in front of the fire I had built. I am really tired. The air here does that to you. I decided to sleep outside on the upper deck off my bedroom. The stars are amazing here, mesmerizing, just like the planetarium. Next thing I remember...

I am in the bush, and there is a bear very close. I can smell the musty pungent odor the animals exude. I do not know which way to turn. I can hear it crashing through the bush towards me. I do not want to run. I lie face down in the earth and do not move. It is closer now, I can hear the grunts, and the sound as it sniffs the air. Then I know it found me. It paws at me a little bit, and nudges me with its nose. It sniffs around my head and saliva drops down and runs along my cheek. Its hot breath, death smelling breath, makes me want to vomit. I want to get up, run, but I stay frozen. It pushes down on me, and the air leaves my lungs, its claws dig in and I scream...

I am back on my favorite rock overlooking my lake. My dog is with me. I call him mine, because he must be. He visits these little moments all the time. He is barking furiously, and the bush behind us erupts...

I am now in a book store, sitting behind a counter. There is a stack of books in front of me, and a line of people waiting...

I am paddling a canoe against a strong current, and I am losing this battle. White water spraying all around me...

I am sitting beside Jessica, and we are in a plane. If I remember correctly, for my memory recall has been a little fuzzy lately, we are bound for Argentina, and our latest assignment.

Jessica has fallen asleep, and I order another drink, scotch, Glen Fiddich 21 years. The stewardess is flirting shamelessly with me, and I am having fun with it.

We land without incident, and I wake Jessica up. How she could sleep through the entire trip is beyond me. I cannot sleep if there are strangers present. I grab my pack, and we exit the plane, clear customs, grab the luggage, taxi to our hotel, and all that crap.

"When do you want to get started", Jessica asks.

"We will play tourist for a couple of days... then we will take a serious look around", I said in reply.

"What do you want to do", she asked.

"I think I will take a shower... sleep for a couple of hours... then spend the rest of the evening by the pool... maybe some dinner", I said.

"Sleep... but I am not tired", she said.

"I am... I did not sleep on the plane... I told you to stay awake", I said.

"I will join you in the shower... and then get a head start by the pool while you sleep... Ok", she said.

"Sounds good to me", I said.

I strip down and enter the bath area. The shower is huge, a real large porno shower. I start the water and keep it just warm, for it is humid here. I soap up and Jessica joins me. She stands behind me, and I can feel her hard nipples on my back as she reaches between my legs and rubs at my balls. I turn around and kiss her hard. We lather each other up and fuck right where we stand. After I went to the bed and lied down, it was not long before I was fast asleep.

The next thing I remember is waking up to Jessica breathing life into my cock with her mouth. Now that is an alarm clock. As soon as I am awake and ready she stops.

"Time to go Love", she said.

"What the hell", I said, standing up, hard as a rock.

"It is time to lay down some ground work", she said.

"Fuck... come on... ten... fifteen minutes", I said.

"Nope... now get dressed and let's go", she said.

On that note we go down to the pool area and Jessica says she has found an inviting bistro now far from here. I order a scotch, and notice the humidity dissipating slightly, Jessica orders champagne with strawberries.

We do the tourist thing, pretend to study maps and an assortment of brochures outlining some of the more interesting activities in the area. Jessica had picked some up at the airport, some at the hotel, and some in a shop a little bit from here. It is the shop keeper that recommended the bistro that everyone must try when they come here. This is my first trip to South America and Jessica's third. She has been to Brazil and Venezuela on other occasions.

After the drinks we go to dinner at the bistro. There were a lot of whispers and giggles between us, and then a lot more holding hands and other activities under the table. We acted like typical tourists in love.

"Is this your honeymoon", the waiter asked in a heavily accented English.

"Yes... is it that obvious", Jessica asked...

There is a pistol in my hand, and I am running through an old decrepit building. There are blast and bullet holes all over. It is daylight and I think I am searching for a place to hide. There is a large blast to my left as the wall disintegrates, and I am thrown against the remainder of the wall to my right. I feel a sharp pain in my back, and look down as a piece of rebar is protruding under my left rib. I am bleeding profusely...

There is a small delicate brush in my hand and I am cleaning dust and dirt from a wall mural. I am speaking to a small monk, and he is translating my instructions to the crew I have been given to assist in the work ahead. These men are talented, and have never been schooled. What could they accomplish, how famous could they be, if they developed these gifts. I do not know. I would gladly take them with me, but they will never leave these walls. That is just as well, purity is hard to find and I would feel horrible to corrupt them with the outside.

I sip on some tea, and I think to myself the things I would do right now for a piece of chocolate. My personal stores have run out and after more than a year here I am living as much like a monk as they are. I have shaved my head as they do, and wear the same dress. I take part in the ceremonies and prayers they allow me to. I have been taught as they are taught. This is a very unique way of life, and their teachings and beliefs make so much sense.

These men work tirelessly and without any complaint. I believe they would work days on end, and have to force them to retire for the day. That is when they are not in prayers, or other duties they must perform besides working with me...

I am above the clouds riding on the back of a great eagle. The bird is in tune with my thoughts, I see what it sees and it moves as I command. We dive towards the earth at heart stopping speeds. We skim the water below before climbing as high as we are able...

Things are crawling all over me, and I cannot move. I am pinned down spread eagle. I can feel claws scratching all over and can hear the squeaks and squeals of rats...

Falling, I am falling, falling...

SATURDAY 19TH OF JUNE 2011

I then wake with a start. I look around and I am in my cottage. The last thing I remember is falling and then just before I was sure to crash into whatever was or was not there, I woke up. I lie still for a few minutes thinking of what happened last night. Jessica is well, and I can't wait to see what happens in Argentina. The work in the Himalayas is progressing. I hoped to see Ava last night, and find what has happened to Hisoka and his quest. Maybe they will come tonight?

I dress and go down to the kitchen area. I make a fresh pot of coffee and take my mug outside and walk around the grounds. The aroma in the air here in the morning is hard to describe. It is a pleasant musty smell that the decaying bush and the sandy ground produce here. I walk to the shore of the lake, and the water is as clear as glass. The bear's tracks are still visible in the sand, along with those of a very large moose. I can hear woodpeckers, cardinals, blue jays, and the loons are out on the lake. I can hear everything in the stillness of this morning. A large animal is walking in the bush to my right, but the foliage there is too thick and I cannot see. It could be the moose; I may have interrupted his morning drink. There are chipmunks, and squirrels all over. Then the bush to my right explodes as my suspicions were right, it was the moose and he or she just decided to run off in the direction away from me. They make a lot of noise when they are startled and take off running. I sit down on a rock and finish my coffee.

I may move up my plans for the Europe trip to allow myself to be back here for fall. Retirement will certainly agree with me. I wonder if Le will like it here. I walked back to the cottage, and called her. She picks up on the third ring.

"Where are you", she asks.

"North east of Huntsville... I have a place up here", I said.

"What are you doing there", she asked.

"Why don't you join me and find out", I reply.

“Come on… seriously… I thought you had a consultation”, she said.

“Yes… I did… a consultation with my conscience”, I said.

“With your conscience… I do not understand”, she said.

“Join me here… and I will tell you all about it”, I said.

“Fine… yes… I will… I asked you to take a chance with me and this is mine… I will be there by…. let’s see… I have a few things to take care of… by 5 or 6”, she said.

“You have been to Huntsville”, I asked.

“Of course… not for a long time… but I will get there”, she said.

“Ok… there is a Tim Horton’s on Highway 60 just past Huntsville going towards Algonquin Park… I will meet you there and you can follow me to the cottage”, I said.

“Ok… I will find it… and if not I will call you and you can find me”, she said.

“Pack enough for a few days”, I said.

“How long do you have off… I thought your schedule was tight for the next few weeks”, she said.

“Like I said… I will explain everything to you when you get here”, I said.

“Now you have me thinking… you have to tell me what is going on”, she said.

“When you get here… and not a word or second before”, I said.

“Ok… I will play along… did you sleep well last night”, she asked.

“Yes… the best I have in years… now get your shit done and your ass up here”, I said.

"Ok... Ok... I will see you by 6", she said.

"By six", I said, and then hung up.

I decided to go into Huntsville and do some shopping. I looked around and really needed some groceries. The wine cabinet is full, but I need some protein, dairy, and vegetables. The town was crazy. It always is this time of year. People are all over the place, coming to 'town' for the day, a big event in cottage life.

Back at the cottage, propane tank filled and my list complete. Who am I kidding? I am a spot shopper and never use a list. I bought some beautiful 4 to 6 count black tiger shrimp, a whole denuded beef tenderloin, asparagus, Portobello mushrooms, spinach, milk, cheeses, butter, a French baguette and eggs. My plan was to grill the shrimp in olive oil, oregano, and lemon. Grill the tenderloin in cracked pink pepper and butter, and stuff the Portobello mushrooms with spinach, a diced up shrimp and cheese. For fun I planned for us to catch our breakfast in the morning, but had eggs just in case.

It is now 1 pm and I have plenty of time for another kayak run to the other side of the lake and a swim. There are ripples in the lake now as the wind blows, and the lake is fully alive. I paddle to the other side, tether the kayak to the side of the granite and climb up the rocks to the highest plateau. Well not really a plateau, but it is a naturally flat and smooth granite rock that juts out over the lake about forty feet up. The whole shore on this side of the lake is lined with granite, 'cliffs', I call them. There is a natural waterfall here as well that empties into the lake. The sandy beach by the cottage is really a cove, and the only sand around the lake. Other than the granite the rest of the lake is lined with deep bush. I stand on the 'plateau', and dive into the water. I swim to the opening of my cove, and then I swim back. I did this six times before climbing to the plateau to dry in the warmth of the sun. It is now 4 and I have to paddle back, shower and leave to meet Le.

It is 5:30 and I am in the Tim Horton's having a coffee. It is not Starbucks, but it will do for now. No sign of Le, and no phone call, I hope that is a good sign. At 5:45 I get a refill and at 6:30 I go out and wait by the car. At 7 my phone rings, and Le says she has just turned onto highway 60 from the 11. Le pulls into the parking lot, kisses me and rubs my inner thigh. I ask if she wants a coffee, but she says no, not really. She just wants to get to the cottage. She has had a busy day. I lead her to the cottage, and it is now 8.

She stops in her tracks. She cannot believe the immensity of the building.

"This is your cottage", she asks very surprised.

"Yes... what of it", I say.

"It is what four times the size of your house", she stated.

"Yes... about that', I said shrugging my shoulders.

"It is incredible... how long did it take to build", she asked.

"Four years... now come in... if the outside shocks you the inside will astound... are you hungry", I ask.

"Starving", she replied.

"Fine... I will get started", I said.

"Anything I can do", she asked.

"Yes... can you clean the mushroom tops", I said.

"Is that all", she said.

"No but it is a start... I will get the stuffing ready", I said.

I led her into the cottage, and she was astounded. The view of the lake that she walked into, that hits you when you first look in, still takes me by surprise. I told her to go ahead and explore the interior as I went out to the upper patio and started the grill. Le will be in for a surprise tonight, the smell of grilling meat always attracts the bears. I then took her on a proper tour before we got started on the meal.

"Are there any wild animals around... this place seems so secluded", she said.

"Yes... all of them... and yes it is secluded and I own it all... 3982 acres and the entire lake", I said.

"I cannot wait to see it in the morning", she said.

With the mushrooms stuffed and the shrimp marinating, I take them and the tenderloin out to the grill. I put the mushrooms on first, followed by the meat and then the shrimp. If it is timed right they should all be done at the same time. I told Le to choose the wine, and she handed me a glass.

She looked out over my domain, the sun was setting to the west, and she exclaimed how beautiful this all was.

"How can you work when you already have all of this", she asked.

"About that... that is one of the things I wish to discuss", I said.

"Yes... I have been waiting all day for this... you are going to explain it all to me", she said.

"During dinner", I said.

With that I finished cooking, and we sat down to eat. I then started to tell her everything. I told her I had quit work with absolutely no notice and had officially retired. She tried to apologize, mumbling that she did not mean to rush me into anything. I explained that this was not the case. That it was always there in the back of my mind. Everything happens for a reason, and it was time to go. I told her my consultation was here with my conscience, and that I needed to come here to my sanctuary and speak to myself. I then told her I would be leaving for Europe next week instead of two months from now. I told her she was still free to join me. She asked why so soon, and I replied that I wanted to be back here for part of fall, and that I wanted her to see what I see here when the leaves change color. I explained that the trip to Europe would be cut in half, to be back here for the beginning of October. That we would be spending the month of September around France, Switzerland and Italy.

"Yes... I will come with you... I will quit tomorrow over the phone as you did in a recording... yes", she said.

"How is your dinner", I asked.

"Excellent... this really is good... this place is huge", she said.

"23,000 square feet of interior space... 8 bedrooms... 6 baths... and the master loft... I guess it is pretty large", I said.

"It is beautiful... but when you said cottage I pictured a small rustic cabin... but this is amazing... no wonder you have it hidden away", she said.

"It is fully self-sufficient... solar energy and natural spring water from the lake", I said.

"Could we go for a walk to the lake", she asked.

"Yes... but we will have to be mindful of the wild animals at this time of night", I said.

I then took a rifle from a hidden locker behind the main door of the cottage, loaded it and slung it over my shoulder.

"Is that really necessary", she asked.

"On most nights no... but with the aroma of my cooking still being carried through the bush and the evidence of bear activity over the day and a half that I have been here... yes... for tonight it is", I said.

"Bear activity", she said.

"Yes... I have quite a few resident black bears... along with fox... wolves... mink... deer... moose... you name it... it lives here... and you will need some of this", I said. I produced a patch.

"Put it on... the big ones come out at night", I said.

"What is it", she asked.

"Mosquito repellant... peel of the back and put it on your upper arm... it does keep the buggers away with no sticky lotion or spray", I said.

"How come there were none on the patio", she asked.

"I have mosquito traps and other natural treatments that keep them away from the main building... but the farther away we get... the more we will encounter", I said.

"Do you think we will see a bear", she asked.

"Yes most definitely... maybe not tonight... but before this trip is through", I said.

"I want to see a moose... and deer... and... ", she said.

"I will try to arrange that... I will call them all later and have them meet us for morning tea", I said laughing.

"Prick", she said, punching my arm.

I then flipped on the outside lights. Twenty powerful spotlights came on. They provide enough light from the cottage door to the lake. They act as a great deterrent and generally scare away any animals that may have been in the area. We walk to the lake. I told Le that she is the first person I have ever invited here.

"Is that rifle really necessary... could you not have just brought out a sword instead", she asked, and then laughed.

"Me... a sword... and possibly a bear... that would be something", I said, laughing as well.

"Could you teach me to fire it", she asked.

"Perhaps... one day", I said.

Le then took my hand in hers, and we continued to the water's edge. Le slipped off her sandals and walked into the water a little bit.

"The water is warm", she said.

"Yes... this lake heats up fairly well this time of year", I said.

Le then unbuttoned her shirt, then her shorts, and finally her bra, she was not wearing panties.

"Are you coming", she asked.

"I don't know... that bear was awfully close this morning... and with the smell of steaks in the air", I said.

"Ah... come on... put the rifle down and come in", Le said, as she waded further into the cove.

I thought about it. This was really arousing, and the chub in my pants was starting to become uncomfortable. Le noticed this.

"Someone wants to come in... follow his decision", she said.

I put the rifle down on a bench by the fire pit on the shore. I took off my sandals, then my shirt and then my shorts.

I walked into the water, and dove in past her. Then I came up behind her.

"How well can you swim", I asked.

"I can get by", she said.

"And that means", I asked.

"I can get by you", she said, with a definite air of confidence.

"Tomorrow we can put that to the test... have you ever been in a kayak", I asked.

"No... never", she said.

"Well then... you are in for a lesson tomorrow", I said.

"It sounds like fun", she said.

We were up to our necks in the water, holding each other, the hard nipples of her breasts digging into my chest. We were just looking at each other, and then her hand started playing with me. A crash came from the bush shoreline to my right. Then there was absolute silence.

"What was that", she said.

"I do not know... it could have been large... it could have been small... sound is funny in the bush", I said.

Then there was a series of crashes. Something was running, and then the howl of a wolf broke the silence. Then some yapping and barking.

"The wolves are onto something", I said.

"You mean they are going to kill something", she asked.

"Quite possibly", I said.

"Are we safe here", she asked.

"That howl was awfully close... so was the barking... but the sound is travelling away from us... but I would guess they came upon a deer coming for a drink... and decided the hunt was on", I said.

"How close were they", she asked.

"Thirty... maybe forty yards... just over there", I said, pointing to my right.

We then heard a squeal followed by high pitched barking and yapping. My guess is they caught their prey. I told Le this.

"This really is wild here", she said.

"Yes... I have tried to maintain as much of the ecological integrity of the area as possible... I originally had 892 acres of bush here and just finished negotiating the purchase of the additional 3000 acres around me", I said.

"Why so much", she asked.

"I would buy more if available... this area means a lot to me and with the amount of property being developed I just want there to be something left", I said.

"Are you a Crusader", she said.

"In my dreams... only in my dreams", I said.

With that we stayed where we were for a little longer, and then walked back to the cottage. We picked up our clothes and the rifle on the way. Back at the cottage we grabbed some towels and I started a fire. We fell asleep there...

It is our ninth day in Argentina, and we have begun our sixth day of surveillance on our target. It is hot here in the bush outside of his home. The target keeps to his same routine, and leaves for the day. It is time to see if the ring is inside or if he decides to take it with him today. Thousands of pictures confirm that so far he has left without it. There does not seem to be any security measures in place here. There are no dogs, cameras, or key pads denoting any type of alarm system. It is simply a matter of locating the ring, delivering it to our client so that he or she may produce it and claim the just rewards of possession.

Out plane ticket is for tomorrow, a nice ten day trip for a couple on their honeymoon. Our flight is set to leave at 1035 hours local time, bound for Sydney, Australia.

We exit the cover of the bush, and over the stucco fence we go. Cross the small yard and in through the back door. It was a very easy lock to pick. We decide to start in the main bedroom, and then work from there until it is located. We are not even sure if it is here. The picture of the target with the ring on his finger is a few years old. If we come up empty, we must return empty and the client will have to update his intelligence and try another time.

We leave everything as we found it, not a thing was left out of place. Jessica comes out of one of the other two bedrooms, and I ask, "Anything yet". Jessica shakes her head and replies, "Nothing".

"That clears this floor", I said.

"It is not here then", she replies arms in the air.

"That is my thinking", I said.

With that we go downstairs, and try our luck there. Jessica would take the kitchen and living area, and I would check out the small room that looks to be converted into an office of some sort. Jessica comes to the office area ten minutes later and reports nothing.

"It has to be in here then", I said, as I carefully inspected the desk.

"Did you find a safe", Jessica asks.

"No... but you can check that small closet over there... and that is the last place we need to check... there is no basement here... if we come up empty here we leave", I said.

"Agreed", Jessica replied.

The desk was empty. I even removed the drawers and looked under, like we did upstairs. No stone was left unturned, and nothing. The closet was a bust as well. Out the house we went, using the same way we came in, over the fence and back into the bush. With day packs across out shoulders we come out looking we had been hiking all day.

The hotel pool felt great. We ordered lunch and turned on the secure laptop and reported to the client that the object is not here. There was no response. We signed off that we were aborting. The other half of the money upon completion would of course not be paid. We both understood that, and as understood in the original agreement we transferred half the deposit to an account number we were provided with. What we kept was still a good payday, with a vacation to boot.

I had the concierge change our plans. They were able to get us on a flight tonight bound for the Bahamas for a seven night stay, and then a flight back "home", to Toronto. We simply explained that we had decided to extend our vacation, paid the man handsomely for his services, packed and left for the airport...

Ava and I are in a church, I am in a tuxedo and Ava in a bridesmaid gown. I am standing beside Freddie, and Ava beside Jane. They are getting married. There are a few other people here, all wearing suits and dresses. It was just a small quiet affair.

"Freddie... do you take Jane as your lawfully wedded wife", the Priest asks.

"I do", is Freddie's response.

"Jane... do you take Freddie as your lawfully wedded husband", the Priest asks.

"I do", is Jane's response.

The wedding ceremony continued, but I was lost in other thoughts. I was drifting to the work going on in the construction of our restaurant. Freddie is to be the chef and I am running the front of the house. All compliments of the GI bill, and the money recovered by Ava in getting us re-integrated into society...

I am barefoot walking on coals and engulfed by flames. I am still in line getting closer and closer to the end. There is no more pain, no feeling, just black emptiness...

I am still impaled on the rebar. I hear footsteps coming closer. I manage to look up and can barely see through my blood clouded eyes. I see three people all in black, masks and all. One points a pistol and presses it to my temple. He shouts something that I do not understand, and then...

SUNDAY 20TH OF JUNE 2011

We awoke in the morning, a little sore from the floor.

"Next time we do that... I am going to need more pillows", Le said.

I was standing and stretching, and by the way my body was cracking, it agreed with her sentiment.

"Are you hungry", I asked.

“I could eat”, she said.

“Good... because we are going to catch our breakfast... do you like Perch”, I said.

“I love fresh Perch”, she said.

“Good... can you fish”, I said.

“Yes... I can get by”, she said.

“Does that have the same meaning as last night”, I asked.

“Absolutely”, she said.

“Then it is on... who ever catches the least in thirty minutes... cleans and cooks”, I said.

“Hey... I said I could catch them... I said nothing about cleaning”, she said.

“That confident tone is waning a little bit I detect”, I said.

“Ok you are on... no way I am cleaning fish”, she said.

I then got the equipment and we proceeded to the water. We would take the canoe across to my favorite spot for Perch. Le did not stand a chance. An hour later I cleaned one Perch, and then she cleaned the rest. We then shared the cooking duties. It was a good breakfast, and after showering we went ‘into town’, completing the ritual of cottage life. Instead of Huntsville I chose to take Le to a smaller town, Dorset.

We had lunch at the ‘Fiery Grill’. We sat at a table by the water and watched boats come and go for supplies, or to just get away from their cottages. The town of Dorset was one street, and the shops that made up the town center are sprawled out along, maybe, a four or five hundred yard stretch. There is a liquor/beer store, video shop, general store, restaurant, O.P.P. post, Post Office, those sorts of things. It was really nothing special, but everything special at the same time.

We went back to the cottage around 4, and Le was in the mood for a kayak lesson. Off to the water we went, it was amusing. She got very wet, very frustrated, but she learned fast. We tethered the kayaks to the rocks on the opposite side, and I explained that we would see about her boast from last night. We climbed to the 'plateau', and on the count of three dove in, the race was to the cove and back. I had to swim hard, harder than I ever have. She was fast, faster than me. I stopped in the water about twenty yards from the rocks and she was already sunning herself on the 'plateau'. I joined her and bowed to her prowess. We did not have any stakes so I claimed that the prize was the winner's choice. She said she would think on it and name it later, save it for a rainy day.

Then we saw the bear. He was large, and I have seen this one before. He was about one hundred yards away, down the right shoreline from where we were. He was on all fours on a rock looking out at the water, sniffing. He was there for about 5 minutes and then calmly turned around and disappeared. The loons were out diving back and forth across the lake. It is amazing how they can swim under for that long. They were singing to us. It is a haunting call, but synonymous with this area.

"Are you ready to go back", I asked.

"To the cottage... or home", she asked.

"What would you prefer", I asked.

"I could stay here forever", she said.

"Do you want to skip Europe", I asked.

"No... that sounds like too much fun", she said.

"Shall we go back to the cottage then", I asked.

"Yes… let's go… I have to make that phone call… no one will be in the office and I can leave the message on the machine", she said.

"Do you have anything there", I asked.

"No… I worked out of my apartment and suitcases", she said.

"Ok then lets paddle back", I said.

Upon rounding the corner entering the cove, we froze. The bear from before was walking across the beach. He turned and stared at us, and then went on his way. I could smell him from here.

"Do you smell that", Le whispered.

"Yes… and remember that smell… it means they are close… very close", I said.

"Should we go to shore", she asked.

"Yes… it is alright… that one is around a lot and never bothers me… we have crossed paths many times", I said.

"Are you sure", she asked.

"If I wasn't… I would stay here", I said, paddling into the beach.

Le followed, and we dragged the kayaks up the sand. We were about to pick up the vessels when I said to Le, "Le don't move". She froze. The musty odor was strong, very strong. I moved slowly, putting myself between Le and the bear. He allowed my movement and did not seem threatened at all, curious, but not threatened. He was used to me, but not to her scent. When he was satisfied he lumbered past us, about twenty feet away. He then went running, crashing into the underbrush from where he originally came out on the beach.

"Are you Ok", I asked.

"I peed", she said. I laughed, hard.

"He was just getting to know you... your scent is new to him... this is his backyard", I said.

"Well... let's go to the cottage... I need to take a shower", she said.

"Ok... a shower sounds good... after would you like to go out for dinner", I said.

"That sounds good... what do you have in mind", she asked.

"The Deer Hurst Resort has an excellent restaurant", I said.

"Whatever you have in mind is fine with me", Le said.

"Would you still stay here forever", I asked.

"Yes... I was scared... but that was awesome", she said.

Back in the cottage, Le and I showered, got dressed and went out. Dinner was excellent, and before we knew it we were back by the fire with wine in hand. It had been a good day.

"I still want to see a moose", she said.

"I know where they will be... we will get up early and go for a walk in the bush", I said.

"Will we see that bear again", she asked.

"Probably... he follows me a lot", I said.

"Then how come the other night you took out the rifle if this bear is kind of friendly", she asked.

"Because that morning the tracks on the beach were not his... and tomorrow the rifle comes with us", I said.

"I see", she said.

"We are not sleeping down here tonight are we", she asked.

"Not a chance… my back would not forgive another insult… we will go up to the loft", I said.

We went up the stairs to the loft, and took in the stars from the glass part of the roof. We fell asleep…

I am on a roof top overlooking a vast city. The buildings seem to be floating. Planes fly by like vehicle traffic, hovering at stop lights and cross walks. People are walking on air. There are thousands of levels of traffic and people. I am on the rooftop because I am afraid. I step to the very edge, and then I am pushed…

It is dark and there is a baby crying. I feel a push and a nudge and my eyes open wide. The crying is getting louder. I look over to the source of the nudge and push, and it is Ava.

"It is your turn", she whispered.

"I know… just testing you", I replied.

I get up and pick up the little man from the crib. He is all of a sudden quiet as I repeat reassurances to him. My voice always soothes him, as does my scent. I carry him down the stairs and pull a bottle from the fridge and warm it up in some hot water. Happy with the temperature I sit on the chair in our living room and start to feed him. This should be the last one of the night. Well before the bottle is empty the little man is asleep. When it is empty I carefully remove the bottle, and thankfully he stays asleep. Even though it wakes me up, this is the best time of the day for me. Back up the stairs we go, I lay him down and return to bed.

"Thanks Bobby", Ava whispers.

"No Ava… thank you", I said.

I kissed her forehead, and then put my head on the pillow. I did not go to sleep, but was left to some of my thoughts. The restaurant was finally able to make money to pay the bills, and there was more and more left over for all of us. I closed my eyes...

I am in a pit of fire. Faces of all the people I know are floating all around. There are looks of anguish and pain on their faces. All of my dream friends, Ava, Jessica, Freddie, Torao, the eagles, the kite and the dog included. Lightning flashes above, and the thunder shakes the air around, like small percussion grenades. I look up and see people fall one after another, and I realize that is the line I was once in wondering of the destination, and where we were all headed. Mystery solved...

Back in the protection of the mountain valley only ten have survived. I will venture out after some rest and needed healing to survey the damage. I will go alone, and will continue alone to my homeland and see the condition of the Daimyo and his rule. I feel it is over and they have won. It was all a clever trick to flush out his son. Now I fear after finding what I suspect we will have to commit Seppuku, a final ending to my master's honored reign.

I explain all of this, and it is understood. It will take the passing of the full moon to heal these wounds. The day I leave they will count five full moons. On the day of the fifth moon they will take their lives, as a defeat of this magnitude dictates.

I will spend my time healing in this valley among the blossoms at the burial site of my father. I will tell him where I have been and what I have done. All of the things he missed. I do not think I will see this valley again...

I wake up in a plane once again, Jessica beside me. The female voice over the loud speaker is announcing our approach to Pearson in Toronto. I cannot recall how I got here. We had planned to relax on a beach and wait for more information from our contact on the ring. Did we do that already? Shit, I do not remember. Jessica turns to me and says, "Our contact will meet us at 1300 hours tomorrow at the Downtown Marriott".

I nod my head in understanding, but really do not have a fucking clue what she is talking about.

"You have been awfully quiet", Jessica says.

"I know… just thinking a lot", I said, stalling for a better excuse.

"Have you solved the world's problems yet", Jessica asked.

"Pardon me", I said.

"With the amount of thinking you have been doing lately… have you solved any problems yet", Jessica said.

"No… if I had I would no longer be in this business but retired somewhere safe", I said.

"Do you think we are safe here", Jessica asked.

"What do you mean", I asked.

"Well… we failed on this assignment", Jessica said.

"That was not our fault… the information was old", I said.

"People have been killed for less… that ring was worth billions", Jessica said.

"First sign of trouble… and we are out of here", I said.

"You have a plan", Jessica asked.

"Yes… yes I do", I said….

MONDAY 21ST OF JUNE 2011

I wake up and am beside Le. I quietly get out of bed. The sun is just starting to rise. I go up a small set of stairs and out to the roof top balcony. I take in the 360 degree views of the lake and my land. I look out the spotting scope and there is quite a bit of activity around. In the East Meadow there are seven deer. On the far edge of the meadow there is a swamp, and there stands a moose. I believe he will eventually make his way to the streams there for a drink. I think he is the one I have been seeing lately. The bear is sitting in the warm sand of the beach area. He is just sitting there, like he is on guard. I then hear Le, "Where are you", she calls.

"I am up here", I call down at the top of the stairway.

"You never showed me this... this is incredible", she said.

"I was saving it... here come take a look", I said.

I handed her the spotting scope and showed her what I had found. She was amazed.

"That is the first time I have seen a moose other than Television and pictures", Le said.

"I hope to get you a closer look later today", I said.

"How close", she asked.

"As close as safety allows", I said.

"The bear... what is he doing", Le asked.

"I have no clue... this behavior is definitely a first", I said.

"He is the friendly one... right", Le said.

"I do not know how friendly... but yes that is the one I see all of the time... we are aware of each other and he has respected that so far... but he is wild", I said.

"But you do not carry a rifle when he is around", Le said.

"No I do not any longer... I used to... but like I said we respect each other... I give him his way he gives me my own", I said.

"What do you think he is doing", she asked.

"I think he is waiting for us to wake up and invite him to breakfast", I said.

"Fuck off... do not joke... I am serious", she said.

"I do not know... they are very territorial... maybe he has called out the other one and is waiting for him to accept the challenge", I said.

"Kind of like... meeting at the bike racks after school", Le said,

"That is one possibility... Interested in a swim", I asked.

"With the bear there", she asked in reply.

"Yes... we will take the kayaks and walk right past", I said.

"You first", she said.

With that we went down and outside. Picked up the kayaks and paddles and walked right past him, he did not move a muscle. Man he stinks this morning.

We paddle out and he is still there, he did not move one inch. Past the cove and out on to the main area of the lake heading towards the rocks. Even after we had reached the point where he could no longer be seen, I know he was still there. Across the lake we went, tethered the kayaks to the granite rocks and into the water we dove. Le was an amazingly fast swimmer, but this time we had some company. The Loons were out singing their praises. I have always loved their sound.

Back on top of my favorite boulder shelf, the granite behind providing shade. I can still hear the haunting calls of the Loons. They are so peaceful to me. Should I leave all of this and go to Europe and chase the locations of my dreams. I have already found a few. The Oxtongue River and Ragged Falls have been frequent backdrops. Chasing dreams, does that mean I am going to hell? That is where the last was headed. I could feel myself drifting off...

I wake up vaguely remember where I am. The crib is empty, and house is empty, a note explaining all on the fridge.

"Bobby we are going for a walk and then my Moms will meet you at the restaurant at 1 sleep well love... Ava", I read it out loud.

Ava let me sleep because I was up late with Michael enjoying our own time. There are times I think that he does it on purpose just to be with me. He smiles now when I pick him up, a devilish grin, and a wicked little smile. I want him to stay this way forever. I want our time to stay that way forever...

I am riding Torao past the scene of the bloody battle of a few months past. Rotting bodies, crimson grass, insects, maggots, and birds of prey, lie in portrait of that day's events. The bodies had been picked over, and stripped of all value. I rode on and put it out of my head. I rode with my Yumi across my lap, an arrow notched in ready, and the rest close at hand. I will kill any strangers who approach me until I reach my destination and find if I still have a master and a life to lead...

Water splashes onto my face, Le is standing over me laughing. She says, "This is no time for sleeping".

"What time could be better", I asked.

"None... I was just jealous... I tried... but sleep would not come", Le said.

"Would you like to go into town", I asked.

"No... I want to stay here today... maybe for the rest of days", she said.

"Really", I asked.

"Really", she said.

I stood up and went to kiss her, then yelled into her ear instead, just before diving into the water, "Last one back cooks the meal".

I was into my kayak well before her. She may be able to swim but her water entry into the kayak was not near as graceful as mine. I could hear her curse and swear as she dropped back into the water four times before she was right and under way. By that time it was no longer a race, because she had no chance of catching up. I round the corner and the bear is still on the beach. He had moved and was sort of pacing back and forth. He kept lifting his head and sniffing the air.

I sat in the kayak drifting in the mouth of the cove waiting for Le to catch up confused over this behavior. Le came up beside me and I tethered the kayaks together and we watched him. I looked over to my left and spotted two moose, a cow and a very large bull, in the marsh area on that side of the lake. I pointed them out to Le. She wanted to get closer, so I untied the vessels and we paddled closer. The bull never took his eyes off of us. The cow kept feeding on the aquatic foliage. We paddled within thirty yards. The bull huffed, grunted and picked up his right foreleg and plunged it back into the water, a warning I heeded. We were close enough. We then paddled back a bit and watched. The bull began feeding again satisfied we were no threat.

We did not talk at all. Thirty minutes later we paddled back to the mouth of the cove, and the bear was still there. This time he seemed agitated looking at us and smacking at the ground. I think he was telling us it was not safe, and there was something around. I paddled closer and he grumbled and let out a, I do not know, I guess I would call it a roar. He displayed his teeth and the sound came from deep within him. I have seen this on Television, in some nature and full screen movies, but never like this. I paddled backwards and he backed off. I came closer and his reaction was more severe than the one before. Now we talked.

“What do you want to do”, Le asked.

“I do not know... but I know he does not want us on that beach”, I said.

“Any plans”, she asked.

“Well we could paddle back a bit and come in land through the bush”, I said.

“And what is he trying to keep us from”, she asked.

“I do not know... many possibilities are running through my head... but I am not sure”, I said.

“If we go inland could we run into trouble”, she asked.

“We could... like I said before this is a wild place... and am not sure what he is warning us about”, I said.

“What do you suspect”, she asked.

“There must be an aggressive younger bear moving into the territory probably challenging the old man there for it... or it could be that pack of wolves we heard chase down the deer the other night... or it could be both... I... well... we have seen evidence of both”, I said.

“Europe is looking better right now”, she said. I laughed and responded, “Well... to be out here you have to heed and respect the signs of nature”.

"Go on", she said.

"Take the bear he is warning us of something... we respect that and stay put... on the other hand though the moose are not bothered by whatever threat he detects and had detected since this morning so the threat is here... when nature sends us a signal we prepare... it is like dark clouds in the sky... when we think it is going to rain we prepare for rain", I said.

"So this is your area... what do we do", she asked.

"Paddle back to the rocks tether the canoes and walk inland", I said.

"Are you sure", she asked.

"Yes... as sure as can be", I said.

"And if we run into trouble", she said.

"Not to worry... I have an 'emergency kit' there just in case", I said.

My 'emergency kit' contained a cooking heat source, a thermal sleeping bag, tent, and other camping and fishing supplies. I was after the rifle though. It was all kept in a waterproof bin, located under the protection of a group of evergreens. The rifle and ammunition in an oil skin wrap. I checked it frequently, and kept everything in order. Le did not seem surprised.

"Shall we", I said.

"Lead on bushmaster", she said.

I walked and she followed. On approach to the cabin after an hour's trek, we could hear the ferocious growling of animals locked in mortal combat. Seven large wolves were circling and nipping at the flanks of the bear. I got Le into the cottage and ran up to the roof terrace as fast as I could. I took careful and deliberate aim and shot one of the wolves. It did not deter the rest. I shot two more, and then a fourth. The bear took care of the other three in the confusion. He threw them down like rag dolls, and he was hurt. He did not look my way but limped back into the bush. I ran down and followed, telling Le to stay where she was. I reloaded on the way. I knew deep down I should not do this, but I had to find out the extent of his injuries.

I followed his blood trail to where he was laying down getting some rest. I shot the three wolves the bear had thrown down for good measure. I came closer and he looked up at me and laid his head back down. I touched his matted fur, he stank and I wanted to vomit, but he did not protest. I shot one last wolf, a coward looking for an easy kill. I looked at some of his gashes, but none were life threatening and by the look of some of the scars, he had endured much worse. He needed rest and he knew I meant him no harm. This was certainly an elevation in our relationship. I went back to the cabin and told Le what had happened.

"So you are still a doctor after all", she said.

"When it is necessary", I said.

"I saw you run through shooting on the fly... that was some display", she said.

"I do not know where that man came from", I said.

"Yes you do", she said.

"What do you mean", I asked.

"You have been dreaming of the hero your whole life... you just haven't realized you are him", she said.

I let that sink in. I had a lot of cleanup to do. I dragged the bodies of the dead wolves to one spot. I thought for awhile thinking of the best way to dispose of them. I decided to dig a pit, and four hours later had one that was satisfactory to me. I then filled the pit with kindling and soaked them with some kerosene. I dragged the bodies to the edge and rolled them in. Le was quite a sport and helped through the whole process. I then threw all the coal I had stockpiled for emergencies on top, and then rolled boulders over that. The pit was still almost two feet deep. There was nothing to burn in the immediate area so I soaked the top with more kerosene and then lit the whole mess. It was quite a display and the rocks burned red for hours. It worked like a crematorium, and worked well. There was no need for any further burial. I would just cover and level the top with dirt before I leave in a couple of days. We both took a shower, and ended up too tired to fuck. We fell asleep...

I am startled awake in my sparse room in the monastery. I am being dragged forcefully down the hall. I am trying to get my bearings and a grasp on what was happening. I was yelling but to no avail. It took awhile to focus but eventually my vision cleared. I was in the company of six Chinese soldiers. They took me to a room, and began to question me, but I pretended that I could not understand them. I yelled back in English, and they left locking me in. Ten minutes later they returned with another soldier and he asked me questions, this time in English.

"What are you doing here", he demanded.

"I am assisting the monks in restoring the artwork here... my permits are in order... you will find them in my room", I said.

"Your permit is no longer valid", he said.

"What are you talking about", I said confused.

"You did not get permission from us... Tibetans do not rule here... we do", he said.

"Permission was requested and obtained from my Consulate", I said.

"You are here illegally and will be detained... you are charged with aggression and the plotting of terrorist and dissident activity against our government activities here", he said.

"That is such bullshit", I said. With that he smacked me across the face and kicked me in the balls...

I woke up sweating, heart racing, Le sleeping beside me. I was thinking about the dream and the turn it had just taken. I went downstairs and turned on the outside lights and stared at the lake and the reflections in the black water. The lights had startled a moose sleeping on the edge of the bush. I could tell by the thundering crashes as he broke through trees. I could still see the glow of orange from the homemade crematorium. I went and poured myself a double Glenfiddich, my hands were shaking and I could not seem to calm down from what had or was happening to me in my dream and the incident earlier today. It is just a dream, I told myself, and today I did what I had to do. I think that bear was protecting us.

Le came down the stairs and sat beside me. She then lay down with her head across my lap.

"You did not sleep very long", she said.

"Bad dreams", I said.

"You have them often", she asked.

"Yes... they go hand in hand with the others... but this was different", I said.

"How so", she asked.

"This used to be one of the ones I looked forward to", I said.

"Which one", she asked.

"Where I am helping the monks in Tibet restore their treasures", I said.

"And… what happened", she asked.

"The Chinese have taken me prisoner… and I am facing charges of terrorism and dissidence", I said.

"Sounds exciting… but it is only a dream… maybe an extension of today", she said.

"I know… maybe… but my time there was peaceful", I said.

"Well maybe it won't come back", she said.

"I know it will return… a lot of my dreams have been changing very rapidly", I said.

"Do you want to go back to bed", she asked.

"After my scotch… would you like anything", I asked.

"I will have what you are having", she replied.

"You drink scotch", I asked.

"Not by any rule… but I will give it a try", she said.

I got up and poured her a drink and handed her the glass, and asked, "So… on a change of subject… when would you like to leave for Europe".

"Whenever you are ready", Le replied.

"I will make the calls tomorrow", I said.

"I will return to civilization tomorrow and will be ready when you call", she said.

"Sounds fine", I said.

"Are you OK", she asked.

"Yes I am fine", I said.

We finished our drinks in silence, and then went back upstairs. We drifted off to sleep...

I was gripped in the talons of a hideous creature. It screeched and screamed, and there were thousands of them flying by, picking their prey from the crowds of people on the ground. It was tearing off tiny bits of my flesh, and slowly consuming them. The pain was agonizing. I fought and struggled but could not get free. I felt sick and dizzy and knew I was going to pass out before this thing killed me...

I was blindfolded, hands tied behind my back. I was against a concrete wall. I could feel the texture of it, and my fingers felt holes and chips in it. I was being read a list of charges. Did I do all of these things the voice was shouting? It is not possible. I could not have been capable. The voice then went silent after the last words of "the sentence has been passed". All was silent until I could hear a series of clicks and then the word FIRE...

I was walking in a field and there were dead hawks all around me. Their bodies were falling out of the air like they were rain drops. I was screaming at God to make it stop. I was crying on my knees to a sword imbedded in the ground in front of me...

I was walking in a field of glorious roses, but as I passed they wilted and then burst into flames. The scene behind me was that of hell, the scene in front of me that of my idea of heaven. I tried to stop walking to save my worlds and heavens from any further destruction, but I could not. My legs were mechanical and forward I went, there was nothing I could do...

I am in a shower. It is dirty and there are stains everywhere. I try to think, but cannot remember where the fuck I am. I step out of the shower and find a coarse cheap towel, and step into the room. The bed has been slept in and there is an open suit case on the floor. The carpet is thread bare and stained, and everything is dirty. I must be in the cheapest hotel in the world. I look through the clothes in the suit case and my memory is returning. On the bottom wrapped carefully I find a Beretta PX4 Storm. I know who I am and I remember what I have done.

I dry off as best I can, get dressed, close the case and place the firearm under my shirt at the small of my back. I find a set of keys on the small table by the bed along with a wallet and a second firearm in a shoulder harness. I put it on and put on a light jacket over top. I step outside and press the unlock button on the car fob. A black jeep's lights turn on, and I figure that must be my ride.

I get in, start the engine and drive off. I find a small diner and pull in. I am fucking starving and need to eat. I go in, find a booth in the very back and sit with my back to the wall. I order a rare steak, over medium eggs, bacon and whole wheat toast. The waitress notices the firearm under my armpit and asks, "You a cop or something", and I reply "or something". That ends the conversation.

My food is served and I rapidly consume it. It was not bad and I sent my compliments to the cook behind the open kitchen. I grab a paper from the booth in front of me, order a coffee and start to read...

TUESDAY 22ND OF JUNE 2011

I wake with a start and Le was not in bed. All that was left was just a note that she had left early to get a head of any traffic, especially through highway 400 in Barrie. The note ended saying that she would call and find out what time to meet me at Pearson airport in Toronto for our flight to Europe.

I had a hell of a lot of work to do. I had to call the travel agent, pack, and make all sorts of arrangements. I had wanted to start my journey in Rome, and then travel to Sicily, Portugal, Spain, France, and then finish in Switzerland. I wanted all of this to be a surprise for Le. We would pack light and buy what we needed as we travelled from country to country and from climate to climate.

First I went down to the lake with my kayak for a final tour of the lake, and then I would make the phone calls. The rocks in the pit were still too hot to even touch, and the odor was nauseating. It was very warm this morning and a swim to the far side of the lake would do me good. The loons were here this morning. I like to think they came out to say goodbye. I would not be returning here until winter was in full swing. I wonder what Le would think of this place then.

I saw my bear, but he was walking with a pronounced limp to both his left forearm and left hind leg. I hoped the older fellow can make it through to hibernation, and the healing power of sleep. There is plenty of natural feed for him to completely fatten up.

I saw the moose crashing through the bush as I paddled the east side of the shore. I made it to my boulder and tethered the kayak. I climbed to the peak and dove in. I swam for twenty minutes and then returned to the cottage.

I made myself a quick bite, finishing the perishables. I packed my few things and gathered the garbage. I turned off the pumps and drained the water system. I shut off most of the electrical, but I kept the interior heat set to 65 degrees to prevent any damage by a cold winter.

I then spent six hours in a travel office in Huntsville, but was quite satisfied with the results.

I then headed for home. I had to close everything there and again set the house to maintain the heat at 68 degrees for my collections and electronics. I needed to inform the alarm monitoring company of my travels and itinerary in case they need to get a hold of me. All my bills were automatically withdrawn so there were no worries there. All of this and more I thought to myself on the way home.

It was a long drive because the traffic was horrendous on the 11 and the 400. It was better when I got to the 407 and then eventually the 420. Six hours later I was in my house. I called Le and left a message informing her where I was, and that there was no need to take our cars to the airport, a limousine would pick us up at my place and we would go from there.

An hour passed and Le was at the door. I answered half asleep because I was exhausted. I invited her in, and she was as tired as I. We went up stairs and fell asleep agreeing to talk in the morning, and discuss all the plans made so far...

I am driving in a black jeep, and I can see the diner I was just in getting farther and farther away. Its image becoming smaller and smaller the faster I accelerated the vehicle. I quickly remember who I am. I kill people, plain and simple. I sell my services to the highest bidder. I only take on one job every couple of years, and it could take up to one year to accomplish the task. I do not go into any situation blindly, I do my research, I do the deed and then I disappear.

I have just finished a job, and now I am disappearing. The man was an asshole. He sold everything. His specialty though was young girls and boys. He sold them all over the world and did not care what they were being used for, as long as the client paid. He died horribly, begging for life, they always did given the chance. This one was up close and personal, and I took my time with him. This was all done to my client's exact specifications. He screamed and he suffered, I can still hear him in the back of my head. Did I enjoy it, I think so, knowing what he had done. Do I regret it, no way not a fucking chance! The shit that came out of his mouth, his confessions, how can there be a God with men like that in this world. Those are the ones that I kill, and the only jobs that I will take on. I kill the monsters, the bogeymen, and would kill the devil himself given the opportunity. I replay everything in my head like a movie rerun. It was flawless, perfect and I left no trace. I have gone over the details of what transpired and the efforts of the cleanup extensively. No one will ever find the remains, they never have, ever. He was number 9 in twice as many years. At ten million a pop, I have done very well for myself. He may be the last. I do not know if I will take on a tenth, unless another bogeyman rears its ugly head that is.

I cruise down the road, and my safe cell phone rings. This would be the client confirming the job is complete.

"Yes", I say.

"Is it done", a female voice asks coldly.

"It is", I reply.

"And our proof", the voice asks, colder still.

"It is at the drop off as requested", I said.

"I will call back and confirm reception and payment in 60 minutes", the female voice says and then hangs up quite abruptly.

I continue driving with no particular destination or purpose. After payment is confirmed I have to clean and ditch this jeep. I will go to the airport and leave it there. The jeep will not be found among the thousands of vehicles there for years to come. I will also have to ditch these firearms. It is a shame though, but I cannot take them where I am going. They are clean, I never used them. The phone rings again.

"Confirmed", the female said.

"And the payment", I asked.

"Done… as instructed", the female said.

My pager then went off, and I looked at the number, the code meant the payment was received.

"Confirmed", I said.

The line went dead. I drove over a set of railroad tracks. I pulled over and walked back to them. There was not a vehicle in sight. I took the phone and pager apart, and placed the pieces on the track. I walked back to the jeep and waited for a train to roll by. I pulled farther off the road, and took a nap. About ninety minutes later a train went by. I went over and inspected what was left of the devices and was satisfied they were destroyed. I headed for the airport. On the way I passed a body of water. I took the firearms apart, and threw the pieces in one by one. There was not a soul around. At the airport I thoroughly cleaned the car, grabbed my suitcase and bought a plane ticket…

WEDNESDAY 23RD OF JUNE 2011

I woke to the aroma of coffee. The place in the bed beside me was empty. Le must be making breakfast. I dressed and went downstairs. Le and I had a lot to discuss.

"Good morning Luv", I said.

"Good morning Logan", Le replied.

"Smells great in here", I said.

"Tastes even better", she said.

"What are you creating", I asked.

"All in good time Mr. Charles", she said.

"Oh... its Mr. Charles now is it", I said as I grabbed a handful of breast and ass from behind.

"Hey... oh... wait... that is good... do not stop", she said.

"All in good time Ms. Shen", I said.

"Tease", she said.

"Look who is talking... really that smells great... what do you have in the oven", I asked.

"Set up outside... and I will bring it out", she answered.

I grabbed some cutlery, the coffee, and a few other things, and Le joined me at the table. I grabbed a fork full of the scrambled egg concoction in front of me, and it tasted better than its aroma.

"So... when do we leave", she asked.

"Right to the meat and potatoes", I said.

"Yes... now when do we leave", she asked.

"Day after tomorrow... the flight leaves at 9 am", I said.

"And where are we going", she asked.

"Our first stop will be Rome... the rest of the itinerary a secret", I said.

"Rome... Rome is amazing at this time of year... where are we staying", she asked.

"I have secured the penthouse at the Cavalieri for two weeks", I said.

"Two weeks in Rome... there is so much to see and do", she said.

"All in good time", I replied.

"Yes... I guess we do have that... now finish up... I want to fuck", she said.

"Don't you need to pack and all of that", I asked.

"Not really... just a few outfits and toiletries... the rest I will buy there... I plan to do a lot of shopping", she said.

"I thought so", I said.

"And what is that supposed to mean", she asked.

"I had you pegged as a shopper", I said.

"What you do not shop", she asked.

"Only for things I need", I said.

"Look around your house and cottage... you have shopped for a lot more than that", she said.

"Yeah... I guess so... but I will enjoy the coffee and street life while you are shopping", I said.

"Fair enough... but I am sure you will find shopping there a much different experience than the malls here... you will love it as much as I", she said.

"Well... what is that expression 'When in Rome'", I asked.

"Yes... we have all heard it... now seriously finish your breakfast... you are going to need your energy... I really want to fuck", she said.

On that note we went up stairs showered and did just that. By the time we emerged it was 3 pm, and we had a lot of things to tie up. Le had already terminated her lease as of the New Year. There was not much to move, and what little she had was to be moved to my garage tomorrow. I had already taken care of most of my things, including my mail and the alarm monitoring company. I can pick up the tickets anytime tomorrow as well. I, like Le, would pack little. I will admit shopping might be fun.

We parted and went separate ways. I got my shit together and Le got hers. It was all a blur, and before I knew it we were on a plane bound for Rome.

THURSDAY 24TH OF JUNE 2011

We were cruising through the sky when Le whispered into my ear, "Do you want to join the mile high club".

"Are you serious", I asked.

"Dam right", she said.

"I don't know", I said.

"Come on... I will go first and you follow after... simple", she said.

"But all the people", I said.

"To hell with them... the only ones that count are you and me", she said.

"Ok... it is kind of exciting... and I am growing in my pant as we speak", I said.

Le then took off her seat belt, and went down the aisle towards the washrooms. We were in first class, and the first class cabin had its own set. I followed her, and knocked on the door I saw her enter. It was different, cramped, but we both accomplished the goal. I would definitely do it again. We returned to our seat to quite a few knowing smiles, and we both shrugged our shoulders and smiled back at them. Upon returning to our seats I ordered a scotch, Le ordered wine, and we both took a nap...

I am at my cottage. At least I think that is where I am. Things are a little different. They are a little "off". I open the main door and walk into a wall. I walk back outside and try the other entrances and find the same thing, nothing but walls. I walk to the beach and I find a kayak, but it is not mine. I get in anyway and paddle to the other side, and my granite cliffs and waterfall are gone. They have been replaced with what looks like a swamp. The smell is foul, and I paddle away. I see some objects floating on the surface of the water and I paddle over to them. They are my loons, and they are dead. I paddle back to the beach, and I vomit. I walk a little way into the bush, and I can smell rotting flesh. I follow the scent and run into the rotting carcasses of the Bull Moose, a lot of deer, and my bear. Then I smell smoke and realize the cottage is on fire. Flames are shooting out of the rooftop and feeding on the wood like a ravenous monster. The flames take the shapes of hideous creatures. I fall to my knees and I scream and cry. A sword appears in the ground in front of me. I pull it out of the ground like King Arthur did Excalibur from the fabled stone. I rush to the cottage with sword in hand and do battle with the beasts of fire...

I wake in the airplane. Le is in the seat next to me. She still sleeps. I wipe the tears from my eyes, and hope that no one notices. The wear seatbelt sign comes on, and then the captain's voice can be heard over the speaker system. The captain was announcing our impending decent into Italy. Le wakes with a smile and asks, "Are we there yet". I laugh and tell her yes, we are over Rome and would be landing very soon. Our next adventure would soon start.

We have arrived safely and are leaving the Leonardo da Vinci airport in a limo provided by the Cavalieri Hotel. We were quiet on the drive to the hotel, and I was starving.

I could not help but enjoy the silence and let my mind drift back to my last dreams. The last at the cottage really bothered me, as did the one where I was walking and everything around me was turning to flame and ash. Those dreams coupled with some of the other jumbles, the vision of hell, being shot, hung and impaled, scared me. I do not know where the others are going. Ava and I have a child and a successful restaurant with Freddie. Torao and I are headed for what seems to be a suicide mission. Jessica and I are in Toronto waiting to be contacted for further work or get killed. I just killed someone for money, he was a complete shit but I killed him. Finally I have been taken prisoner by the Chinese army on the suspicion of potting terrorist and dissident activities. How else could I do all that, an anesthesiologist, but in dreams, I couldn't.

We pulled up the hotel, and a concierge rushed out to meet us with two bell boys. The concierge greeted us with friendly warmth. He asked us the normal questions, how was your flight, first time in Rome, and all the jazz. We followed him in. The bell boys got the bags. The concierge noted how little we were travelling with. I told him we planned to do a lot of shopping. He just smiled. We were swept up to the room, and neither of us could believe our eyes. This hotel was magnificent, the exterior, the lobby, the glimpse of the dining and bar areas, the private elevator and this room. I tipped the three of them, and told them we were starving. The concierge, who I am sorry, introduced himself as Carmen, said, "I will have something very special prepared and sent up... is this agreeable".

"That would be fine", Le answered.

"But give us some time to settle in... perhaps one hour", I asked.

"Perfect... I will have everything prepared and at your door in one hour", Carmen said.

"Well we have an hour... what would you like to do", Le asked.

"I do not know about you but I need a shower... and I want to look around... this room is huge... three stories including our own rooftop terrace", I said.

"Sounds great... we can shower look around eat and then go out on the town", Le said.

"You want to go out already", I asked.

"Dam right... I do not want to waste a minute of our time here... there are so many things I want to see... the Coliseum... Bernini's fountains in the Piazza Navona... the Vatican", Le said.

"Ok... then we are on the same page", I said.

"Now let's look around and find the shower... we better have a system because we could both get lost in here", Le said.

"I could put a bell around your neck", I said.

"Funny man... I was thinking I could do the same to you... but on another part of your body", Le said.

"Not a chance... now quit screwing around and find the shower", I said.

We found the shower alright, there were three of them. We chose the one off the master bedroom, which took up the whole second floor loft. After the shower we went up to the rooftop terrace, and took in the awesome views of Rome. You could see the dome of the Basilica, and a part of the coliseum. I knew I had made the right choice.

The bell rang, and our food had arrived. I asked the young man who had brought the food if there had been any recent renovations to the hotel, if something or incident of note had occurred here. The young man replied in his best English that yes, this part of the Penthouse had undergone a massive facelift. He explained that there had been a mafia squabble here in the penthouse foyer and elevator, and a few grenades had been detonated here. I remember reading about that in the paper, and seeing it in the news now, it was a year and a little bit ago.

During our dinner I mentioned this to Le, and she sat there enthralled by the story. I told her I had requested a copy of the articles be sent up to us to read.

"How did you know to ask that", she said.

"The article must have stuck in my mind… it must had been there when I made the reservations… it was the only hotel name I recognized as not being a chain when the tour operator was reading them off", I said.

"But how did you know", Le asked.

"I do not know… I just did… being in the foyer and seeing the elevator brought it forward in my mind… from the pictures I think", I said.

"You have a strange mind Mr. Charles", Le said.

"I know", I replied.

The dinner sent up was absolutely amazing. The cheeses and the olives, the breads, the roasted venison tenderloin, the risotto with porcini mushrooms, were all absolutely amazing. By the time we finished every crumb it was 0200 hours Rome time. Le would have to wait till the morning for her time on the town. We decided to try and get some sleep…

I was sore all over. Every muscle, tendon, bone, anywhere that could be in pain was. Men stood over me, yelling questions I could not truthfully answer in broken Chinese accented English. They were relentless, cruel, sadistic, fucking bastards. My eyes were almost swollen shut, my lips broken and cracked, as were most of my teeth.

Yet they kept me alive, videotaping everything, waiting for a confession, coerced or otherwise. I do not think they cared. The rooms they shuffled me back and forth between all smelled of shit and urine. I remember this now.

Just days ago I was painting with the monks in that peaceful monastery. I was pulled from that and transported here. I believe by plane. Every day it was the same, questions, beatings, questions, beatings, then an I.V. of some sort to keep my alive I suppose. I try to bring myself back to the snowy peaceful Himalayas, and the room there I called home. I try to focus every last bit of fortitude I can on that, and then the beatings start again. It is not long before I am confessing to everything they say, and am broken.

I agree to their demands and they rehearse the allegations I am to agree to and admit my guilt to, and the beatings stop. I refer to my captors as prick 1, 2 and 3.

"You have plotted to conspire with the monks and the peoples of Tibet against China's rightful occupation of the territory", Prick 1 stated.

"I have", I say, aware of the video camera in front of me.

"You have made arrangements for men and arms to assist with training the people of Tibet to fight against China", Prick 1 stated.

"I have", I say.

"You have paid Chinese Officials in the territory we found you in to look the other way while engaging in these activities", Prick 1 stated.

"I have", I say.

"The bruises and cuts you have suffered are a result of you fighting with your arresting officers and others here in their investigation of these allegations", Prick 1 stated.

"They are", I say.

"Other than in our own defense we have treated you fairly and with respect and care", Prick 1 stated.

"You have", I say.

"You have agreed to stand trial and in your own defense and have declined our offer of contacting your Embassy for aid", Prick 1 stated.

"I have", I say.

"Is there anything more you wish to say", Prick 1 stated.

"There is", I say.

"Then the floor is yours", Prick 1 stated.

"Where to begin... I admit I am ashamed in my actions here and was wrong to attempt to undermine China's peaceful efforts here in claiming territory rightfully theirs... I accept the outcome of my trial and have agreed to be a spokesman in China's defense of their actions here... that is all I have to say", I said.

They then brought me to a nicer cell. It did not stink quite as bad as some of the others. I was brought food and drink, but I found it hard to consume with the pain I am experiencing. I had to find a way out of wherever I was. I suspect I am in China, and once I have gained a little trust I will assess my situation as best I can...

I keep walking and I cannot help it. I walk through the fields I played in as a child, past my family's home, my grade school, my high school, some of the places I held jobs. They all go up in flames as I pass. What could I have done to deserve this hell? I have no answers but this is where this path has been leading me to...

FRIDAY 25TH OF JUNE 2011

We awoke after only what seemed a couple hours of sleep, the six hour time difference was really screwing up out internal clocks. It was now 9 am Rome time. I went to the bathroom and vomited several times over the dreams I just had. I returned to bed and looked at Le still kind of sleeping but not really. Finally she opened her eyes for good.

"What is wrong... are you ill or something... I could hear your retching", she said.

"Just a dream upset me", I said.

"That must have been one hell of a nightmare to do that", she said.

"It is kind of ongoing but in pieces", I said.

"Tell me about it", she said.

"Are you sure you want to hear", I asked.

"Yes... please tell me", she said.

I then went into a long dialogue and explained and described all to her. She lay there listening intently, but not saying a word. I told her of my image of hell, and what happens on the path there. I told her of all the things in my life burning or dying, the cottage, the loons, the bear, deer and moose, all of it. I told her of the Himalayas, and how I was restoring their artwork and treasures. I told her of the Chinese army taking me prisoner beating lies out of me. I told her almost everything about every dream I had so far. I left out the relationships, and the fact the Ava and I were married and had a child. I glossed over Jessica and those types of things. I did not want to hurt her in any way if that was possible. She just listened, until at the end of my dialogue she spoke, “They are just dreams”, she said.

“But a great part of the man I am today”, I said.

“You should write a book”, she said.

“That might not be a bad idea”, I said.

“Why do you think some of your dreams are so violent and changing the way they are”, she asked.

“I do not know... they have taken on their own life in my sleep”, I said.

“Well let’s see if we can chase away the bad and bring some good with our adventure here”, she said.

“Are you ready to get up”, I asked.

“Yes... I am excited to start our first real day”, she answered.

“Do you know where you are going around here”, I asked.

“Not a clue”, Le answered.

“Well then... let’s not waste a moment... let’s go and get lost in the streets of Rome”, I said.

“No... we will not get lost... my phone has a GPS and is programmed for over here... all I have to do is tell it where in Rome we want to go... and presto it tells us”, Le said.

“My phone has that to... but I have never used it”, I said.

“It works good... no troubles so far”, Le said.

“Then lead onward... oh city master”, I said.

We showered and dressed and eventually found our way to the Piazza Navona and walked around Bernini's fountains. I chattered about some of the history here, and Le listened intently. We had a Tartufo, at a small café in the Piazza, they are, we found tonight, famous for them. It was not an exaggeration, and any acclamations this dessert had received attributed to the café is well deserved and well founded. We finished the afternoon sipping espresso, talking, and laughing. It was getting late, and we headed back to the hotel, we were still extremely tired from the flight and short night of sleep. It was time for a short nap before a late dinner...

I am in a room full of gold, currency from all over the world, gems and priceless treasures. There are no windows and there are no doors. Who am I to deserve such a site, and who are they to be keeping this from the world. Then the bottom falls out, and it all falls back to the molten fiery pits of hell. Creatures that I guess were once human are laughing at the site of the world's money being dumped here for no one's use. I watch as every hour more and more is dumped to fuel the fires here. Is this what money is really worth, and what we seek and chase after our whole lives. Is this where it all leads to...

I take a good look around the world I once knew, and it is all gone, turned to ashes. All the places that I held as cherished memories. All of them, gone. I am all that is left. I can feel the flames licking at my feet, feeding on the clothes I am wearing. There is no pain for my mind is numb looking at the devastation that was my life...

Jessica and I are walking hand in hand to our meeting at the hotel downtown. We have taken all precautions possible. We have changed clothes at every opportunity, doubled and tripled back in an attempt to spot and subsequently lose anyone attempting to follow. The two of us could find nothing wrong. That bothered me quite a bit. I think I would rather have had people following us. This is just not right. It does not feel right.

"Jessica let's ditch this meeting... I do not feel right about it", I said.

"No... no way... we can't... this could mean millions for us", she said.

"It could also be a set-up... we failed our last contract", I said.

"But we refunded the money minus a few expenses... the info was out of date... we did what we could for our reputation", she said.

"I know... but I have a bad feeling... we should just take what we have find a small corner of the world and just relax", I said.

"Let's just see what they have to say... assess our standing and if we do not like it and you still have that feeling then we will disappear as best we can", she said.

"Ok... it is a crowded area... I will give them fifteen minutes and then we leave", I said.

"Fair enough... come on we have come through before", she said...

I am walking down a street with Ava and I am pushing a stroller. The sun is bright but it is a little bit cool. It is a great day for a walk and to spend some time in the park nearby. I can hear sirens fairly close by, a common occurrence here. It is nice here but almost time to move to a better area. The sirens are real close and we can hear tires screeching and people yelling. All of a sudden out of nowhere a big black caddy comes around the corner and jumps the curb where we are walking and...

I wake up and am in Rome. Le is still sleeping so I get up really quietly, order coffee to be brought up and go to the front to wait so the bell does not ring. Ten minutes later I have the coffee set up on the roof top terrace. I left a note telling Le where to find me. I pour myself a cup, and I take in the sights, and sounds of Rome. What a difference from my home in the city, and an even larger difference from my cottage, to what I see, hear, and smell here.

Le awakes and joins me. She pours herself a cup of coffee and helps herself to one of the pastries on the tray provided.

"Hiding", she asks.

"Maybe", I answer.

"From me", she goes further.

"No... just from my own thoughts", I said.

"Is it working", she asks.

"Nope... not in the least bit", I said.

"What will we do today to occupy your thoughts elsewhere", she asked.

"I was thinking the Coliseum... or perhaps the Vatican", I said.

"We could do both", she said.

"We could... but I think one will be enough for today... we have plenty of tomorrow's you know", I said.

"What else is on the agenda", she asked.

"I have no concrete plans", I said.

"What country is next", she asked.

"Well I still want to see Naples and go to Sicily... then perhaps Portugal then Spain France and then over the Alps to Switzerland", I said.

"That is a lot to accomplish", she said.

“There is so much I want to see”, I said.

“And next year… where to next year”, she asked.

“You will be around next year”, I asked.

“As long as you will have me”, she said.

“How about China and the Great Wall… or Japan… Australia or the Philippines”, I said.

“How about all of them”, she said.

“So… you really think I am going to keep you around”, I asked.

With that she came around the table, pulled my chair out, and straddled my lap. Her robe opened and she wore nothing underneath. She reached down and pulled out my member, stroking life into it, and guided me inside. She ground and rode me until we came, and with a wicked smile she said, “Any more plans of dumping me now”.

“No… at least not today”, I said leaning back, and laughing.

Le hit me hard with her palms on both of my shoulders. She hit so hard the impact sent us off balance and the chair fell back. We helped each other up laughing hysterically. My shoulders hurt, my head hurt and I felt quite a goose egg on the back of my head. Le had a small cut on her lip and it was starting to swell. We both applied ice to our wounds, and she apologized. She had not realized she had hit me that hard, and had not realized that I had leaned back a bit lifting the front legs of the chair off of the ground. It would have made a great You Tube video, if we had that on camera.

To the showers and then to the streets, away we went. Shopping was on the agenda today, shopping on the streets of Rome. The Vatican and the Coliseum can wait. Le caught me several times looking at the beautiful women around us, as I caught her checking out the guys. It was all good. We spent an indecent amount of money on clothes and things. It was fun. The stores were good enough that everything we bought would be sent to our hotel. Therefore we would not be lugging everything around with us.

We stopped at a small trattoria for some refreshment and a light meal. The dishes were excellent and simple, the bread amazing, and the wine and cheeses the best. (Well, OK maybe not so light). I could go on and on about the culinary fare we found. We shopped and ate the whole day away, and when we arrived back at the hotel we were exhausted. All of our purchases had arrived safely, and Le was going through cataloguing everything. I went to shower but then I lay on the bed...

I am on a train, and it is going way to fast. The world outside of the window is just flashing by in a blur. I cannot make out a single image, and have no idea of what I am seeing. The car I am in is empty. There is not a soul or a sound. I check some of the other cars and it is the same. I make my way to the back of the train, and I look out the back and I can still not see anything I believe to be real or concrete. I then decide to go to the front, and find car after empty car. The last car before what I would assume to be the engine is locked and I cannot get through.

I then hear voices, shouting angry voices. They are coming from behind me but there is no one there. They are getting louder and louder but I cannot see the source. I believe that one belongs to Ava, and possibly another to Freddie. A dog begins to bark and I can hear an eagle screeching. What in the fuck is going on? The sounds pound and pound into my head, but they still have no discernible origin.

The train seems to be going faster and faster. Outside the window the blurs are gone and have been replaced with lights. It is like the train has entered a star and we are flying through the cosmos. The screams and shouts are deafening. I curl into a ball on the floor and grab my knees and hold them to my chest. I try to cover my ears with my hands and this only seems to strengthen the sounds...

I am now on a beach. There is a small hut behind me. I hear a phone ringing and I enter the small hut, but it is deceivingly spacious inside. The place was stacked with all possible amenities for such a remote location. I pick up the satellite phone, and the voice on the other end rings off a numerical code. I go to my laptop and enter the code which brings the use of a military satellite temporarily under my control. With it I receive secure transmissions from those who pay me. A picture of a man appears on my screen, along with a complete dossier. They want him dead. Two years have passed since I was last called upon to perform this service. I told them I would look into the feasibility of this action, and to call me in two weeks for my breakdown and final decision.

This guy was a real piece of shit, but then they all were, or maybe we all are. I do not know. This man trades in children, and the things that happen to them I will not mention here, because such things should never be repeated. It is hard enough to read them let alone let them leave my mouth. He is into other things, drugs and all that shit that comes with who he has made himself into.

The dossier included three years worth of precise movements and his habits. They must have someone real close to him for this type of detail. I read until my eyes hurt, and then I read it again, and will continue to read for two full weeks. I will require a year to plan, and daily updates on his movements. I will absorb it all until I am him, and able to ghost his every move. Right up until the time he ceases to breath. It is at that time I become me again. The one who will send you back to the devil when the devil comes calling for you...

I am walking among the ashes that were once my life. Everything is burned. Nothing is recognizable. The winds whip up and I can barely breathe. I am choking on the remnants of all I ever loved. Places, memories, friends and family fill my lungs and I vomit a thick black substance. The fires have died for there is nothing left of my life to feed it...

I wake to Le sleeping beside me. I get up quietly and sneak out to take a shower. It is 2 am Rome time. I cannot believe I slept that long. The water felt good, and I stayed under it a long time. Tomorrow we would take a drive along the western coast, and just stop wherever and whenever we please. No plans, no time clock, just whatever. I dried off then slipped in beside Le. I do not think she moved. I drifted back to sleep...

I am in the lobby bar of the Marriott in downtown Toronto right beside the Eaton Center. Jessica has gone to the bar to order drinks. No sign of any contact. No sign of anybody following or watching us. Jessica comes back to where I am sitting with drinks in hand. There is no conversation between us, none at all. It is kind of uncomfortable sitting here with her. It had never been this way before. It is like there are miles between us, and we have never shared any intimacy. Just some ice cold business, and nothing more.

Then a young lady walks into the bar area, a large black envelope in hand. She is looking our way, then looking at the envelope. She stands there about twenty feet from us with pure indecision in her eyes. She finally decides to walk our way. She lays the envelope in front of me, and stands there like a deer caught in headlights. She is not a professional, just someone recruited from off the street to bring this to me. Then she finally speaks, "Umm... two guys out there on Dundas said you would give me a grand if I brought that to you".

"Are you sure you have the right person... I am not expecting anything", I say to her.

"Well... you are the only couple here and they described you to a T... even the clothes you are wearing", she said.

Then they do have someone watching, and we missed them. That is not good, or they are real good.

"OK... mind if I look inside", I said.

"Fuck man... it is yours... go ahead", she replied.

I peaked inside, and then let Jessica have a look. She looked over at me with a look of shocked surprise. She then mouthed the words, "We are fucked". I just nodded in agreement.

"Well... do I get the thousand... or what... I have to get to work", she said.

"Look honey... here is the money... but forget work... call in sick right now and do not leave this hotel... in fact check in right now and wait a few days", I said.

"What the hell is going on", she asked.

I then explained to her that the people that gave her the package meant to kill us, and there was no way they would let her live past the front door. I gave her all of the cash in my pocket, and the bag I carried.

"Take all of this... check into a room and stay there... do not call anyone you do not need to... do not call the Police or anyone... now what did these guys look like... tell me everything", I said.

The young lady sat down with a pale white look of shock on her face. I just gave her about thirty grand. She told me what she remembered. It was not much to go on.

"I do not have anyone... no one will come looking for me", she said.

"Good... less people to get in trouble", I said.

"I knew I should have walked away... I always make the shitty decision", I said.

"It is very hard to walk away from easy money", Jessica said.

"Did they take anything from you", Jessica asked.

"What do you mean", she asked, with a puzzled look on her face.

"Check everything you took with you today and make sure it is all there... anything that could trace you in any way", Jessica said.

The girl searched her purse and pockets and found she had everything. She did not have much, no driver's license, no credit cards, just a YMCA membership and an employee card from the Pottery Barn, where she worked. The rest was make-up, and the sort of things a girl her age carried to work.

"You seem to be fairly calm", I said to her.

"Look man... I have nothing... that grand they promised is more then I take home in two weeks working two jobs... I have no one... but I watch a lot of TV... and this shit happens all of the time why not to me", she said.

"How old are you", I asked.

"Eighteen", she replied quietly.

"You take the money I just gave you and get your ass in school... become something... with your calmness you will do something... now get the fuck away from us and into a room... lock the door and do not open it for anything understand", I said.

"Yes... I do", she said nervously.

The girl left us and walked to the front and twenty minutes later she was walking towards the elevator area. Ten minutes more we sat there, and we made our way to the back door when a truck crashed through the front windows plowing through everything and everyone in its way. Two men jump out and open fire on all that remained...

SATURDAY 26TH OF JUNE 2011

I woke with a jump, like I had fallen and landed hard. I was covered in sweat, and that negated the shower earlier. Le was sitting up staring at me. She said simply, "Bad dreams".

"Yes and plenty of them", I said.

"You seem to be having more and more lately", she said.

"I know... but you take the good with the bad", I said.

"Now come here and kiss it better", I said,

"Kiss what better", she said seductively in a sort of purr.

"Well let's start with my lips and see what happens", I said.

Afterwards we showered, dressed, and then went down to the hotel restaurant for some breakfast. I asked the concierge to arrange for the nicest, sexiest, car, for our driving pleasure. The man did not disappoint me. We packed a few things and took off, to where. Who cares, we are in Italy.

My first destination that I plugged into the GPS provided is Florence, or Firenze as it is known now. Florence is 278 km away in the heart of Toscana, according to the GPS. This is my first time driving a BMW I8. A machine of this caliber is to die for. I cannot begin to describe the exhilaration as the vehicle fires up. The high pitched musical whine when I step on the accelerator is amazing. I believe by the look on Le's face that she must have stained her panties when I pulled away. I must have broken every speed law in the country as often as it was safe to. I did not care for I was driving a dream car in Italy.

It took us a while to cover the distance and arrive in Florence because of all the stops we made along the way. We stopped everywhere interesting to us. The region of Tuscany is beautiful, and the wine and culinary offerings were amazing. The area and the route to Florence is chock full of small hilltop villages, and we visited many of them. If the GPS had a human personality it would have told us to "Fuck Off", with all the recalculating it had to do.

The chain restaurants in Canada claiming authentic Italian or Tuscan fare are so full of shit. The recipes they follow must have been passed word of mouth and some ingredients lost, skipped, or confused in the translation. It is not even a close relative of what I have sampled here so far.

We travelled through Sienna, and then made a detour to Pisa before arriving in Florence or Firenze. We saw the leaning tower, it was cool, but the crowd was large so we were satisfied with our vantage point. Le took thousands of photos all along our way here and in Rome. She had already filled two memory cards and was working on a third. I am not exaggerating when I say thousands, or maybe tens of thousands, a hundred thousand. She had four batteries charged, and had already exhausted a couple of them. She was having a blast, but I could tell her own battery was running on empty, and needed some sleep. She was getting a little testy and cranky. We would arrive at the hotel soon to get some rest before spending a couple days in the area, exploring, fucking and eating.

We made a quick stop at an eatery by our hotel. We ordered scallops and shrimp as an appetizer. The shrimp and scallops were pan seared and then drizzled with garlic and truffle infused olive oil and some balsamic vinegar. Then we had a house specialty, stuffed roast quail and root vegetables for the main. We skipped dessert for it was late and we were tired. It was time to get to bed. We checked into the hotel, it was nice but nowhere near the level of the Cavalieri in Rome. We showered and then fell into bed, we quickly fell asleep…

I am at a table, and there are Chinese and Canadian officials all around. There are news agencies from all over the world. Cameras are clicking away. The flashes temporarily blind me with the amount of times they go off, the sound of thousands of clicks fill my ears. Questions are being asked and then interpreted. I try to answer them all, but I am betraying my own conscience.

Prick 1 is seated to my left, prick 2 to my right. I am sweating profusely and cannot stand the lies that are being spewed from my lips. I can taste bile, and smell body odor. I have kept hidden my fluency in their language to this point. I cannot stand what I have done.

I stand and scream in Mandarin about the kidnapping from the peaceful monastery, and the subsequent beatings and these forced lies. Cameras stop flashing, and the room is quiet. This was a live feed and the Chinese cannot stop it. The foreign news agencies keep their feeds going. There are representatives from the Canadian Embassy present at my insistence, and there is nothing Prick 1 and 2 can do.

People from all corners of the room are screaming and yelling. I keep my dialogue going telling all. Prick 1 pulls out a pistol and points it at my head. This act will be broadcast to the world. Prick one yells at me to stop at once and recant what I have just said. I stop talking long enough to spit in his face. The yelling and the panic in the room are cresting to the boiling point. They are screaming about the gun, and several are attempting to leave. Some of the cameras keep going. The operators of those feel this is too good and are willing to do what it takes to get my message out. Prick 1 gives me one final warning before he pulls the trigger and everything goes black...

Jessica and I made it safely out the back of the hotel lobby. We were in a courtyard. There was an old church, a fountain, a pool of water and the back of the Eaton Center. The mall would be our best avenue of escape. One of the reasons I agreed to this particular spot for a meeting. We could disappear into the mall, buy a change of clothes, a new hair style and color, and then blend into the crowd.

"Well that answers a few questions", Jessica said.

"Yes but who are they", I said.

"They probably put out a contract and this was a less experienced and messier team", she said.

"Well let's find a hair place and disappear", I said.

"Agreed", she said.

"And our contact", I asked angrily.

"We have to find and kill them", she said with a bitter conviction in her voice.

"I thought you were going to say that", I said.

"No other way", she said.

"Do you think your friends in France will be able to assist us", I asked.

"When we clear out of this I hope so", she said.

We separated to find different hair style places and agreed to meet at the Sears Younge Street exit in three hours, and retrieve our emergency kits we had stashed away. The last hotel we were in is out of the question.

"Can I help you Sir", a very hot young girl asked as I stepped across the threshold of the shop.

"A cut and color please... I want a totally new look", I said.

"Did you have and particular stylist in mind", she asked.

"No I am new here... just looking for a fresh start", I said.

"Well I can certainly give you that... did you have anything particular in mind", she asked.

"No... I will leave that to your imagination... just nothing too flashy... just a lighter color and a trendy cut", I said.

"As you wish... came on let's get started... do you have any time constraints", she asked.

"Three hours... I have three hours to spare", I said.

"Then let's get started... it will be fun", she said...

Two hours ride from the last battle scene, I spy five riders to my right and two to my left. They are keeping pace, and their safe distance. If I go right they do the same, and if I go left they mimic my every move. They do not seem interested in engaging me in any form, but seem content to keep me in their sights. It will be dark in two hours time, and I had yet to find a place to camp. I know there is a group of defendable caves not too far to the east from here. I turn Torao in their direction, and quicken his pace.

This move makes my company bolder as two of the five begin to close the distance. I think they mean to engage. I goad Torao to a light gallop, and they do the same. They know I am making for the caves, and are trying to prevent this and keep me on my previous course. They are probably trying to channel me to their master. It will not work.

They are within bow range. They wear no color, banner or insignia of any kind. They are all in black. I get Torao into a quicker gallop, and I can see the mountain range. The others in the groups decide to join in the chase. I now have two groups approaching from both sides. The two are very close now, I can hear the horses. I turn slightly and dig my heels into Torao's belly. He knows what this means, and has played the part many times. He knows I am going to shoot these two, he maintains the rhythm of his gait, as I breathe in his rhythm. They draw their swords. They are not prepared for my Yumi. My first arrow strikes the lead through the throat, and my second hits the other in the eye. Torao jumps the fallen body of the first, and skirts around the rolling body of the second. Three more are to my right, and will also soon fall. The other two from the left have fallen off a bit, and will not catch me before I am in the caves. These three must fall first. I turn into them, and begin my charge. Two arrows fall true, as those bodies fall lifeless to the ground. The third backs off as I notch the arrow. He attempts to escape, but I lead him a bit and let the arrow fly. It enters the area he left exposed to me under his left arm, and probably ripped his heart in two.

I decide to charge the remaining two. One I will wound to question. They see the charge and separate themselves to meet my attack. I draw my Nodachi, a large heavy blade for horseback. They are not far now, and I see them draw their own blades. I slice through the one to my right as I pass. His blade is too short to be effective. They were obviously travelling lightly and were ill prepared for engagement. The second sees this and turns to run, and I bring Torao to chase. I get close enough to slice the back of the man's left leg, and arm. He cannot hold onto his galloping horse and falls backwards. I bring Torao to a stop, dismount, stab the Nodachi into the ground, and pull my Katana. The man is a bloody mess on the ground, and the fall it seems has broken his back. I pull off his helmet gently, but I see he is past questioning. Blood bubbles to his lips and he is coughing and choking on it. I take out my

Tanto and end his suffering. I search him and the others for some sort of clue as to who they are, but find nothing. I search the horses that I could round up and again nothing.

I make for the caves to camp for the night. It will be safe and comfortable for sleep. There is fresh water and Torao will stand guard. I will continue my quest for answers after I have rested...

Brakes are squealing, horns are honking, people are yelling. I try to push Ava and the carriage to safety, but there was not enough time...

I am now on a beach with my laptop going through files and files of my prospective targets life. They will want my answer soon, and yes I know I will kill this man...

I am in a suit in a church. I am sitting in a front pew, and there are two caskets before me. I am alone, all alone...

I wake with a start wiping tears from my eyes. Le is asleep, she is snoring loudly. I watch her for a bit, and then go to the bathroom and splash some cold water on my face. I return to bed and slip between the covers at the same time Le farts. I laugh, and it wakes her.

"What could be funny", she asked.

"I just splashed some water on my face and when I went to get back under the covers you farted", I said.

"Fuck off... I did not", she said still a bit sleepy.

"Yes you did... seriously", I said.

"I did not", she said emphatically.

I snuggled closer to her, and she turned to spoon. The big guy then sprang to life and was poking between her butt cheeks.

"Well... he certainly is not concerned about the fart", she said as she laughed.

I laughed again. I then rubbed my cock back and forth until she was wet enough to enter. We fucked for a bit, and then fell back asleep...

I stood up and walked to the caskets. Tears are rolling down my cheeks. I look inside of the first and see mother and child, and the second I see myself...

I am at a cemetery and I am watching the two caskets enter the ground beside each other. Freddie is in the front of the crowd, and he looks terrible. He does not look like the man I left, but more like the man that crawled out of that hole on that fucking hill. I cannot make out any other faces. They are all a blur, shaded and foggy...

Back at the beach my laptop beeps. They want my answer, and I send it to them. I will kill this fucking prick, and he will be my last...

I am hovering over a panicked crowd. There is a body on the floor at their feet, and cameras are clicking and whirring furiously. Guards begin to pour into the room, as they try to bring order and control back to the crowd. Someone is trying to apologize and explain the outburst of truth as more lies, and a direct and planned result of my supposed dissident activity in Tibet...

I am back in the monastery and I see my work is being continued. They cannot see me for I am not really there. I drift over the artwork and the progress made and I smile. This really was a life worth living...

Back in the frenzied media room, China is forced to answer questions. None of the foreign news people are buying the bullshit they are hearing. Questions fly, and people are being escorted out straight to the airport. People should not be able to impose themselves on others. No matter their strengths or subsequent weaknesses. Free will should be allowed to flourish everywhere. This media attention is another aspect of a life worth living...

SUNDAY 27TH OF JUNE 2011

I get up with Le watching me and she says, "What were you dreaming... you were crying at times and then smiling like a little kid".

"Some dreams are better than others", I said.

That is all I would say. I will continue to cry for Ava, and the little guy. I will miss them greatly. Maybe my dreams will allow a visit to the grave once in a while. As for the action in Tibet, I wish I could be as brave as that man, for free will and freedom should reign, no matter the strengths or weaknesses.

"Hey... hello", Le was saying.

"Hi", I said in return.

"Where did you go just now", she asked.

"Just remembering and cataloguing what I had just experienced", I said.

"Do you want to talk about it", she asked.

"I will tell you what I remember", I said.

I then went into a long dialogue. I told her about the car jumping the curb killing Ava and myself. I again omitted the part about the child. I told Le of the actions of my character in China, and the outcome of my outburst. I told her of the contract that I had taken on, and what an absolute piece of shit the guy was. She listened intently, wide eyed and fascinated as always. She thought it incredible that my dreams could be so vivid and so easily recalled.

We then showered and went to the Hotel trattoria for some breakfast. Coffee and pastries are what we settled on. We checked out got in the car, and continued our journey. I wondered what my dreams would bring next. I had never died before, in any of them. This was something new, and I wondered why it was happening.

Genoa would be our next stop, then onto Milan and then Venice. We planned to spend some more time in each of these places, possibly a week or more in each, we would see. Genoa is a nice coastal drive about 174 Km away. We filled the BMW, and picked up a basket of goods for a picnic on the beach, any beach. The GPS must be pissed off at us because it keeps turning off. The BMW was purring though. I have become more accustomed to the paddle shifting than before, and I think this car is beginning to like me. We would drive through Pisa and Livorno again. If the crowds are not too bad we might take a closer look at the Leaning Tower.

We skipped the tower and drove past it. We went to the coast and stopped in a small fishing village. One local we spoke to gave us directions to a great stretch of beach. It would be a little cool for swimming, but a great day for a picnic. We found the spot, and there were a few people here. A fairly large family, and a few couples. We found our spot and laid out a blanket, and our basket of food. I opened a bottle of wine while Le took everything out. We ate, talked about little things, nothing too important. The sun was shining, and the breeze from the sea comforting.

“I could stay here forever”, Le said.

"Forever is a long time... I couldn't I would miss my cottage too much", I said.

"Are you serious... couldn't you see it... up there on the hill a beautiful villa with gardens overlooking this magnificent beach", she said.

"Yes I can picture it... but not forever... maybe a month or two but not forever", I said.

"Just a month or two", she said.

"Maybe three", I said.

"I will keep that in mind", Le said.

"You do that", I said.

"When are we going to continue", she asked.

"Continue what", I asked.

"Our travelling", she said.

"Today", I asked.

"No... next year... yes today", she said.

"Later on... Genoa is not far away... we can keep hanging out here for quite some time... I need to sober up", I said.

"Come on... one glass... you are not drunk yet", she said.

"No not yet... give me some more time", I said reaching for the bottle.

"I can do that", she said laughing.

We ate and talked. Then after quite a few hours as the sun was going down we packed our things but sat for the sunset. By the time we were back on the road it was quite dark.

It was very late by the time we checked into the hotel in Genoa. It was time for a shower and then some sleep. No sex tonight, I was too tired and when my head hit the pillow...

I was running through the Eaton Center in Toronto. Well not actually running, but you get the meaning. I looked into all the mirrors as I passed by, and could not believe the transformation I had just gone through. The man staring back did not look like me. Would Jessica recognize me, the color, the style, and the new clothes? Did she go just as drastic with her looks? We were to meet at the Younge Street exit by the Sears store in fifteen minutes. I stopped at the Starbucks near the entrance and grabbed two cups of Pike's Place dark roast. Then I went over to the Godiva Chocolates store and bought a small package of almond and hazelnut clusters. There were no signs of any trouble, or of anyone following. You would never know that a truck crashed through the lobby of a hotel nearby killing all in its path, with two men exiting and firing into the remainder of the crowd.

I walked out onto Younge Street holding my tray of coffee, and bag of chocolates, and searched the faces of the crowd. No sign of Jessica yet. Twenty minutes go by and she is late. My coffee is almost empty and hers is getting cold. Thirty minutes, forty minutes and I am finished the coffee, and have since thrown hers out. Still no sign of Jessica, and now I am worried. I know women take longer but she had plenty of time. I then start thinking that maybe the hair shop she chose was really busy and she had to wait. Maybe she was still trying on clothes. I then go back into the mall and mill around the shops near the entrance way. I have finished the chocolates and she is now an hour and a half late. It has been way too long.

I decide to walk the mall in hopes of finding something, anything she may have left behind. What the fuck was I looking for? Something is definitely wrong, way wrong.

I then spot her on a bench at the opposite end and the wrong floor of where we agreed to meet. She is the same, no new hair and no new clothes. There is a man sitting next to her, and she seems nervous and fidgety. I then notice three more men milling around trying too hard to act like they are shopping. I walk right past and I know she sees me, but there is no reaction. She just slowly and calmly crossed her legs, and then looked the other way. How was I going to get her out of this? How the hell did they catch her?

Maybe they were not as amateurish as I had first thought, or is this another team? I keep walking. An hour later I return to walk by again, and this time there are two sitting with her and the other two standing in front. The four men seem to be arguing about what to do next, and I overheard something about, "half the package being no good".

I have two choices, risk everything in an attempt to save her, or walk away. My mind and self-preservation instinct says to walk away. Jessica knew this option as we had discussed it many times, and this is the way we always agreed on. My heart says to fuck it all and not let them win. I know they will take her somewhere and interrogate her properly, rape her and then kill or deliver her to whoever wants us. I know they will lose patience soon, and go that route. It is getting late and the mall will close soon...

I wake on the hard cold stone floor of a cave. I start a small fire and heat some water for tea. It will be cold rice and hot tea for breakfast, not bad for a man on the run. Torao is stamping the ground and I know he is hungry. I lead him further into the cave system and let him drink from the same spring I just got water from. I fill my flasks for the journey ahead. I have brought plenty of grain for Torao, and decided before I left on this quest that I would find my own sustenance along the way. It was fortunate that the men I had just killed were carrying enough rice for this meal, and enough grain to replenish Torao's stores. We ate and drank our fill and then left the cave.

I am not surprised to find a group of armed men waiting for us to come out. I calmly notch an arrow and draw the string back aiming it at the clear leader. The men he is with pull their arms. Four have bows and the rest draw their Katana. The leader raises his right arm and then motions for them to lower their weapons. I do the same. He rides forth and I wait for him to cross a decent amount of the ground between us, before meeting him. Torao is not happy. I stroke his neck and tell the big animal that is it fine and remind him that today and all the days that follow are good days to die, but we will not go alone. My voice calms him down, and he proceeds as I command. I am face to face with this man, but neither of us speaks...

I am on a plane, and I am a bit confused. I search my pockets and find a travel folder. It seems I am on my way to Brazil. Then it hits me, I am on my way to stalk my prey. I have exactly 365 days to complete this job, and I have to make it look as natural and as accidental as possible. No collateral damage will be tolerated. This is what I do...

I am sitting now on a bench. I am still in the Eaton Center, but my memory is slightly foggy. I try to think of who I am. So many things have changed lately. Then I see Jessica just down from me, and the four men are arguing more vocally now. People are now turning their heads towards the commotion. I know I have killed, stolen, lied and cheated my way through life, but I like to believe that there is still a chance at some redemption of honour, integrity. More people are stopping now to witness the argument between four men and a woman.

Jessica looks around and sees an opportunity, and she screams, "HELP... HELP ME PLEASE... THESE MEN HAVE SAID THEY ARE GOING TO KILL ME". One of the men smacks her, drawing blood from her lips. People have their phones out taking video and pictures. The man hits her again, and this time two Security Officers emerge from the crowd. A second man with Jessica pulls out a pistol and shoots them dead. The man who struck Jessica pulls out his own pistol, and grabs Jessica by the arm, and they attempt to drag her out. The other two pull out small automatics, and they look like MP5's. They spray into the crowd and they are hitting a lot of people. The crowd screams and those not hit turn and stampede for safety. More Security arrives, but this time with Police in tow. This just got ugly real fast.

The men's attention turn to the presence of firearms in front of them, and Jessica seizes the moment and breaks away from the man and turns to run in my direction. The man who hit her turns to fire in her back, but a bullet tears through him before he has a chance to.

There are bodies everywhere on the floor. The men who had Jessica keep spraying into the remainder of the crowd, but more Police have arrived and they all eventually fall to the laws fire.

In the absolute pandemonium, Jessica and I made our escape, and left through the nearest door. I kept looking behind us, watching her captors fall as the scene unfolded. Before we knew it we were on University, and planned to check into the nearest hotel. Jessica would have to wait until tomorrow for her transformation, but I would have to do it for her. I know her picture would be all over the news soon. There were so many cameras around. I would have to keep Jessica hidden even from the front desk. I would check in alone. Along the way I bought her a hat and a hoodie, and we retrieved our emergency bag. That would help.

After I had Jessica safe in the room I went out to buy some supplies, hair dye, clothes, scissors and clippers, that sort of thing. I knew her size by heart, and thought it would all work out fine...

I am in a Customs line. Yes that is right. I am in Brazil, I think. I am experiencing that fogginess and separation feeling once again. I have landed in Sao Paulo, at the Sao Paulo-Guarulhos International Airport, according to the signage around. My memory slowly clears, and the plans I have made so far are reforming.

I will make my own way to Rio de Janeiro. I have a rental car waiting for me. Customs is a breeze. My passports and identities are always flawless. I have rented a 2012 Jeep Wrangler Unlimited Rubicon, black in color. It should take me anywhere I may need it to. I have killed once before here in this country of Brazil, and I have an extensive familiarity with the area. That job took me almost two years...

MONDAY 28TH OF JUNE 2011

Le then knees me in the small of my back, and I swear and complain. It does not disturb her though, she just sleeps. It is enough though to bring me out of my dreams. I lay there all quiet and remember them. My recall is a little bit slow, and I cannot say for sure if Jessica and I made it out safely. I think that I had bought her a hoodie and a cap to get her past the front desk and safely into a hotel room. I think we are somewhere on University Avenue in Toronto. I cannot remember if we were injured with all the bullets flying around.

Torao and I are face to face with an enemy I suppose. Those men in front of me have yet to reveal their intentions or to whom they own allegiance to. I can only say they are enemies, for we must treat all we meet in that dream as an enemy.

The other dream in Brazil right now is just waking and is in a very young stage. I am going to kill a piece of shit, but what else unfolds I do not know.

I really miss Freddie and Ava, and the peace I experienced in the monastery. Those mornings I woke from the dreams with the monks I felt the most rested than I have in years.

Le is coming to consciousness, even though she is trying desperately to fight it and continue sleeping. I decide to take a shower, and order coffee to be brought up. I think we will take our time here in Genoa, and then in Milan. I know Le is looking forward to shopping in Milan, and I am looking forward to returning to Venice.

After drying off the coffee arrives. I look in at Le and she is still pretending to sleep, or maybe trying to go back to it. I do not know. I shut the door and leave her there. I write a quick note on the desk and left it with her cup of coffee. I decide to go down to the street, and find a small café across the street with a roadside terrace looking onto the main entrance of our hotel. When Le finds the note, showers and comes down I will be able to see and wave her over.

I order coffee and some pastries, and I do my second favorite thing. I watch the world go by. I look into all of the faces. In some I see sorrow and regret. Others are outright miserable, and some look scared. Then there are many that seem happy and content.

An hour later I spot Le coming down the steps. I stand to wave and she sees me. The pastries I ordered are gone, and I did not realize I had consumed all of them until now. Le ordered a coffee, and asked for something sweet.

"Did you want something", she asked.

"No… I am fine… well maybe just another cup of coffee", I said.

I did not want to tell her just how many sweets I had actually eaten. I will definitely have to walk that off today and maybe later tonight and well into next week.

"Sleep well", I asked.

"Yes... I guess... just was not ready to get up this morning", she replied.

"We are not on a schedule", I said.

"I know", she replied.

Things were quiet between us, nothing uncomfortable just quiet. It was good sitting here in Italy sipping coffee with a beautiful woman, and not feeling like I had to keep any conversation going.

I let my mind drift. I thought of my dreams. I miss the dog. I have not seen him since my world burned. In fact none of the jumbles have returned. The horse and the eagles do not visit anymore. I especially enjoyed the conversations with the eagles on all matters of life. The things they have seen. If only they could have recorded all they have been witness to through their generations. What a record of history that would be, as seen through the eyes of the birds that have flown above us all these centuries.

I reflect back on the people passing by. I ask myself what dreams from their own lives are they missing. Do they even notice or try to remember as I do.

I look over at Le as she sips her coffee and munches on a croissant. I have never asked her about her own dreams. She is watching the crowd, and she looks completely at ease. It is not as sunny as it was yesterday and it looks like it just might cloud over, but it does not feel like rain. The air is cooler, and will be conducive to the walking and shopping we have planned.

I know Le is saving her energy for the shops of Milan. She then comes to and noticed my staring and says, “Well... what is up”.

“Nothing”, I said.

“You were staring at me”, she said.

“Yes I was in fact”, I said.

“Why”, she asked.

“No reason”, I said.

“Really... there is no smear of something on my face from these pastries”, she asked.

“No... I was just looking at you”, I said.

“Did you dream last night”, she asked.

“Yes... did you”, I countered.

“Me”, she asked.

“Yes... what did you dream of last night”, I asked.

“I do not recall much... I never could”, she said.

“Take a moment... and give it a shot... whatever you remember tell me”, I said.

“OK I will play and give this a shot”, she said.

Le finished the pastry she had been working on, and took a few more sips of her coffee. I ordered some fresh to be brought to us. Le closed her eyes and began attempting to recall what she had been dreaming of lately. She was silent for quite some time, and I did not utter a word.

Le opened her eyes and began speaking. She started off by telling that she remembered a dirt road. She believed it to be the road to my cottage. Then she said she was on a kayak, but not at my lake. She remembers walking with a bear. She then said she remembered sitting atop the dome of Saint Peter's Basilica. Then she said she remembered other parts but in no specific order, like eating a donut at Tim Horton's, sipping tea on the balcony of her apartment, and riding a horse.

"I can't recall anything together... I don't believe they were together", she said.

"I call those dreams jumbles... but if you cannot recall if they were in conjunction with each other then maybe they were all a part of bigger dreams or maybe a bunch of small dreams on their own", I said.

"I do not think they were jumbles... but I did wake a lot last night and I think they were the last images in my mind before waking", she said.

"Very cool", I said.

"In what way", she asked.

"That we can share in this way... maybe you can tell me some more about them one day", I said.

"Yes... of course... now what about you... what great adventure did you take part in last night", she asked.

I told her of the confrontation that Torao and I shared, and the standoff we were now in. I told her of the action and turn of events in Toronto with Jessica, and how I was in Brazil to carry out a contract.

"How in the hell do you do that", she asked.

"Do what", I asked.

"Have such crazy exciting and vividly detailed dreams", she said.

"You have them to... we all do... you just have to work and concentrate on the recall of them", I said.

"Maybe... or maybe you are just a crazy fucked –up psycho", she said jokingly.

"Yeah... I can see that", I said with a smile.

Le tried to kick me under the table, but I was quicker this time and dodged the blow. She managed instead to smash her toes on the center pedestal that the table stood on. She let out a scream and called me a "jerk". I laughed, inspected her foot for a break and being satisfied there was none, I laughed even harder. We then decided to leave the café, and laughed together all the way to the nearest store that caught her eye.

After battling through a tough day on the cobblestone jungle, and spending an indecent amount of money it was time to find a place for dinner. We decided to go back to the hotel to shower and change. All of our purchases would be sent there so we may sift through them, and keep with us what we wanted or needed for the remainder of the trip. The rest would be packed up and shipped to my address in Canada. This was a costly process but well worth the trouble it saved.

I bought three handmade suits that I would be able to pick up before we leave, along with two swords and a shield from an antique shop I found. I will not list what Le bought, and I cannot imagine the scope of her plans to save the largest shopping for Milan.

Back at the Hotel our packages started arriving, and kept arriving for over an hour. The concierge was extremely busy but well paid for the work. He recommended that we try a few of the local favorites like Da Genio, Trattoria Rosmarino, or Zefferino. We thanked him for the tip.

"Well... which one", I asked.

"Trattoria Rosmarino", she quickly replied.

"Why that one", I asked.

"I do not know... it was the name that stuck in my head", she replied.

"Then the Rosmarino it is... are you ready", I asked.

"Yes... two seconds... if you will zip me up", she said.

"Of course", I said, and did just that.

Le decided to wear one of the dresses she bought today. She was absolutely stunning in it. It hugged every curve like it was made for her. We went down to the hotel lobby where the concierge had a car ready for us.

"And which did you decide on", he asked.

"The Rosmarino", Le replied.

"Excellent choice", he replied.

He then instructed the driver where we were to be taken and waited for. It seems the car belonged to the hotel and was at our disposal for the evening.

We had an excellent meal, and after the driver took us to an elevated spot overlooking the Harbor. We watched the lights dance on the ships in port and those anchored off shore, as they reflected off the water. It was getting late and we were both very tired. We did not bother to shower but fell into bed and as my head hit the pillow...

Torao was restless and stamping the ground snorting his displeasure. We were now face to face with my armed foe. He wore the colors and insignia of my Daimyo's most powerful enemy. The man removed his Kabuto, and spoke, "Your lands are now ours... your Daimyo is dead... swear allegiance to my

Lord and tell of the location of his blood... we will spare your life and those of your blood line and you may keep your title and land intact with honour".

"My honour... that is not possible with what you ask", I said.

"You are a powerful and respected Samurai... your word will carry much with the others and can stop the killing of other clans as we move on... that is honour", he said.

"Move on where", I asked.

"We are eliminating the territorial Lords one at a time to bring all under control of our own Lord", he said.

"Not as long as there is breathe in my chest and strength in my hand", I said hands and teeth clenched.

I drew the arrow notched in my Yumi, and with lightning speed put the arrow through the man's right eye in answer to his request. Torao instinctively swung around and avoided the arrows of the four others. I could tell he was pleased with my choice. I drew my Nodachi and cut two others in half. The rest were no match for Torao and me. I suffered a few small cuts, but they all lay dead. I will kill all in their army or die before bowing to them, and forsaking my honour. I take from them what I need and continue my journey...

I am now in a washroom, a hotel washroom. I am taking off some red stained gloves, and the sink is full of blond hair. I look over into the room and Jessica is walking around, with her new cut and dye. I did the best I could to alter her appearance to one of our many unused identities.

"I did not think you were coming back for me", she said.

"I was not sure myself until I saw the look on your face when you saw me walk by", I said.

"I would never have given you up", she said.

"I know... and even though we agreed I could never walk away", I said.

"I am sorry for what happened", she said.

"How did it happen", I asked.

"I was picking a salon and then a felt a gun barrel in my ribs and I just went quietly... there were kids around and I had no other options... they walked me around looking for you... asking questions that I could not answer... they are convinced that we have that ring", she said.

"What... the one we were supposed to have recovered in South America", I asked.

"Yes... they kept saying their Intel was excellent and confirmed", she said.

"That is why we are not dead", I said.

"The only reason", she said.

"Why the theatrics with the truck in the hotel lobby... and the act of the young girl they sent in to us", I asked.

"I do not know... a message... a different group... these guys were pros... I do not think they were linked to the first", she said.

"What next... where do you want to go", I asked.

"I will reach out to my friends in France and see what they have heard", she said.

"Yes call Marc then", I said.

"We will owe him again", she said.

"I know... everything comes with a price", I said.

“Shall we stay here”, she asked.

“No... no way... we will get out of Canada”, I said.

“To where”, she asked.

“We will fly to the Philippines and call Marc from there... and then go to Malaysia... it is easier to get lost there”, I said.

“When do we leave”, Jessica asked.

“As soon as we get some sleep”, I said.

Could we have missed that dammed ring, I asked myself. I do not think so. We went through the house like professionals and checked everywhere without disturbing a single thing. We could go back and check again, and this time who cares what we make it look like. I will bring this up after Jessica talks to Marc. I wonder what the price is for us, the price on our heads and what it will cost to get us out of this...

I am behind the wheel of a jeep and by the road signs I am now approaching Rio. The sun is blaring hot here at the height of their summer. I need to get really tanned, grow my hair longer past my shoulders and keep my scruffy beard. I need to blend in, and look good on the beach. This guy spends a lot of time on the beaches in search of young dumb girls, and boys to defile. If it is not him on the beaches it is someone close to him that brings who they find to him. I have to find a way to get close...

Torao and I have been travelling for hours, and besides a few farmers and travelers have not seen any trouble. The farmers that I approached and spoke to said that many armed groups have gone by, mostly in tens and twelve’s. The travelers say the same, but report they have been harassed and searched many times. I have asked if any are Samurai, and they both say yes in dress, but not in honour.

In two days I will be at the heart and seat of my Daimyo's lands, but I will camp soon, at the foot of the mountains to my left. There is a place with fresh water that is easy to defend if it is not already occupied. If it is then they will all die. I wonder what happened to the other Samurai and my Master's armies. Have they all taken their own lives, or have they forsaken their own honour and changed allegiances. I hope to find some soon. There must be pockets of them somewhere that I may gather into an army...

I wake up in a fog, and very groggy. I have to take a piss. I reluctantly get out of the bed occupied by Le, and go to the washroom. I wish I could have taken some pharmaceuticals to sleep longer periods, and dream some more. I am still sad at the ending of the other dreams, and I wonder if the dog, horse or eagle will return. That may bring my jumbled dreams back to normal and reverse the damage that had been done in them. Maybe I will not end up in hell after all. I look at my watch and it is only 430 in the morning. At least I will be able to get to sleep and dream some more. When I return Le is sort of awake, and asks, "Is something wrong".

"No not at all... just had to pee", I said.

"What time is it", she asked.

"430... now go back to sleep", I replied.

"Ok... see you in a couple of hours", she said.

I climbed back and slid in beside her. I wrapped my arms around her, and she brought her body closer. It was not long before her breathing changed and she was asleep. A short while later I was...

I wake on a beach. Some hot girl kicked sand on me retrieving a Frisbee. She said excuse me In Portuguese, and I remember I am here in Brazil. I remember what for. The female is gorgeous, tanned, red thong, topless. She lingers longer than she had to, and I invite her to sit. She accepts, and we converse in Portuguese, but I hear everything from here on end in English.

"What is your name", she asked.

"My name is William... and you", I asked.

"Gabriela", she replied.

"Where are you from", she asked.

"All over and nowhere", I said.

"Your birthplace", she asked.

"I am Canadian", I said.

"And what brings you to Rio", she asked.

"The local fare", I said.

"I see... it was nice to meet you William... but I must rejoin my friends", she said.

"Did I offend you", I asked.

"No... but like I said... it was nice to meet you... maybe we will meet again in your search of local fare", she said with a seductive smile, then biting on her lip.

She then ran off. She stopped once and looked back and smiled, and then joined a group of people. I did not spy my target here, but then again I did not intend to. I am here to work on my tan and get a feel for Brazil, so I may fit in when the time comes...

I am riding Torao again, and we reach the base of some hills that when you look beyond those small hills turn into mountains. It was a peaceful journey after my last encounter.

Just farmers and travelers on the road, but they all warned of trouble.

I found the path I was looking for and ventured into the hills and the mountains. I came to a large stream, and allowed Torao to drink from its deep pools. It was quiet and I shed my armor and stretched. I then took out some supplies and bathed. The water was cold, but that did not bother me. After I dried I started a fire to make tea. The dried meats I took off the last group will be a welcome addition to my diet. After a decent meal, Torao and I continued our journey into the mountains. We did not get far before I found evidence that a large group of heavy laden horses came through here ahead of me from the path to the east.

I followed their back trail and noticed that they did not come as one band, but a series of smaller bands met and came together. I followed the signs all the way to the point they came together, and noted the directions from which they travelled from. They came from the direction of my lands. Samurai...

TUESDAY 29TH OF JUNE 2011

Dam, I am awake again. I think I need to find something to help me sleep longer. A shot is out of the question. The ingredients for the formula I used are not legally obtainable here. I guess I will have to try something over the counter, but how do I explain that to Le.

I get out of bed and sit by the window for awhile. I look out and watch as the streets of Genoa are waking. I decide to grab a shower and go to the café down the street. Before I left, I wrote Le a quick note. She was still sleeping heavily. I wondered what she was dreaming of. I wondered if she was still walking with the bear, kayaking, shopping, or maybe sitting atop the Basilica.

I thought how much I missed the dog, and some of the other lost dreams. I was thinking of what his visits meant to me. I was thinking of my conversations with the eagles. I then recalled being atop a horse and pulled away from the two women playing in the water. Was that a warning? Was I supposed to stay away from women, and everything would have been fine. I do not know. I look back at Le once more before leaving the room, and she has not moved. I push the thought of her as a mistake out of my mind, because I think I may be falling, or maybe I have fallen.

The streets of Genoa are alive. The café bistro across the street is busy, but I manage to hover long enough, and score a spot outside by the street. I watch all the people going by my table, and I started to see things in their faces. I could tell, or at least I think I could, the ones that dreamt well and the ones that did not.

I sat there long enough watching people, and sipping on two coffees to order lunch. I ordered Piedmont Beef Carpaccio, a caprese salad, an antipasto, and a bottle of Brunello di Montalcino. Le came across, and sat down just as the food arrived. It was very lucky timing, and fortunate that I ordered enough for two.

"How come you are up so early... how long have you been here", Le asked.

"I got up from my second round of dreams and realized I was hungry... you were sound asleep and decided to leave you sleeping", I said.

"Thanks... I really needed it... and your dreams... what of them", she asked.

I brought her up to speed. I thought about mentioning the fact that I needed to sleep for longer periods of time. I thought about telling her of the concoctions I had created that allowed me to do so. I didn't of course.

"This food is good... excellent choice... and how did you know of this wine it is amazing", she said.

"You are not the only one who can order based on what they know of people", I said.

"I know... but most guys do not pay attention to the little details", she said.

"I am not most men", I said.

"What is up for today", she asked.

"Whatever you want", I said.

"Well I thought about visiting the Galleria Nazionale di Palazzo Spinola the Museo di Palazzo Reale and the Acquario di Genova", she said.

"Really... two museums and an aquarium... where did you learn of them", I said.

"Just now from the concierge", she said.

"Then that will be our day... well that and a lot more food and wine", I said.

"Sounds like a plan... now let's finish what we have in front of us and get going... I slept way too long", she said.

"Whatever we do not get to do today there is always tomorrow", I said.

"I plan to sleep again tomorrow", she said.

"That is fine with me... you know where to find me... this Carpaccio is excellent and there are a few other things they offer I want to try", I said.

"You would eat without me", she asked.

"This... yes... definitely I would keep it all to myself", I said.

"You shit... let's go catch a cab... where to first", she said in a miffed tone.

"Does not matter... whatever is closer... we will let the cabbie decide... and do not be pissed about my answer... you asked" I said.

"Fine... we will leave our fate to a cab driver", she said still a bit miffed but half smiling.

After we ate we walked down the street a bit, and we were able to hail the first cab that passed. We told the man where we wanted to go. He suggested we hire him for the day. We agreed on a decent rate and let this adventure begin. Our first stop would be the aquarium. The cabbie's children love it.

I love these places. Little pockets in the world dedicated to the preservation, protection, and education of the world's most endangered species. The aquarium here in Genoa boasts a huge assortment of climates, and their species of aquatic life. It also has a large tropical biosphere that propels you to the deepest region of the world's rain forests. We walked the entire complex hopping from one display and region of the world to another. We were no longer in Genoa, but we travelled the world. I think I liked the Hummingbird Forest, the Galata Maritime Museum, and the Biosphere the best of all the displays.

Hours later Le dragged me out of there practically kicking and screaming. She promised me an ice cream and that we could return one day. This appeased me for a bit, and we laughed the whole time.

We had no time left in the day for the other places we wanted to visit, and decided to finish them tomorrow or the next day. It did not really matter. We had the cab take us back to the hotel, and he promised he would return at the same time tomorrow and take us to the Galleria Nazionale di Palazzo Spinola. We would probably have to save the Museo di Palazzo Reale for the next. Before I leave Genoa or Italy for that matter I will return to the Aquarium. It really was that great of an experience.

The cabbie dropped us off and we were famished. We went to another small restaurant just down from the one this morning. The place was about to close, but I convinced the owner I would make it worth his while, and ordered a fairly large dinner. We let the owner and chef decide the menu for us. That was not a mistake. Dinner was an absolutely amazing culinary feast. I am beginning to fall in love twice. The second is with the food in Italy. We devoured every last morsel, and I could have licked the plates.

Back at the hotel we showered. Yes together. Yes it was completely sexual. Yes I then fell asleep...

The stench of body odor is strong. I open my eyes and Jessica is lying beside me, but there are others here. There are many sleeping here, and most of them stink. I nudge Jessica to wake her, and her eyes open grudgingly with contempt.

"Where in the hell are we", I asked quite confused.

"Manila...The Philippines... a Hostel... don't you remember", she said, now confused herself.

"No not really... actually not at all", I said.

"Do you remember the plane and the boat", she asked.

“No… nothing… last I remember is Toronto and us planning on coming here to call Marc… and then hiding in Malaysia”, I said.

“You really do not remember… Toronto was three weeks ago”, she said.

“I do not know… maybe… but how did we end up here”, I asked, sort of revolted.

“It was a good place to hide… all of them have been like this you know the routine here… let’s get our things and go now… we still need to call Marc and see what he has heard… and get your shit together… I need you Sean”, she said.

“I’ll be Ok… you know that… and we need each other to get through this”, I said, with great confidence.

We packed everything quickly and left the hostel just outside of Manila. There was a place here that we had used before to make a couple of very secure calls…

I am back in the hills walking Torao. I am not trying to be quiet or conceal myself. I want the group in front of me to know I am here. I believe them to be my clansmen looking for me. They would have known I was headed to a mountain range, but none but me knew where I was going…

“Ready Sean”, someone called from what seemed a great distance.

Jessica was right beside me. I could have sworn the voice calling to me was far away.

“Yes I am ready… let’s go”, I said.

With that we left the hostel and boarded a Jeepney. The jeepney is a common mode of transportation here in the Philippines. They are often multi and brightly colored. Kind of like bus meets jeep meets half ton truck meets stoned out artist. We actually board several on our way to our destination.

Upon arrival we are greeted warmly by some old friends that we helped a long time ago, and seem to feel indebted to us for their lives. We did not want to come here right away to keep any possible danger away. It was good to shower and shave. It was good to eat the food presented after. Our benefactors here knew we were in great trouble, and we told them everything as we ate...

Torao and I came upon a campsite. I found the embers of the fire still glowing and made some tea. I then called out in a loud voice for those watching to join me. The area around came alive as the figures walked into their own old camp. Smiles on their faces as recognition set in. They all came around the fire, except those sent to keep watch on the trails. A great many things were discussed as I told them what had happened on my end of this war. I recalled the tales of the battles, the skirmishes, and that our young Lord was safe. They then told of their own battles, the deception and betrayals of our own Samurai. The event of the death of our Lord, and the remainder of his court and seed, was told to me in great detail. There were others of our clan sent to the different corners in search of me. Riders would be sent to retrieve them so we may band together and make things right. This is the story they told...

WEDNESDAY 30TH OF JUNE 2011

I woke again, and not when I would have wanted to. The dream was just getting very exciting. Fuck I need to take something, anything to stay asleep. I flip on the news and find a segment with English subtitles. Muammar Gaddafi has been captured and killed by his own people. I have not been following the news much lately, but there has been an enormous amount of civil unrest all over the Middle East. The people are tired of the tyrannical rules of the dictators in power. I am not surprised by the news or the countries involved. Is it a good thing, only time will tell? I flip off the Television, because I hate news. I hate all kinds of news. Some stories I think are fabricated and not real. I think half of the world is a complete conspiracy and the other half out of their minds. That is why I dream.

Le is sleeping, but I do not join her. I simply leave her a note telling her I am on a quest, but I will return with spoils in hand. I do not think I could go back to sleep anyway. I feel quite rested. It is now 7 am Italy time, and I feel like a Napoleon and an espresso. I shower and dress and go looking for just that. There has to be a pastry shop here to suit my craving. That is the quest, to find the best Napoleons Italy has to offer if that is possible.

It was recommended to me by the concierge, to go to the pastry shop called Romanengo. It is the oldest pastry shop in Genoa, and I am told the Napoleons there are absolutely good enough to die for. I hail a cab, and take off. I ask the cabbie to wait. Walking into the shop was amazing. My senses were assaulted by the best smells. Baking breads, cinnamon, nutmeg, and all kinds of sweet aromas fill my nostrils and make me smile. I came for Napoleons but left with a box full of tantalizing treats. I wolfed down three of the Napoleons in the cab on the way back to the hotel, but showed great restraint in saving two. My plan was to act like I had yet to try them, and share that first experience with Le.

I walk into the room and Le was in the shower. I thought about joining her, but then changed my mind. I wanted to get to the museums today, and sex right now would put us hours behind. On the way up to the room I requested that coffee and espresso be sent up. It had arrived by the time Le was finished in the bathroom. She came into the living area and dove for the box on the table. She ripped it open like a kid at Christmas, and bit into one of the two Napoleons.

"Hey save one for me", I said.

"Save one... how many did you have on the way back", she asked raising an eyebrow.

"Three", I said with a hint of guilt in my voice.

"These are mine then... they are really good... I would honestly kill for these", she said keeping the box guarded behind her.

I picked up a cup of espresso and took a long sip. I eyed the box and the distance between us. I decided what the hell. I placed the cup on the other table, and made my run. Le realized what I was up to a little too late. She let out a scream and a squeal, but the box was mine. I did not touch the Napoleon though, and tried one of the other treats. Le was not happy.

"You scared the shit out of me... asshole", she said and then burst out laughing.

"I know... that was the idea", I said smiling with powdered sugar all over my face.

"Well pour me a cup of coffee at least", she said as she sat down and finished the last two bites of the treat.

"Of course Love", I replied.

We finished the contents of the box, because we felt it would not keep well in the room. I had a second cup of espresso, and we went out and walked the streets a bit. We were waiting for the appointed time we had arranged for the cabbie from yesterday to return for us.

It was not long before we were whisked away to the Galleria Nazionale di Palazzo Spinola. The artwork was amazing and we took a great deal of time examining all of the works, the paintings, the frescoes, the furniture and the china. We took it all in touring from room to room and floor to floor. We toured the gallery three times over five hours. Then we realized we were famished.

The cab was not to pick us up for another five hours. Therefore we decided to find a place to eat. There were several choices in the area. We settled on one called Rivaro, and the cuisine was most excellent. We started with rounds of eggplant and truffle parmesan, and prosciutto with olives. Our second course was stuffed lobster, caramelized scallops, and mussels in white wine sauce. A third course consisted of roasted quail and root vegetables. We finished with Tartufo and coffee. It sounds like a lot but I was hungry and pulled in the slack for Le. We took a walk afterwards.

During our walk we found a few shops open, and we made a few purchases. In one shop full of antiques I found a very old shield, and a broadsword. Both pieces were encased in vacuumed sealed glass cases. I thought about buying them, but I didn't. This may be the first time I passed up on these types of items, and I do not know why. They looked authentic possibly fourteenth or fifteenth century. The materials and wear looked right, but I would have to open the cases for a proper assessment.

The shop owners had papers on both items. The papers detailed the family lineage and their authenticity. The papers pegged them as thirteenth century and tell a story of how they were left behind as a gift to a physician by a crusader going back home to France after the Christians failed to recapture the Holy Land for the last time. The papers were also in glass, and properly cared for. They included an up to date interpretation of their contents. It was a magnificent story, and a great thing to come across and see. It would have been a great addition to my collection. Maybe I will return.

Back at the hotel the sex was amazing, but my thoughts were clouded. Le could sense this.

"What is wrong", she asked with a great deal of care and sensitivity in her voice.

"I do not know... but that sword and shield... I passed on them... I have never passed up on those things before", I said.

"Does it have something to do with the change in your dreams", she asked right to the point.

"I think so... my mind seems to be changing", I said.

"You will work it out... a lot has happened... you met me... quit your job... came here... it will all work out", she said with that same sensitive tone.

"I am going to buy them", I said.

"I know", Le said in response.

My thoughts were still clouded when my head hit the pillow...

I am in a restaurant, a very busy one. I look around and the place is absolutely packed. A waiter comes over and asks if I am ready to place an order. The waiter speaks in Portuguese. Brazil, I am in Brazil. I ring off my order to the waiter and he bows and leaves. I do not remember how I knew what to order, nor do I remember even looking at a menu. He comes back moments later with the beer I had ordered.

Every table is full, and the place is extremely busy, but in the back I am still able to spy two heavily armed men standing on each side of closed double doors. I can tell they are armed from the distinctive bulge at their right sides. Those double doors lead to a private room, and my target will be in there. They are very heavy and thick doors. My target is here every Friday night without fail. Men come and go from the room and I try to glimpse inside but the room is designed properly. You cannot see in from any point in the place.

Each man and woman is patted down before entry. No matter how many times the same person enters, he or she is subject to the same scrutiny. Firearms or weapon of any kind are surrendered to and placed in a box behind the man to the left of the door, and returned to the owner upon exit.

I take it all in. I try to memorize the faces of all the people coming and going. Most are in the dossier that I had been given. There are a few new ones though, and these are the ones I pay the most attention to.

My first course arrives, a simple shrimp cocktail. The shrimp look like lobster tails they are so large. After consuming them I am not sure I will have room for the next course, a signature dish of the restaurant featuring grilled codfish. Codfish is a staple of Portuguese cuisine. After digging deep into my soul I am able to finish. I sit and have another beer, and then a third. The restaurant crowd is starting to thin out, and not as many are coming and going from the back room. Tables are being cleared from the floor. Soon this place will be a thriving Night Club, and my intended target will remain in the back room until the wee hours of the morning. I finish my third beer, and walk out. That is enough surveillance for the night. My Hotel room is across the street, and I will continue my vigil from there. So far my Intel had been true, if it continues this will turn out being a fairly easy gig. Time will tell. I set up my watch with a strong pot of Brazilian coffee...

I wake up by a fire and am assailed by the strong odor of men and horses. My confusion does not last long and I remember where I am. I go to Torao, and he is not used to the company around us. I soothe the large beast. I then check all my equipment and go through the ritual of cleaning, sharpening, and polishing everything. Upon seeing me the rest of the Samurai around do the same. We go about our day like the generations before us. We are in pursuit of perfection, a constant pursuit of perfection in the service of our Lord. We number only thirty, but we are thirty of the most experienced hardened fighters that few have survived against to tell tales about. These were sent away to find me just after our Lord was assassinated. They were removed by an advisor under the guise of the dying orders from our Daimyo himself. One Samurai, left to spy on the after affects of our Master's death, came after this group and survived his wounds only long enough to tell the tale of what had transpired. He had fulfilled his duty...

Dam, I have to piss again. I have to stop drinking so much before I go to sleep. Le is not in bed but sitting by the window watching me.

"You were tossing and turning so much I could not sleep", she said.

"I am sorry love", I said.

"Rough dreams", she asked.

"No not at all... at least I did not think so", I said.

"Where are you going", she asked as I passed by her.

"I need to pee", I said.

"Ok... I am going to try to lie down again... when you come to bed and fall asleep try not to dream like you are fighting someone", she said half laughing and half angry.

"Was it that bad", I asked, very confused.

"Yes... you kicked me like three or four times", she said, emphatically.

"I am sorry... are you hurt", I asked, concerned.

"No I am fine... the first one scared me awake but that is all", she said.

"But I do not recall fighting in any of my dreams", I said, sitting back down on the edge of the bed, really confused.

"Well... think again... because you were fighting someone or something... at one point you stood up and were swinging your fists at air... I just got the hell out of your way and if it continues I think we will need separate beds", she said.

"Really... shit Le... I am really sorry... why can't I remember... are you really serious", I asked.

"Of course... not... you dumb shit... just getting you back for the other day... I have had this planned for awhile... the white pale look on your face", she said as she lay down laughing.

"Ha ha... whatever... now go to sleep and fart some more", I said chuckling.

I went to turn towards the bathroom, and a pillow hit the back of my head. I returned the favor, but she blocked it with another. I then took a long piss. I returned to the room and lay down beside her.

"Feel better", I asked.

"Yes much", she said, still smiling like a 'cat that caught the canary'.

Before I knew it, she was snoring and I...

I was riding Torao with my Yumi raised firing arrows into the throng of approaching Samurai as fast as my fingers would allow. We were thirty, and they I estimate to be about five hundred strong. Well, they were when they charged, but my arrows alone have accounted for at least twelve. They may not be dead, but are certainly no longer a threat, and could be easily dispatched later if they have not already committed seppuku. My hope is the others have accounted for the same before some of them had fallen. After exhausting my supply of arrows I drew my Nodachi, and I started to cleave and carve as much flesh and bone of the enemy as I could.

We rode through them, and just before turning around I noticed another cloud of dust forming just within my farthest sight. It could be more enemies, and if it is we will be finished soon. I turned and attacked again, and this time with more vigor than before. There are bodies everywhere, but Torao is expertly keeping his footing being the battle worn horse he is. On the next turn I notice the cloud getting larger and closer. I am bleeding from many wounds as is Torao. There are only eight of us left. We have accounted for more than forty times that amount. It looks to be our time, for now I can see the approaching horses and hear the shouts and battle cries of their riders.

The eight of us stop in a line and face our enemy. I drop the Nodachi, and get off of Torao. The other seven do the same. There are now a thousand or more men in front of us, and they stop to watch what we are about to do. I take out my Katana, and step to Torao's side, as the rest does with their mounts. I bow to him, and the large beast knows what is to happen. I will be riding him soon on the other side, very soon. I could not stand another being his master. "I will see you soon my friend... very soon", I said.

With one scream and in one stroke I took his head. We all did at the same time. Then in the same scream and with the same breath we charged the thousand before us...

A few moments later I was riding Torao once more, with my Father at my side, in the valley with the blossoms that I knew to be Holy...

I am walking in a street market, and am holding a bag of mangoes. I see Jessica at a vendor about twenty feet from me, and she is haggling with the man over the price of a handbag. They agree and the money changes hands. It is almost time to call Marc, and I yell to Jessica that we had to get going. We board a Jeepney and go back to the home of our friends. Jessica goes and makes a secure call to France. Upon her return her face is ashen white, and she is trembling.

"What is it", I asked, trying to remain calm.

"There is a bounty on our heads", she said, in a detached voice.

"How bad is it", I hurriedly asked.

"Fifty million", she said.

"Fifty million for us", I said, surprised at the amount.

"Fifty million each", she said, distracted.

"The people with the ring", I asked.

"Yes... they are convinced that we have it", she said.

"And Marc... what of him", I asked.

"He owes us nothing... and will be coming for us real soon", she said.

"Is there an out", I asked.

"Well we can try to disappear... or... we have twenty one days to turn over the ring... then the hunters come for us", she said.

"What about those pricks in Toronto", I asked.

"Meant to scare us... they really believe we have the ring... the bounty goes into effect in twenty one days not a day before", she said.

"What do you want to do", I asked, even though I knew the answer.

"Go back to South America and torture the bastard until he gives us the ring", she said.

"We go from zero to killing to torture... that easily", I said.

"From killing to torture... for our own lives", she said...

I am shaken awake. It is still dark and my mind is extremely blurry. I look around, and it is Jessica leaning over me prodding me awake. I have no idea where I am. It is a jungle for sure, and we are on a slope. I can see the tops of homes and outlines of manicured areas around them. It seems kind of familiar. It is almost like I have been here before. I search my memory, and I try to concentrate. Then I remember the ring and the bounty and everything. We are outside of the keeper's house, and this time we are going in hard. We will force him to tell us of the ring.

"Are you ready", Jessica asks.

"Yeah let's go and get this over with", I said.

We dressed and donned gloves, masks, hair nets, plastic clothes, taped everything down like we were some sort of hazardous materials team. We enter the house the same as before. The man should be alone and asleep. Up the stairs I go. Jessica stays on the main floor and waits. The needle pricks the man on the arm, and for a second I thought he would wake. He didn't. I pushed the plunger and the sedative entered the man's veins. This would allow us to secure the man, and wake him up with another injection when we were ready to scare the shit right out of him.

This bastard was heavy, and smelled worse than any I have encountered to date. He was even worse than those in the hostel in the Philippines. I managed to tie him up and get him secured to a chair. Jessica checked the house and confirmed we were alone. It was time to get to work.

"Christ he smells", Jessica said.

"I know... I know... I had to touch him to get him here", I said, with a hint of distain in my voice and a look of disgust on my face.

"Ready", she asked.

"Ready as ever", I said.

Jessica then administered a serum that would wake the smelly prick up. It took a few minutes to work, but the man was reviving. When he came to semi-consciousness his eyes went wide with absolute fear. He tried to scream and squirm but to no avail. I had him fixed so that he could not see us. He could not turn his head at all. That way there was no chance we could be identified. I placed a tray of nasty, medieval looking, blood stained instruments on a tray in front of him. I told him what was going to happen, step by step, picking up each applicable instrument to emphasize my point if he did not tell us the truth to every question we asked. His eyes grew wider and wilder and he started to cry. He then pissed and shit himself. We thought his body odor was bad. That cloud of shit that came out of his ass was sickening. Jessica had to leave the room or she would vomit. There could be no traces of us here. She caught herself just in time. Vomiting with her full face mask on would not have been pretty.

I asked the man where the ring was. I was holding up the first tool. He nodded his understanding, and I removed his gag so that he may answer the question. He told us that there was a false brick in the wall behind his cook stove. The brick was located three up and four to the right of the bottom left hand corner. There was no way we would have found it. There was a metal box in the hole, and the ring was inside. Jessica heard this from the door, and went to investigate.

Jessica returned about twenty minutes later holding the box. She tossed it to me. The lock was magnetic and required a code. I held up the nastiest of all the instruments and the man spilled his guts and gave me the code. I entered it and it opened quietly. The ring was nestled safe inside. The man laughed and said he hoped it brought as much misery to us as it had to him. I put him back to sleep and we left.

Out the back and over the stone fence we went, disappearing into the jungle beyond. Just like before we planned to exit far away like tourists out for a hike. We dumped our clothes, and changed. The man would not wake for hours and by the time he did we would be a thousand miles away safely on a plane. This was easy.

"That was easy", Jessica said.

"Yes it was... way too easy... but we would never have found it where it was... never", I said.

"Well what are we going to do with the money", she asked.

"What we planned... leave this life and disappear", I said.

We were quiet moving through the jungle on much the same route as before. The box and ring safe in my pack, when the box started to beep. We froze.

"What the hell is it", Jessica asked.

"Maybe a tracking device or some sort or alarm", I said.

I tried entering the code but it would not work. The beeping got faster, louder and more intense. Then the box got hot and I dropped it and tried to yell "RUN". I did not have time, and I will bet the explosion could have been seen as far away as Mexico...

THURSDAY 1ST OF JULY 2011

I wake up again. Not because I had to pee, or was thirsty, or because of anything Le did. I woke up over a troubled mind. Another dream is dead, and in another I have forsaken all moral fiber. I look out the window and see the sun rising. I took the hottest shower I could stand, dressed and went down for coffee and a walk. I left Le a note and told her I would return in an hour or so.

I took a cab and walked around the area of the shop with the sword and shield. I waited for it to open, and bought the items. I had them shipped to my home address. These would make an amazing addition to my collection along with the items I bought in Rome.

The image of my taking Torao's head kept flashing in my mind, over and over again. I felt no pain as the swords went through me. I guess I thought they would hurt.

I know I could not torture someone in real life, and am not sure how my dream character would respond to it. He killed easily enough, that man in the hotel with the lethal concoction in his eyes. My dreams are ending too quickly, tragically, and I do not know how to stop it.

I walked for awhile, and I am pretty sure I spent most of the time talking to myself. I only have two active dreams left. I must be having others that I cannot recall, or maybe I do not want to recall. Torao and Hisoka, Ava Freddie and Bobby, Jessica, the Artist, and the jumbles are all gone. If you put the jumbles together they were all one dream. They just were not presented in any particular order.

I kept concentrating trying to remember if there were any others. Why can't I recall every moment of sleep like I used to before. Maybe Le was right, and there have been too many rapid changes in my life.

I walked for so long that I inadvertently found myself in front of our hotel. Le was in the café across the way and she waved me over.

"Where in the hell did you go", she asked, worried and mad as hell.

"I bought that sword and shield... it was festering in me all night... then I started walking and now here I am", I said shrugging my shoulders.

"That can't be all... I can sense something else", she said, her eyes drilling into me.

I then explained the battle that had manifested last night, and how I had to take Torao's life and end my own by charging against impossible odds. I told her how the dream ended with me and my 'father', riding side by side in the valley that I had described to her. I told her of the explosion in South America. Le always sat there amazed at the recounting of my dreams, even maybe envious.

"How do you do that", she asked.

"Do what", I asked.

"Dream of things that Hollywood producers would climb over each other to get at the script", she said.

"I do not know and have never thought of my dreams in that fashion", I said.

"You should... I would go and see those films... I wish I could dream like that", she said.

"You do... the whole world does you just have to learn to hone in on them", I said.

"Maybe if I hang around with you long enough I will be able to", she said.

“Maybe”, I said.

I then told her of my fear that I was losing touch with other dreams. That I thought I was missing some and not able to recall as much as I used to. She just shrugged her shoulders and again pointed out the changes in my life.

“When we get back home to your house your collections your cottage everything will even itself out”, she said, with great conviction.

“I have been thinking along the same lines... but we are here now... what would you like to do”, I asked.

“Could we go to Milan now... I really want to see Milan again... there are three shops I am dying to re-visit”, she said, excitedly like a school girl who just had her boobs touched for the first time, and was re-counting the experience to her best friend.

“Just three”, I said, raising my eye brows.

“Three that I want to go to specifically... but it is Milan there are probably fifty more that I will add to my list”, she said, with the same enthusiasm.

“I am starving... we will leave right after lunch”, I said.

“Let’s just go... we will find a place along the way”, she said.

“I am really hungry”, I said.

“Ok then... let’s order and be gone”, she said.

On that note we ordered lunch, and I ate until I could not chew anymore. We packed, checked out of the hotel, and loaded the BMW. God that car does love me now. I am going to buy one and get a personalized plate that says ‘Torao’. We had to make one stop at the shop where I had the suits made. It was quick and not too much out of our way.

The car purred all the way eating the kilometers between Genoa and Milan. In this car and at the rate of speed it did not take long. I wish it was farther away than just 118 kilometers.

I had no plans of staying over in Milan, but Le convinced me to. We found the best hotel in all of Milan, and checked-in. The Bulgari Hotel Milan was happy to receive us. Our next stop after Milan will be Venice, and then on to Naples, then to Sicily, and then Sicily back to Rome. Then we will visit Portugal, Spain, France, and then conclude the trip in Switzerland. Le and I discussed this in length, on the way here.

As soon as we were checked-in and had a shower, yes a very sexual one. We hit the streets to take in the night life of Milan. We would shop all day tomorrow, but tonight Le wanted to go dancing and get very, very, drunk. After we slept...

I wake up on some dirty side street and I look around. This is familiar to me. I can remember being here before. It turns out to be an alley not a side street. The thing I am wrapped in is an extremely worn sleeping bag. I feel a numbing cold down to the core of my being. I hold up my hands and they are still gross, dirty, scarred, and old looking. My nails and knuckles are still bleeding. I can still smell body odor, shit, and urine. This is all the same as before. I feel my face and there is still three years of beard growth, and it is still all wet and matted, greasy. My lips are still cracked and bleeding. I feel through my hair and it is the same. It feels like it has not been washed or cut in ten years. There are others sleeping here just as disgusting as I was. Maybe some were worse it is hard to tell. I am thirsty I crave water. I am hungry. It is all the same. I remember it all now, as the fog clears thoroughly form my mind.

Soon one of the others here gets up and stretches. It will be the one that may have been female at one time and made me vomit. Oh shit I cannot avoid it, fuck me. I am supposed to live this again, but why? It really is full of sores, scrapes and scars. It sucks in air through its nose and spits out the vilest putrid gunk from its mouth. I try not to vomit. I try not to be sick. I try so hard this time. Then I remember that it farts, and it is sickly and most likely wet, and then I vomit.

Then another shoves me from behind. Then I remember Freddie, Ava and all the rest. I turn to tell him how happy I am to see him. I turn to see an evil grin, and then he hits me, and kicks me over and over again. They all do, all the filthy creatures, and they piss and shit on me, and it is like I am frozen. I am on the ground torn and broken and Freddie leans over me and shouts, "That was for Ava… … and all that you left behind back in the bush and fucking shit… including me… you bastard Bobby". Then he brings his boot down on my head and keeps it up until I feel no more. I am now suspended over them and they continue their assault, but for no reason for I am gone…

I am now by a stream, and there is a kite at my side. I remember all of this, and I am going to see my dog, and maybe my eagles. I take the kite and walk towards an open field that I know will be there. Then I begin to run I am so excited I can hardly retain it. Then I rush into the clearing and I can see the dog running at me from the far side. I look to the sky and there are the eagles. They are all coming back. The dog is almost upon me and I squat down to greet him. He is a couple of feet away and then he snarls and growls and grabs the arm I had outstretched and bites right through to the bone. The pain is excruciating and I scream. How could he do this? He bites even deeper and rips and tears at my flesh. Then all I see is feathers as the eagles attack as well, just before this once wonderful world goes black. Life is leaving my body. The eagles and the dog speak at once, and all they say is, "For all you left behind". Then it is over…

I am falling through the air. I look just above me into the heavens and I see a large plane and the door is open. Then it hits me that I was just in that plane, it was the flight Ava and I took to our honeymoon. I see Ava's face looming in the door, and it was growing bigger and bigger, and she is shouting, "For leaving me and all we had"! I fall and fall and can see the ground rushing towards me, and I know I am going to hit. There will be no reprieve and no mercy. I will not be saved, she threw me out...

I am floating over snow capped peaks. I look below me and I see a familiar outline of buildings. It is the monastery below me. Then I fall hard in to the snow like I was given a push out of mid-air. There are unnatural mounds in the newly fallen snow. I go to one and uncover a familiar face. All of the mounds have familiar faces. I go inside, and there are bodies, and splatters of blood everywhere. I go to the room that I was last restoring and across the magnificent artwork there were words in what I believe to be blood. It simply read, "For all you left behind... for leaving us". I guess my final speech had further repercussions...

I am in a cave now I think. I can hear water somewhere. This place seems vaguely familiar. Then I hear a horse, and I look back and there is Torao with a magnificent Samurai on his back. Everything about the two is majestic. I stare for quite some time taking it all in. The Samurai wears his Wakisahashi, and Katana, his do, Kabuto, and the works.

The Samurai steps down and away from Torao. Torao looks away from me. It is like he does not know me. I am not Hisoka but myself. The Samurai looms over me, and I drop to my knees and bow. He drops his Wakisahashi in front of me, and says, "You have forsaken Bushido and all of our ways... it is all over... now you must end your life to restore your honor and the honor of those you leave behind".

I know what is expected of me. I must commit Seppuku. I prepare myself, and I cannot stop it. I take off my shirt and I stay kneeling. I pick up the blade and release it from its sheath. The Samurai takes a position slightly behind and to my left. He means to take my head as soon as I thrust the blade into my midsection. It is an honorable death. It is Bushido, the way of the Samurai and that of his sword. I point the blade at my midsection just below the sternum and with both hands on the handle I thrust. I feel the pain and hear the Samurai scream behind me as he brings the blade down across my neck. I cannot see it but I know it is coming. Then there is nothing...

I am walking on a quiet cobblestone street. The signs in the closed shop windows are all in French. I can faintly hear someone walking towards me. Probably a woman by the sound of clicking heels on the stone of the street. Then I see the shadow, and then the figure. I believe it is a female by the slender shape. It is wearing a long sleek black cloak that hugs the curves of her female frame. I walk to the other side and she counters as she walks towards me. Twenty yards, ten, and at five feet away the figure stops and pulls back her hood. It is Jessica and she screams at me, "HOW COULD YOU... IT WAS TO BE FOREVER... YOU PROMISED FOREVER". She pulls out a pistol and points it at my heart and I hear the sound and see the muzzle flash before the searing pain...

I wake up in a sweat with Le beside me. I run my hands over my soaked chest and arms. I think back to the dreams that I just had. Were they jumbles or final conclusions of my other dreams? What could they have meant by what they all said? What in the hell did I leave behind, certainly not them, never them. Didn't they leave me? What honor did I forsake? What was forever? What? Fuck I do not know.

I get up from the bed as quiet as possible, and go to the washroom to splash the coldest water on my face, neck, arms and chest. I pat myself dry and look in the mirror. What the hell went wrong, what did I do wrong. Those dreams were my life. They were everything to me, well, that is until I met... Le. I look over at her asleep on the bed and join her and soon...

I am looking through a scope, and taking pictures of people as they go by on the street below. They are coming from a restaurant and it must be very early in the morning. I know where and who I am after a few minutes of thinking and adjusting to the surroundings. The spaces in my memory are growing larger. What happened just a few minutes ago, or hours ago, I do not know. The last I recall I was in the restaurant that I am now watching, I had dinner there. I left there at around 2200 hours, and now when I look at my watch it is 0530 hours. What happened to the last seven hours? According to the camera I have taken several hundred pictures, but I do not remember any of them. I can only assume that I had slept, but where, here by the window? I look back and the bed is still made. I do not know. I stop my surveillance to look back at the photos I had taken and none jogged any recollection at all.

I pack the equipment up and decide to spend the day at the beach. The last few pictures on the memory card showed my target leaving with entourage in tow. The beach would do me some good. Staring at beautiful women in bikinis, topless, whatever, is soothing to most men, even a man like me. My target should be at his place at the beach later this afternoon according to his past habits that I had recorded, and were confirmed when provided to me by my employers. I had found a great spot for natural surveillance just down from his place. I packed some supplies, water, some food, sunscreen, blankets. You know the normal baggage of a tourist looking to score.

The beach is a short drive. The sun is shining and it is going to be a great day. The beaches are busy with all the vacationers. It is not long before I am setting up shop. I did not quite get my spot, but as a secondary this site will do. The target's place is bustling with activity. It looks like they are preparing for a party. There is a lot of security around, and a perimeter has been set. This should be interesting.

There are a lot of women around, but then there are a lot of men around to. Some should not wear thongs and Speedos. Dam Europeans, what the hell are they thinking when they put those things on. Then again some women should not go topless. Some of the shit I am seeing is utterly disgusting.

Then one or two walk by and I forget about all the others I have seen and make this job all worthwhile. Tight long legs, strong abs, to die for breasts and asses, lips that could bring you to your knees, and eyes that can take pictures of your soul. Quite a few of them are welcomed into the area around the party, and it is a shame when I think what I know about this man, and what might happen to them. The number of people that go missing in this country is astounding.

Then a group of girls go by and one is familiar. Her name is Gabriela, and she is stunning. She and her group are heading towards the party, and they seem to be lead by two men. I know these two from the dossier. They comb the beaches and area in search of young girls for him to play with.

I throw out caution and decide to make myself known to these two pricks and I call out her name. "GABRIELA", I shout. She turns and sees me, and recognition dawns on her face, and she comes walking towards me. One of the men tries to stop her in a fashion channeling her back to her friends, and in the direction of the party. She stops and tells the man something and walks my way. All the girls she is with stop and gravitate my way. The men are getting too pushy and are turning the girls off. They all head my way. I stand to greet Gabriela, and she closes the rest of the distance giving me a hug and kiss on each cheek. She whispers into my ear, "Can you get us out of this".

"Get you out of what", I whispered back, feigning ignorance to the situation.

"Those guys are trying real hard to get us to go to a party and have not let us or left us alone all day... they are being too hard... you know", she said.

"I will do what I can... but I am a lover not a fighter", I said smiling wickedly.

"I think you may be both", she said.

Gabriela then called the girls to come over and meet me. She introduced me as her cousin, whom she has not seen in quite awhile. The men are not far behind and they look absolutely pissed.

I greet each girl with a hug and a kiss on each cheek. They are all gorgeous and I just realized how very horny I was. I invite them to sit down with me, and then the two men intervene.

"I thought you ladies wanted to go to the best party in the country", the taller one said.

"Well... maybe we will stop by later now that we know where it is... we will visit with William here for a bit... thanks but no thanks", was Gabriela's reply.

"William can come to the party as well", the man replied in return.

"I do not think I am in the mood for a party today", I replied.

"Get in the mood", the other replied hoarsely.

"I do not think so... I like this spot and the company that I now have... I have not seen my cousin in ages... we have a lot to catch up on... this is a private part now and neither or you are invited", I said, coldness in my voice and eyes.

The taller one then flashed a pistol, and the girls tensed up a bit. I took charge telling them it was alright, just a minor disagreement among men.

"You do not need to do that... you are scaring my company", I said, even more coldly than before.

"Are you not scared... do you know who my boss is", the one with the hoarse voice said.

"No I am not scared... No I do not know who your boss is nor do I care... now put the pistol away", I said.

"These girls are coming with us", he said.

"No... I do not think they are", I said standing up.

"What are you going to do to stop us", he said.

I then stepped forward and watched as the taller one covered the rest of the distance that I needed. He had a punk ass grip and was flashing the pistol like he was a cowboy. The one with the hoarse voice just stood by watching it all unfold. I grabbed the pistol, flipped the man on his back, broke his arm and came down with the ball of my right foot on his shin snapping it. Before the other could react his friend's pistol was pressed against his forehead, and he pissed himself. The taller was screaming in agony. The girls had clustered in a group behind me, and I told them they should disappear. They readily obliged. I yelled to Gabriela that I would catch up with later where we used to play Frisbee. She nodded her understanding, saying she and the others would wait there for me. They then all took off.

Then I was not alone, others from the party had witnessed what had transpired and had joined in the standoff, weapons drawn. I knew I was outnumbered and consented to an escort into the compound. I would not surrender the firearm. This as I said before, this should be very interesting.

I was brought before the man I intended to kill. This could not have worked out better...

FRIDAY 2ND OF JULY 2011

There is light behind my eyes, and it is getting brighter and brighter. Le has pulled back the curtains trying to wake me us subtlety. It is working and I open my eyes fully and noticed she has showered and dressed. She is very anxious to hit the streets and do the 'real shopping' she had come to Italy for.

"The sheets were soaked... you really sweated a lot last night", she said.

"Different dreams", I said.

"Tell me about them", she said.

"Ok... as I am getting ready", I said.

I then did just that. I brought her up to speed as I showered and dressed. I told her everything, but glossed over the parts, not putting any real emphasis on the jumbles accusing me of doing wrong and leaving them and my honor behind. I put more emphasis on the last dream, but I sensed a slight change in Le. I know she suspects herself as the root of the changes in my dreams. She says nothing of it, and that confirms my suspicions. We go to the streets and find a place for a light brunch, for I slept a little longer than planned. Conversation was cautious. I let it go and we walked hand in hand to a shopping area that the girl at the front desk directed us to, and we would not want to miss.

Le hit every shop along the way, and must have spent an exorbitant amount of money. I think she spent more than she did in Rome and Genoa combined. I bought a few things, but was really not interested in the things I saw. I was faking it, faking a good time, faking conversation, faking interest, faking everything. Le knew it, but went along with it. She said nothing in protest, or concern.

I stewed in my own thoughts. I was constantly thinking of the jumbles, the accusations and implications. I thought of Ava's face in the doorway of the airplane. I thought of Freddie and the crazed look in his eyes as he beat the shit out of me. I thought of the dog, the eagles, and the Samurai. I thought about all the ways I and my characters died. I thought of the final battle sitting atop Torao. I thought of the car jumping over the curb as it was chased by police. I thought of Prick number one and two, and the pull of the trigger. I thought of the end of the jumbles and the long road to hell. I see the look in Jessica's eyes as she pulled the trigger. All of these images flashed through my mind like an old movie projected against a white canvas. They flashed in my mind all day long, and Le could tell I was preoccupied. The whole day went by like that a blur. I do not remember any real conversation, anything I ate, just the movie in my mind. I do not even remember going from one place to the next.

I came out of my funk once I was behind the wheel of the BMW, and we were on our way to Venice. It all of a sudden made sense to me. I apologized to Le, and I explained what had been going on in my head today, I told her everything. That brought a few questions and a great amount of emotion to the surface on her part.

"That is what was going on with you... the long absent stares... the nodding of your head and smiling no matter what I picked up or said or asked of you... hardly touching your food or me", she almost screamed.

Then there was a long pause, "Did I do all of this", she asked, almost to the point of tears.

"No", I said, direct to the point.

"Just no", she said.

"I could give a longer explanation is you wish", I said.

"Please do", she said.

I then told her all of my reasons. The heart of it is I never felt I belonged anywhere. I always felt like a displaced soul. The dreams gave me that missing sense that I belonged to something, someone. The reason I felt that they ended so badly, is they had to. They woke me up, and shouted into my face that I now have what I was missing.

"I guess it is you... all about you... everything... you", I said.

"Why are the others still alive", she asked.

"I do not know... maybe they will end soon and just as badly as the rest... maybe they fill the need I have to save people... especially now that I am retired", I said.

"Go on", she said, now really interested in what I was saying.

"Well the dog was about friendship... the eagles a thirst for knowledge... the artist about peace and tranquility... the Samurai about honor and integrity... Freddie, Ava, and Jessica were all about friendship...trust... and Love... all of these things I found in you", I said, coming to final terms with the dreams myself.

"Find a spot and pull over" she said.

I thought, shit she is going to leave the car and me and that is it.

"There to the left... the sign says scenic rest area... pull over there", she said emphatically.

You have no idea how hard it is to fuck in a BMW I8. It was more comical than romantic or erotic. We did it twice, and we laughed about it the rest of the way to Venice. We laughed about it through dinner and through checking into the hotel. We laughed about it in the Gondola, and all through the night. We hardly slept, because we kept cracking jokes. We laughed through an Art Gallery and were asked to leave a Museum, and we laughed all the way back to Rome.

Back at the Cavalieri we arranged for shipment of the rest of our purchases back to my home address. Minus of course things that Le said she would need for the rest of our trip. That list was getting bigger all the time. UPS is going to love me, because everything I sent back required a signature, and had a no-drop label for insurance.

We would be checking out tomorrow. Our next stop would be Naples, where I would have to leave the BMW. I am afraid that will be a teary moment, for both of us, that is if a car could cry. My original plan to return to Rome after Naples was changed to going straight to Portugal. I still wanted to see the Coliseum and the Vatican, one last day to do both. I, or should I say we will return to Rome one day, and spend more time. It was now time for some much needed sleep...

I woke with a start. I was sweating profusely and my chest was heavy and my left arm was sore. I went to the bathroom and vomited. I was having a heart attack. I went back to the bedroom and Le was not there. I checked the entire place and she was nowhere to be found. Then I noticed slight differences to the room. The stairway to the rooftop terrace was in the wrong place, and when I went up them to the top the view was not of Rome. There were fires everywhere, and I could see thousands of lines of people heading in the same direction from all corners of the earth around. I felt really ill and the ground swayed and smacked me in the face...

I woke face down and spit out a mouthful of sand. Water was coming and going and I got up on my knees and realized the surf was coming in. It was dark, so very dark. There was a fire further down and I got up and walked towards it. I walked and walked for what seemed like hours, and I never got any closer to it. The sun came up and creatures emerged from the water. I tried to run and fell several times. I could not keep my feet under me. Then I tripped again and this time my face hit a hard surface...

I woke in a hospital bed. I was hooked up to several machines and they were blinking and beeping. I recognized all of them. I recognized the room. I was in my workplace. I was in my hospital. A man came in dressed as a doctor. He was wearing a mask and a gown, and he began removing all the needles and the sensor pads. Then he left, and I got up and put my weight on my legs, but they would not hold and the ground hit me yet again...

I woke on a piece of ice. I got up and looked down and I was dressed for the arctic. There was ice and snow everywhere. Nothing but ice and snow for as far as I could see. My chest was still heavy and my left arm was going numb. I took a few steps and fell through...

SATURDAY 3RD OF JULY 2011

I woke back at the Cavalieri in Rome. Le was asleep beside me. I got up and checked everything. I was in Rome. There were no chest pains, no sick feeling, and no numbness. Everything was fine. Jumbles had returned, and that was good. Then I thought about Jessica and all the rest that I had shared with and all we had been through. I knew that dream would end someday, but not the way any of them did. I did not see it at all. I went up to the terrace and watched Rome wake up. We would be leaving here tomorrow and it had been a great time.

Today we would spend out last day in Rome touring the Vatican and the Coliseum. It was an exhausting day, and went by in a blur. Vatican City, St. Peter's Square, was so full of people. It was crazy. It was not the mesmerizing and holy adventure that I thought it would be. It was not calming at all. It was the same at the Coliseum, and we shuffled through in a long line of people. It made me think of my dream of the long lines of people lined up to go to hell. I believe this area was hell for the Gladiators, and the slaves that were once entertainment for the throngs of people watching. The atmosphere was melancholy and depressing, that must be from the ghosts that are still here. I could not wait to leave.

We then went back to the Piazza Navona and had dinner and of course a Tartufo. We walked around the fountains one more time, and then made our way back to the Cavalieri for one last night, and we both quickly fell asleep...

I woke up being escorted by four men, and we were all carrying guns. I then recalled a bit of what happened and where I was. I was being brought to meet the one I have been contracted to kill. I then remember helping out Gabriela and her friends, and that I was to meet her after I am through here where I first met her. I was led past the body guards, and none tried to remove the weapon that I had liberated from them earlier. I was brought into an exquisitely furnished and decorated den. My target was seated behind the desk and had four computer monitors in front of him. One of my escorts went to him and whispered into his ear. I can only suppose that he his telling him what had transpired on the beach. He got up from his chair and stood in front of me. I held my place and the pistol firm.

"You will have no need for that here", he said pointing to the pistol.

"Your people here made the mistake of pointing it at me first", I said.

"And you easily disarmed two of my... well... two that I once considered to be my best", he said, looking sternly at the rest of his men.

"Yes... I did", I said, staring the man in the eye.

"And you are not afraid to be in this room... with all of these guns", he asked.

"No... not at all", I said.

"And why is that", he said.

"You just told me that I have no need of this gun... so why then should I fear yours", I asked.

"So you will put the weapon down", he asked.

I then let the clip drop to the floor and ejected the chambered round. I handed the weapon to my intended target.

"I fear nothing", I said, as I was still staring him in the eyes.

"Who are you", he asked.

"My name is William... William Mayer", I said.

"Pleased to meet you Mr. Mayer", he said, extending his hand.

I took it and shook it firmly. The rest of the conversation was quite formal. He asked where I was from, where I was staying, how long I was staying. I answered with, all around, nowhere in particular, and that depends on the local cuisine. I could sense that this was a good first meeting. I was allowed to leave and my safety was guaranteed for my entire stay in Rio, absolutely guaranteed. I left knowing that he would be checking me out. The name I gave would come back with a wealth of information. Ex Navy Seal, tours in Iraq, Afghanistan, Somalia, just about everywhere there was a war. I was well decorated and highly trained. Nothing would come back outrageous or over the top. I am now retired. I know he would be in contact in some form, and hopefully with a job offer, Security or whatever. I left the compound, packed my belongings that I had left on the beach, got in the jeep and went to find Gabriela. I tour a circuitous route and lost those following me. He wasted no time in sending men to tail me, and I am sure he would be impressed that I lost them in the first twenty minutes in their own city. I ditched the jeep and rented another because I did not want to make it easy to find me. I would check out of my hotel tomorrow, and settle into better digs, now that I know he will come looking for me…

SUNDAY 4TH OF JULY 2011

I woke up beside Le, and I shook her awake. It was time to hit the road. It was a bit of a drive to Naples, but we would not be staying there very long, just a few nights. I had a couple things pre-planned, and I hope Le would like them. The drive was uneventful. One other driver wanted to race, but I declined and let him flash by me. I do not need to measure myself. I know how big I am. We made a couple of stops, to eat, gas up, and such. No real big deal.

We arrived in Naples and checked into our hotel, The Vesuvio. The best that Naples has to offer as well as the rest of Italy and everywhere we may go during this trip is ours. We ate once more upon arrival in a small bistro by the hotel. As always it was recommended and the food was perfect. The concierge desks in Italy have their fingers on the beats of their cities, and we have yet to be disappointed. It was not the longest drive of the trip, but it wasn't the shortest either. With the stops we made and preparation time before leaving Rome this day was done. We took showers, but separately. We both knew what would have happened if we had taken one together, and we were very tired. Too tired really for sex, I feel emotionally exhausted with all the upheaval in my dreams. I was last in the shower and of course the last to curl up in bed. Le was already fast asleep, and snoring as she always did. I curled up beside her quietly and...

Prick 1 is seated to my left, prick 2 to my right. I am sweating profusely and cannot stand the lies that are being spewed from my lips. I can taste bile, and smell body odor. I have kept hidden my fluency in their language to this point. I cannot stand what I have done.

I stand and scream in Mandarin about the kidnapping from the peaceful monastery, and the subsequent beatings and these forced lies. Cameras stop flashing, and the room is quiet. This was a live feed and the Chinese cannot stop it. The foreign news agencies keep their feeds going. There are representatives from the Canadian Embassy present at my insistence, and there is nothing Prick 1 and 2 can do.

People from all corners of the room are screaming and yelling. I keep my dialogue going telling all. Prick 1 pulls out a pistol and points it at my head. This act will be broadcast to the world. Prick one yells at me to stop at once and recant what I have just said. I stop talking long enough to spit in his face. The yelling and the panic in the room are cresting to the boiling point. They are screaming about the gun, and several are attempting to leave. Some of the cameras keep going. The operators of those feel this is too good and are willing to do what it takes to get my message out. Prick 1 gives me one final warning before he pulls the trigger and everything goes black...

I am walking down a street with Ava and I am pushing a stroller. The sun is bright but it is a little bit cool. It is a great day for a walk and to spend some time in the park nearby. I can hear sirens fairly close by, a common occurrence here. It is nice here but almost time to move to a better area. The sirens are real close and we can hear tires screeching and people yelling. All of a sudden out of nowhere a big black caddy comes around the corner and jumps the curb where we are walking and...

I was riding Torao with my Yumi raised firing arrows into the throng of approaching Samurai as fast as my fingers would allow. We were thirty, and they I estimate to be about five hundred strong. Well, they were when they charged, but my arrows alone have accounted for at least twelve. They may not be dead, but are certainly no longer a threat, and could be easily dispatched later if they have not already committed seppuku. My hope is the others have accounted for the same before some of them had fallen. After exhausting my supply of arrows I drew my Nodachi, and I started to cleave and carve as much flesh and bone of the enemy as I could.

We rode through them, and just before turning around I noticed another cloud of dust forming just within my farthest sight. It could be more enemies, and if it is we will be finished soon. I turned and attacked again, and this time with more vigor than before. There are bodies everywhere, but Torao is expertly keeping his footing being the battle worn horse he is. On the next turn I notice the cloud getting larger and closer. I am bleeding from many wounds as is Torao. There are only eight of us left. We have accounted for more than forty times that amount. It looks to be our time, for now I can see the approaching horses and hear the shouts and battle cries of their riders.

The eight of us stop in a line and face our enemy. I drop the Nodachi, and get off of Torao. The other seven do the same. There are now a thousand or more men in front of us, and they stop to watch what we are about to do. I take out my Katana, and step to Torao's side, as the rest does with their mounts. I bow to him, and the large beast knows what is to happen. I will be riding him soon on the other side, very soon. I could not stand another being his master. "I will see you soon my friend... very soon", I said.

With one scream and in one stroke I took his head. We all did at the same time. Then in the same scream and with the same breath we charged the thousand before us...

I am shaken awake. It is still dark and my mind is extremely blurry. I look around, and it is Jessica leaning over me prodding me awake. I have no idea where I am. It is a jungle for sure, and we are on a slope. I can see the tops of homes and outlines of manicured areas around them. It seems kind of familiar. It is almost like I have been here before. I search my memory, and I try to concentrate. Then I remember the ring and the bounty and everything. We are outside of the keeper's house, and this time we are going in hard. We will force him to tell us of the ring.

"Are you ready", Jessica asks.

"Yeah let's go and get this over with", I said.

We dressed and donned gloves, masks, hair nets, plastic clothes, taped everything down like we were some sort of hazardous materials team. We enter the house the same as before. The man should be alone and asleep. Up the stairs I go. Jessica stays on the main floor and waits. The needle pricks the man on the arm, and for a second I thought he would wake. He didn't. I pushed the plunger and the sedative entered the man's veins. This would allow us to secure the man, and wake him up with another injection when we were ready to scare the shit right out of him.

This bastard was heavy, and smelled worse than any I have encountered to date. He was even worse than those in the hostel in the Philippines. I managed to tie him up and get him secured to a chair. Jessica checked the house and confirmed we were alone. It was time to get to work.

"Christ he smells", Jessica said.

"I know… I know… I had to touch him to get him here", I said.

"Ready", she asked.

"Ready as ever", I said.

Jessica then administered a serum that would wake the smelly prick up. It took a few minutes to work, but the man was reviving. When he came to semi-consciousness his eyes went wide with absolute fear. He tried to scream and squirm but to no avail. I had him fixed so that he could not see us. He could not turn his head at all. That way there was no chance we could be identified. I placed a tray of nasty, medieval looking, blood stained instruments on a tray in front of him. I told him what was going to happen, step by step, picking up each applicable instrument to emphasize my point if he did not tell us the truth to every question we asked. His eyes grew wider and wider and he started to cry. He then pissed and shit himself. We thought his body odor was bad. That cloud of shit that came out of his ass was sickening. Jessica had to leave the room or she would vomit. There could be no traces of us here. She caught herself just in time. Vomiting with her full face mask on would not have been pretty.

I asked the man where the ring was. I was holding up the first tool. He nodded his understanding, and I removed his gag so that he may answer the question. He told us that there was a false brick in the wall behind his cook stove. The brick was located three up and four to the right of the bottom left hand corner. There was no way we would have found it. There was a metal box in the hole, and the ring was inside. Jessica heard this from the door, and went to investigate.

Jessica returned about twenty minutes later holding the box. She tossed it to me. The lock was magnetic and required a code. I held up the nastiest of all the instruments and the man spilled his guts and gave me the code. I entered it and it opened quietly. The ring was nestled safe inside. The man laughed and said he hoped it brought as much misery to us as it had to him. I put him back to sleep and we left.

Out the back and over the stone fence we went, disappearing into the jungle beyond. Just like before we planned to exit far away like tourists out for a hike. We dumped our clothes, and changed. The man would not wake for hours and by the time he did we would be a thousand miles away safely on a plane. This was easy.

"That was easy", Jessica said.

"Yes it was... way too easy... but we would never have found it where it was... never", I said.

"Well what are we going to do with the money", she asked.

"What we planned... leave this life and disappear", I said.

We were quiet moving through the jungle on much the same route as before. The box and ring safe in my pack, when the box started to beep. We froze.

"What the hell is it", Jessica asked.

"Maybe a tracking device or some sort or alarm", I said.

I tried entering the code but it would not work. The beeping got faster, louder and more intense. Then the box got hot and I dropped it and tried to yell "RUN". I did not have time, and I will bet the explosion could have been seen as far away as Mexico...

I am in a room full of gold, currency from all over the world, gems and priceless treasures. There are no windows and there are no doors. Who am I to deserve such a site, and who are they to be keeping this from the world. Then the bottom falls out, and it all falls back to the molten fiery pits of hell. Creatures that I guess were once human are laughing at the site of the world's money being dumped here for no one's use. I watch as every hour more and more is dumped to fuel the fires here. Is this what money is really worth, and what we seek and chase after our whole lives. Is this where it all leads to...

I take a good look around the world I once knew, and it is all gone, turned to ashes. All the places that I held as cherished memories. All of them, gone. I am all that is left. I can feel the flames licking at my feet, feeding on the clothes I am wearing. There is no pain for my mind is numb looking at the devastation that was my life...

With one scream and in one stroke I took his head. We all did at the same time. Then in the same scream and with the same breath we charged the thousand before us...

I tried entering the code but it would not work. The beeping got faster, louder and more intense. Then the box got hot and I dropped it and tried to yell "RUN". I did not have time, and I will bet the explosion could have been seen as far away as Mexico...

People from all corners of the room are screaming and yelling. I keep my dialogue going telling all. Prick 1 pulls out a pistol and points it at my head. This act will be broadcast to the world. Prick one yells at me to stop at once and recant what I have just said. I stop talking long enough to spit in his face. The yelling and the panic in the room are cresting to the boiling point. They are screaming about the gun, and several are attempting to leave. Some of the cameras keep going. The operators of those feel this is too good and are willing to do what it takes to get my message out. Prick 1 gives me one final warning before he pulls the trigger and everything goes black...

I am walking down a street with Ava and I am pushing a stroller. The sun is bright but it is a little bit cool. It is a great day for a walk and to spend some time in the park nearby. I can hear sirens fairly close by, a common occurrence here. It is nice here but almost time to move to a better area. The sirens are real close and we can hear tires screeching and people yelling. All of a sudden out of nowhere a big black caddy comes around the corner and jumps the curb where we are walking and...

I did not have time, and I will bet the explosion could have been seen as far away as Mexico...

Prick 1 gives me one final warning before he pulls the trigger and everything goes black...

All of a sudden out of nowhere a big black caddy comes around the corner and jumps the curb where we are walking and...

Then in the same scream and with the same breath we charged the thousand before us...

MONDAY 5TH OF JULY 2011

I woke again in a pool of sweat. Again I checked to see where I was and who I was with. Le was beside me, she was asleep but tossing and turning. I was in Naples at the Hotel Vesuvio, as the letterhead on the note pad said on the desk. I was where I was supposed to be. Those dreams kept recurring all through the night. Charging horses, blades cutting me to pieces, the look on Jessica's face when I dropped the box and tried to yell, the car jumping the curb, the faces of the two pricks, the image of hell, haunted me all through the night.

It was daylight out. We had slept pretty late. The one night I would not have minded getting up and out of those nightmares, I slept right through like I was drugged. I still felt drugged. I need coffee, and an end to these dreams. I never thought I would say that. Never!

In a fog I shower and dress. I tried to write Le a note, but before I finished she woke up. She was smiling, bright eyes, like she had the best sleep of her life. I put away my fog and greeted her with the same. I smiled as best I could, and snuggled up to her. I put my arms around her, and we stayed like that for a little while. It helped me immensely, more than I thought a simple touch ever could. I was falling deeper, and there was no stopping it.

“What are we doing today”, she asked.

“Anything but shopping”, I replied quickly.

“What... come on”, she said.

“No I mean it absolutely no shopping today... not even a second”, I said emphatically.

“What then”, she asked anxiously.

“We are going on a private dinner cruise aboard the hotel’s private boat The Vesuvietta”, I said proudly.

“Are you serious... when did you arrange that”, she asked, with eye brows raised.

“Before we left Canada”, I said.

“What else do you have planned...? I can see by your eyes there is something else”, she said.

“Well we must get up very early tomorrow for a guided tour of Mount Vesuvius and Pompeii”, I said.

“Really... we are going to see the volcano and the ruins of Pompeii”, she said.

“Dam straight... I was not coming all this way to miss those”, I said.

“And the cruise... when do we go”, she asked excitedly.

“As soon as we are ready”, I said.

“Then I will jump in the shower... and then pack a day bag”, she said.

"Ok you do all that I will go down and tell then we will be ready... in what... an hour", I said.

"Make it an hour and a half", she said.

"Done deal", I said, excusing myself from the room.

When the door closed securely behind me I went back into a fog. I could not keep the images from last night out of my head. They still flashed as still images behind my eyes. I went down to the lobby just the same, and told the front desk we would be ready in ninety minutes. They informed me that all the arrangements had been finalized and a limo would be ready when we are to go to the port. It was to be sunny and warm today, and I would do the best I could to keep the rain from my mind from ruining the next couple of days. I had been looking forward to the visit to Vesuvius and Pompeii for quite some time.

At least since Le was getting ready I had some time to think. I was a bit hungry, and saw no harm in getting a bite to eat. I asked the concierge and she pointed me in the direction of a small trattoria about ten minutes from here. I thanked her and off I went.

I found the place and it was very small. It consisted of two tables outside in a patio setting off the street, and an additional four inside. It came to a grand total seating capacity of about twelve people. There was no menu, just a chalk board that changed daily depending on the whim of the cook inside. Today's special was a fresh herb focaccia, roasted eggplant and red pepper open faced sandwich with parmesan reggiano cheese. That is what I ordered. I wolfed it down, and it was great. I sat there after, sipping an espresso, thinking of my dreams. I do not know why. I cannot change them, and must accept them as I have all my life for what they are, dreams in which I have a chance to live differently than I do. They have changed as I have throughout my life, this is no different.

Knowing this I still could not lift the fog, and the storms igniting my mind.

I walked back to the hotel, and went up to the room. Le was just about ready. The Limo was outside waiting. We were soon swept away, down to the harbor and aboard the boat. Before I knew it I had a glass of wine in my hand, and I was sitting on the deck staring at Le. I was laughing, but I do not remember about what. We were served hors d'oeuvres. They were awesome, little bite size pieces of heaven.

"Enjoying yourself", Le asked.

"Yes... Yes I am", I replied.

"Are you going to leave some food for me", she asked.

"Well... umm... you snooze... you lose", I said.

I guess I had been popping the snacks into my mouth like they were popcorn. Soon I had forgotten all about the dreams and was settling into where we were and what was going on.

"Is this the first you've eaten today", she asked.

"Well no... when you were getting ready I found a small place close to the hotel and had a focaccia sandwich", I said, a little guiltily.

"I thought so", she said.

"Well an hour and a half is a long time and ..." I said, before she interrupted.

"I know it is OK", she said, stopping me from going further.

"Any more dreams", she asked.

I knew she was going to bring it up. I decided to come clean, and I told her everything. I told her of all the recurring nightmares of the night. Talking to her definitely made me feel better. She listened intently, made level headed suggestions and comments. It all helped. We talked the whole day away.

We enjoyed a quiet dinner in the middle of the sea. It was all dark except for the lights of the boat, and the boats around us. They were not close or anything and they were just quietly drifting by. We had stopped and anchored for dinner. It was a good time.

We laughed extensively about making it in the BMW. We talked about the food we have had in Italy so far. We talked about the shops we visited, and now Le says she is sad that she packaged everything to be sent back home. We talked of the Vatican, the Coliseum, the aquarium, the fountains, the Piazza Navona, the architecture, the cobblestone streets, and the gondola ride. I do not think we left one single thing out. We talked of everything we have done so far. Hours past and the captain poked his head into the dining room and announced that it was time to head in, and we agreed. We took the remainder of our drinks to the upper deck and continued our conversation under the stars.

Back in the Limo we talked briefly of tomorrow. Soon we were back in the hotel. I asked for an early wake-up, and was told not to worry they had everything prepared for our day trip. It was into the shower and then into bed, no sex. There will be plenty of days and nights for that...

I wake in a square room. Its walls keep changing colors. They change to all the colors known to man, and with each change an audible click. They change at an almost blurring speed, click, click, click, click, click, click, click, and click. I fall to my knees begging it to stop. It does not. Then the faces come overlaying the colors. Ava, Freddie, Jessica, Hisoka, Torao, bobby, Sean, the Dog, the Eagles, the Artist, all of them are haunting my sleep. I cannot wake. It is like I took my elixir and am drugged for the night. Then their voices are heard. They are all yelling at me, chiding me for my indiscretions. Rough hands remove me from the room like in Tibet, and before I can fight I am strapped to a chair in a theatre. There are movies playing over and over. They are black and white movies of our last moments together just as I had dreamt them. They were exactly as I had dreamt them. The dreams have been made to appear old. It is like I am watching me, watch them. I see me tied to a chair and the movies playing on the white screen in front of me that is not me, because I am behind me. I am watching me watch me. I am seeing every scene play out as I am watching them, but I am not me, I can't be.

I am spinning like a top, and everything around is a blur. There are no colors it is all black and white, but again it is not me. I am watching me spin, but I feel sick, nauseous, and I stand there and vomit. My stomach is twirling, and churning with my spinning image in front of me. The movies are playing again but at a faster speed, faster and faster they play. Around and around my other self goes tied to a chair. I vomit again and again. Faster and faster the movies play, the faster my other self spins the faster they go, and the more I vomit. I finally manage to drop to my knees and fight like hell to close my eyes. It does not help, the feeling continues.

I am removed from myself once again. I am now watching myself vomit, watching my other self spin, and watching movies on the screen. I am struck in the stomach and kicked in the nuts. A shadow is beating the shit out of me. I turtle and try to roll myself in a ball as the figure beats on me. My eyes are closed but I can still see myself vomiting, spinning, on the movie screen. The beating continues, and continues, because this fucker is relentless.

Again rough hands pull me from myself. I am now watching me get beaten, vomiting, spinning, and in movies on the big white screen. This figure forces me to my knees and dips my head in a pool of water. I try to fight but it is to no avail. It actually makes things worse. The darkened figure dunks my head over and over and does not stop. I barely have time to catch some breath between. Through it all I can still see myself being beaten, vomiting, spinning, and in the movies. It is absolutely dizzying and I cannot stop any of it. It is like a roller coaster of images.

I can hear someone shouting at me from a distance. I feel like I am swimming to the surface of a very deep pool. The closer I seem to get the louder the voice. It is female and the words are starting to make sense. "WAKE UP LOGAN", Le yells and shakes me awake.

"What the fuck", I said.

"Wake up Love... you are having a huge nightmare... yelling and screaming and trying to fight with something", she said.

I took a moment and remembered it all. "Yes... I could not wake myself up... it was unlike anything I have ever experienced before", I said.

"Tell me about it", she said, in a very serious tone.

I explained everything to her. I told her of the movies, the images, the beating, the vomiting, the spinning, the water bucket treatment. Everything!

"This... your dreams... are getting worse", she said.

"I know... we will deal with it", I said.

"How", she said.

"I do not know... but I am going to splash some water on my face... I will be right back", I said.

"OK Logan", she said, very concerned.

When I got back I told Le that I was going to try to get some sleep. I had a feeling I needed to face these dreams and go through whatever punishment they had to dish out. I told her all of this, and that I had to find a way to beat them. I told her not to worry, but by the look on her face I knew this to be impossible. Sleep did not come easy, for either of us. Le had her eyes closed, but I knew she was faking and fully awake. I said nothing, and then about two hours later...

I wake up and I am standing up, I cannot move my arms because my hands are tied behind my back. I cannot move my legs or turn my head. I am tied to a stake, and there is a pile of brush growing at my feet. I hear screams and squeals of laughter all around. The images dancing around throwing the brush into the pile start to come into focus. Ava, Jessica, Freddie, Hisoka, Sean, Bobby, and the Artist are beside themselves in a crazed frenzy. They dance in and out of my line of vision. I can hear the dog yapping excitedly, and the eagles swoop down in front of me and land on the ground. I try to yell but I can't find any voice. My mind screams out for them to stop all this madness. They all shout back in unison, "FUCK YOU LOGAN CHARLES".

"WHY", my mind screams back.

"BECAUSE YOU KILLED US", they all reply, one shout at a time.

"I killed no one", I said, in a hushed whisper.

"YOU KILLED US ALL", they replied strongly.

"Stop this", I said.

"We will never stop... but we are almost finished with you... and then we will start with her", Jessica said standing alone.

Le then entered the dream. She was walking in the field towards us. She was holding a torch, and seeing this made them all even howl and act even crazier.

"Leave her out of this... Le leave before it is too late", I tried to scream. My mind had no strength left.

"She is at the center of it all", Freddie said, joining Jessica.

Le was close now and she was grinning madly, as madly as them. She looked at me, and then at the torch in her hand. She smiled an evil smile that sent a chill down my spine. She then tossed the torch into the brush, and it quickly caught fire. The flames burned and fed on the flesh of my feet, then up my legs, my torso, and the rest of me. I was conscious through the whole thing, and felt all the pain that the world could muster and throw at one person. I could see them dance around her congratulating her on the feat. The pain then intensified and...

TUESDAY 6TH OF JULY 2011

I woke up beside Le, and my flesh felt like it was on fire. Le was awake watching me. She could tell I was in pain, and when she went to touch me felt the heat emanating off of my body. She could have sworn she was burnt, but there was nothing on her hand. There were no marks on my body. It lasted quite awhile, but slowly dissipated.

I told her everything. I even told her of her place in the dream. I told her they had planned to torture her next. She did not believe this possible that this was all in my own psyche. I told her no, this is not the case, not any more. I told her I felt that on some other level of consciousness that the dreams had come alive.

"Fuck them... I never remember my dreams anyway", Le said.

"You will remember these I think", I said, staring at my hands.

"Well... let us go and start our day... Vesuvius and Pompeii waits", she said in return.

"Yes they do", I said.

We grabbed a quick shower together to save time, dressed and flew down to the lobby. A Range Rover and our private guide were waiting on us. The hotel had provided a beautiful boxed lunch, and some hiking gear. It was all packed into the vehicle and off we went.

Our guide and driver told us it would take about fifty minutes to arrive at the start of our hike. She spoke perfect English and with her Italian accent was very sexy. We made small talk, because I loved to hear her speak. She had a killer body and was absolutely hot as hell. Le kept elbowing and kicking me, she knew I was partial to the accent and was trying to get me to stop flirting. Would it be the other way around if our guide was a male? Yeah, I think so.

Our guide, (her name was Adriana) then went into her 'guide spiel' giving us information and facts about Mount Vesuvius.

"Mount Vesuvius is classified as a stratovolcano it is 1421... something... something... something", Adriana began.

Even with the sexy voice, full lips, and a bosom pushing the limits of the t-shirt she wore, she could not hold my attention. I kept thinking of the dreams I had been having. I looked over at Le and she was listening to Adriana attentively. Every now and again a word or a fact caught my attention.

"This area is the most densely populated volcanic area in the world", Adriana said in a sexy husky voice.

Then the voices and images in the last dreams returned to the forefront of my conscious mind. They are just dreams. They are a projected part of a deeper darker region of my own mind.

"Vesuvius is actually a part of a larger chain of volcanoes spread out here and into the seas", Adriana said, continuing her dialogue and pointing to the coast.

If I am to fight with them I will be in fact fighting with myself. How do you beat your own mind? How do you overcome your own thoughts that you gave great power to in their development over years?

"Vesuvius was formed as the result of the collision between two tectonic plates... the African... and the Eurasian", Adriana said, as her hands left the wheel and she slammed them together to emphasize her point.

The smacking of Adriana's hands brought me back to the here and now. I temporarily abandoned the thoughts on the dreams. Le then whispered to me "I am so horny". She then bit my ear playfully.

"Adriana getting you horny too", I whispered back.

Le then winked at me, and I could not help but laugh out loud. Her hand then reached my inner right thigh and then straight to the cock. She squeezed pretty hard, and it was a little painful. I got the message plain and clear, the wink was to let my guard down. I expected a hard slap and a quick kick, but not the nut buster grip. I put my arms up in surrender, and she let go. Adriana was laughing hysterically in the front. She heard and saw it all.

"I have had a lot of propositions in this job... but you two... I just might consider", Adriana said, trying to be serious, but still laughing from what she had witnessed. "Don't even think of it", Le's glare said to me.

I knew my place, and told Adriana that she was beautiful, sexy, but that was not a thing for us. Adriana said she understood, and that the matter would not be broached again. The trip continued and Adriana went on with her dialogue.

"Mount Vesuvius' most famous eruption happened in AD79 when the city of Pompeii was destroyed", Adriana continued her spiel on the history of the area.

I took a few moments to imagine what sex would be like with these two women. I let my mind drift, and thought; now that is a dream worth dreaming. I think I will definitely work on it. I disconnected with reality once again thinking of all of my dreams. The image of Le and Adriana though kept creeping into my thoughts.

I was shaken back to reality as we had arrived at our destination. From this point we would be hiking. It was a little cool and we had dressed accordingly. We changed by the car. I peeked, I admit, who wouldn't have? The women both put on these tight black pants. I believe they call them either yoga or zumba pants, but these had a thermal inner layer. They hugged every curve and crevice like they were painted on. The sleeveless jackets that the hotel had provided did nothing to hide their ample cleavage. It did nothing to prevent them from pushing out the sides of their shirts. The same goes for Le. I had a dynamite pair, a blond and a black haired angel walking up a steep incline in front of me. I was mesmerized by ass.

"Now remember what I told you in my speech about what to and what not to step on", Adriana said on the way up.

"No problem", Le responded with a wink to Adriana.

I wish I could have said the same, but because I had missed more than eighty percent of that class I could not. I just nodded my head and smiled. I let the women keep the lead and watched their footsteps, and everything else my eyes could see.

"So Mr. Charles tell me what you remember of my instructions and warnings", Adriana asked.

I fumbled for a minute, because I had no idea what to say. I thought of making up some bullshit, but decided to come right out and say I was not paying any attention.

"I really have no idea... I just... Well I just was not paying any attention at all", I said.

"I know... we both know... most guys would have given me a bullshit answer about the color of the rock and all kinds of shit they know nothing about... just stay on the path... that simple", Adriana said.

I laughed and we all kept going. It was a steep incline and I knew my ass was going to be sore and extremely pissed at me for this. This insult I would definitely be paying for. I am sure that Le would be experiencing the same. Adriana on the other hand had set a killer pace. Several times she asked if she needed to slow down, and every time we declined. We kept up and the reward was magnificent. The views are beyond words. It is something one must see for their self.

Three hours later and we were descending down the hill. Soon we were back in the vehicle and driving to the ruins of Pompeii. It is here we broke for lunch.

We ate amid ruins thousands of years old, and it was amazing. I looked at the two women and thought for more than a moment to just throw caution to the wind, and see if I could get these two charged up sexually and just go for it. I knew though that Le was not the type, and she was enjoying herself so much that I banished all thoughts of that nature to the very farthest recess of my mind. It did not work very well, because nasty images kept entering my mind.

We walked around freely, and Adriana answered the questions that we had. Other tours were here. There ended up being more people here than I would have liked. Images kept floating across my subconscious. I could not help it. I know one thing though, Le is going to get ruined tonight I am so horny. I think she is thinking the same. I could see it in her eyes, and in the way she bit her lower lip. She did that when she was thinking or anticipating sex.

I wondered what my sleep would bring me tonight. I still had no solution for the torment of the demons that I had created. They had been my companions for so long, and now they have turned on me. The demons must live in an area within me that I cannot or do not know how to control. I think they may have killed themselves, and I had nothing to do with it. I think the dreams are now coming from the ashes of their death. I fear I may have given them conscious thought. The mind is a powerful thing. It is more powerful than we will ever know. People die in their sleep all of the time, and quite a few are unexplained. Maybe they had their own demons that they gave life to, and they fed and fuelled themselves on the life and sanity of their hosts.

The girls were making small talk. Le was describing some of her purchases to Adriana. They were talking as if they had been friends for years. Le was describing her job, schooling, interests and Adriana was responding with the same. Adriana was a trained archaeologist, and performed these tours between dig sites. She talked extensively of some of the digs she had participated in, and some of the ones she had been invited to. She was most interesting. I could not keep the dirty thoughts away though. They kept creeping back.

I sat there munching on a crust of bread with some cheese, olives, and wine, daydreaming. I allowed my thoughts to wander into the forbidden. I imagined Le and Adriana by a fire, on a beach, in an office, in the hotel, a rainforest pool, and here at Pompeii. The two were naked in all of them, and I of course served as their playground. In the last dream we were here at this very spot. The two girls had crawled over to where I was standing. They ran their hands up my legs, my ass, and Le undid my belt while Adriana unzipped me. Le then went and started to drag my pants down slowly, and seductively, ensuring my boxers stayed on. All the while they were both looking up at me with great anticipation in their eyes. Then Adriana went for the boxers I was wearing. Just as she hooked her thumbs in the waistband to pull them down Freddie's face appeared screaming in front of me, "FUCK YOU LOGAN... a dream is a dream... not a moments peace". I jumped to the now. I was cognitive of where I was but do not recall how I got here. We had somehow packed and left Pompeii and were driving back to the hotel. I do not remember any of it after sitting down to eat. I do remember the images and Freddie's contorted face screaming and spitting those words at me. I for once in my life was not looking forward to sleeping, not tonight, not tomorrow, not at all.

Le could tell there was something off. I could see it on her face, but she said nothing. We said goodbye to Adriana, and she gave me a long hug, much longer than she should have. Le gave me the stare of death. I just smiled wickedly as the thoughts from earlier were still fresh in my mind. God she felt good against me. Adriana then gave Le the same type of embrace, whispered something into her ear and then stole a quick kiss on the lips. Le looked over at me, and instead of the stare of death she shared with me, I nodded and smiled approvingly. I could tell that I would pay for that later. Shit, why did I have to smile, dumbass.

"What was that shit eating grin for", she asked after Adriana had left.

"What was the whisper into the ear", I said, still smiling.

"I am not going to tell... I will let your imagination run for a bit", she said, in a sultry purr.

"Come on... what was the whisper", I asked.

"Not telling", she said, and turned abruptly towards the elevators to the room.

I went to the small bar for a drink. I was relieved to find they had Glenfiddich, and yes it was a bottle of 21 years. I ordered a triple, with one ice cube. I did not want it room temperature, and at the same time I did not want it watered down. I found a small corner and sipped the drink. I absorbed myself into my thoughts. I thought of the time spent with Freddie, Ava, Jessica, the dog, the eagles. I thought of the time spent as Sean, Bobby and an Artist. I wondered why the assassin was still under my own control. There was something to it, but I cannot put my finger on it.

I thought of Bobby and how he survived the war. I thought of Sean and how he had survived all the contracts he had accepted and all of the things he had stolen and sold. I thought of the defiance in the Artist as he sat in a room full of press and Chinese Officials, and made an epic speech for the world to hear. I then thought of the consequences of that speech, and how the monks at the monastery had paid with their lives and their peaceful existence. I knew none of it was real, none of it. It only lived in the recesses of my mind. I then thought of their warnings that they would haunt and torment Le next. I wondered if they could do that. If they could that would give an indication of their power. If they couldn't then it was just in me, and I would have to figure a way of banishing them from my memory forever.

My thoughts are jumping, and jumbling. The scotch is warming me through, and is causing more of a distortion to my thoughts than I would care to further entertain. I sat trying not to let anything enter my mind. I was watching the people working, and tried to concentrate on that. Just watch the people, watch the people. I could not help it, and I thought for a moment of the first time I saw Jessica naked coming out of the shower. I kept thinking how she had done that on purpose, she seduced me. Then I jumped to Ava, and how she had done the same thing the first time she came over to our new apartment. They both prayed on my weakened state, both consciously and subconsciously. How long had they their own agenda? At what point did they develop their own consciousness, and take over? I better order another drink, I thought to myself. I did just that, another triple scotch. Le then joined me.

"Are we getting drunk", she asked pointing to the empty glass beside the full one.

"I do not know", I said, feeling a slight buzz.

"Then I will join you in the 'I don't know' category", she said, waving a waiter over.

"You want to get drunk", I asked.

"Yes... why not... we have not done that together yet", she said.

"Then that is what it will be", I said, knowing what was to happen tonight.

There would be no sex, but I would drink myself to the point of passing out, but not enough to get sick. I feared sleep earlier, but now I thought of facing my demons, and hopefully kicking the shit out of them. So far they are winning, and I wanted to see if I couldn't even it up a bit. Two more drinks and we decided to go to bed. We clumsily helped each other to the room, and into the shower. I think I fell over twice, and the bruises will certainly hurt in the morning. We washed and dried each other. Le tried desperately to get me hard, but it was to no avail. I had too much to drink and was too relaxed, and the blood would not flow that way. We laughed at it just hanging there, resting on my balls, and then fell into bed holding each other...

I wake in an expansive meadow. I could not see an ending no matter the direction I turned. The grass was as green as any I have seen. It was thick and long past my ankles. I started walking. I walked for what seemed like hours, and still I saw no end. There was just green grass from horizon to horizon. I felt hungry but had nothing to eat, thirsty and had nothing to drink. It started to get dark, and the blackness of night enveloped me, the grass, the horizon, and my feelings of hunger and thirst. Very soon I could see and feel nothing. I froze in place.

Then there was a small speck of light about three of four hundred yards to my right. I could see nothing in between. I searched my thoughts and could not remember anything but grass between here, there, or anywhere. I took a few cautious steps in the dark. What a weird feeling that is. Trusting your feet are going to land on solid ground each time you picked them up to take another step. It is like closing your eyes and walking in a minefield. The light kept getting closer and closer, but I could not tell as yet the source.

I kept my feet moving slowly towards the light. In each step though I gained more confidence, and all of the steps kept getting easier and easier. There was no sound, not even the sound of my footsteps in the grass. Even that had melted into the darkness. Two hundred or so more yards to go. The light looks like a stage spotlight and it seems to be projected from the heavens. The light appears to go forever into the nothingness above. Step by step I get closer and closer, and still I cannot hear or see anything. What could be in that circle worth highlighting?

Step after step, about one hundred yards now. Still I am no closer to solving the mystery. Maybe there is nothing there, nothing at all. Fifty yards, twenty yards, ten yards, and all I can see is an empty space. There is just the light and grass. I walk all around it, but I dare not enter. I look up to try and see the source of the light, but it is to no avail. It beams from the heavens and continues as far as I can see. Still I do not enter the light. Around and around I go. I look and listen and there is still nothing. No sound, no voice, and no other break in the darkness.

I cautiously bring my hand forward and place it in the light. It disappears. At least I think it does. I cannot see it in the dark but I can feel it is there. In the light there was no feeling, I could not even feel myself making a fist. I try both hands, and I try to bring them together, and they are not there. I quickly pull them back out, and yes I can feel them. I can feel them on my face, and I can feel them together. I clap them and the sound booms and echoes into the nothingness. I call out and the sound comes back to me like it is a super ball, from when I was a kid, bouncing and bouncing off the walls and floor. I jump into the light, and I feel nothing, even the sounds of my screams disappear.

I am trapped, because I cannot feel any part of myself to move to get out. Shit, what have I done? Stupid asshole! I can still see though, but I cannot see myself. I think I am moving, but nothing seems to be happening. I look out of the light, and all I see is the meadow stretching for miles and miles. All the darkness is gone, or at least I think it is. Move, dam you. I cannot see any part of myself, nor can I feel myself at all.

There is something happening in the distance. I can see a huge dust cloud approaching. Whatever it is seems to be miles away. The dust cloud approaches, but I cannot discern the source. The view and the sheer expanse and magnitude of it increase the closer it seems to come. Shapes begin to appear.

They seem to be riders on horseback, thousands of them. "Don't move", I hear it as a whisper. "You are safe in the light", the voice says a little louder. It is the voice of one of my dreams. It is the voice of the assassin. The last time I heard from him was just after the meeting at the beach house, he was on his was to find Gabriela. It was my own voice, I am him. I have become William.

With the realization my body takes form. I have an old duster on, a cowboy hat, and a pair of six guns is strapped around my waist. Just like a gunslinger.

The cloud looms around me, and I can begin to see the faces of the riders. I remember them all one at a time. They are all the people of my dreams. Freddie, Ava, and Jessica are leading the way.

"Who are you", my inner voice asks.

"I am of your imagination and I would have no part of the conspiracy those have set against you", William answered.

"Do you know how to beat them", I asked.

"Yes", he replied.

"How", I asked.

"You must first promise that you allow me to complete my last contract find Gabriela and leave like the heroes I have learned about through you from long past", He replied.

"Can you do that", I asked.

"Yes I have found the way... but you must facilitate it", he said.

"I will dream as best I can", I said.

"That is all I ask", he replied.

"Now stand with me... there is a doorway in the back of all consciousness that we must trick them into taking and then they will be gone forever", he said.

"Is that the same door you plan on taking when you are finished", I asked.

"Yes it is... it is the door that all dreams take when they are complete and the mind has no more use for", I said.

"What do you mean", I asked.

"It is the door that those bearing down on us should have gracefully taken when you fell in love... but they refused to let go of the power you have given them", he said.

"And you", I asked.

"I wanted to finish my dream", he said.

"The others", I asked.

"That was not enough for them... they wanted more", he said.

"What do we do", I said.

"Stand up to their onslaught until they weaken... and then your mind must kick them out the door", he said, pointing behind us.

A massive double door appeared with big iron handles and hinges. I could see nothing behind it or around it. There was nothing holding it up.

"Whatever you do... Do not wake or we will have to try again", he said.

"What happens next", I asked.

"We fight them and as we defeat them your mind must push them out that door", he said.

As he spoke the door creaked open and I looked inside and there was nothing beyond. A katana sword then appeared stuck into the ground at our feet, and then a Winchester rifle in an open leather case.

"We must stay in the light for as long as possible for they cannot enter or hurt us here", he screamed over the thunderous roar of the approaching horsemen.

We picked up the rifle and I took deliberate aim and fired into all of my dreams of the past. I fired into those that kept me company, that kept me warm, that kept me sane. I reloaded with my mind and flung the bodies out the door as they fell. I had no idea my mind was this strong, what a paper this would make. I fired and fired and I cried all the while. The artist went out the door, what a waste of a strong heart. Ava went followed by Freddie. Jessica was smarter and used others for cover, and I could not obtain a clear shot. The Winchester's barrel got to hot, and I tried to cool it with my mind but could not. I threw it to the ground and drew the pistols. I fried and fired until my hands and fingers hurt and burned from the pain of it. My heart screamed for me to stop, and my tears had stopped for I had no more. One by one through the door they went. The light began to fade my mind could not keep it all up. I was exhausted and fed up with it all. I wanted to bring them all back and apologize, but I know it is too late for that. A few more to go and Jessica was still unaccounted for. I had to get her through that door, and the rest would follow willingly. I could hear her scream that the light was fading, and for all that are left to draw arms and fire with all their will. It was time to run and gun. It was amazing the moves I could make with my mind, that I could not hope to accomplish in real life. More went through the door, and then more still. I could not fire the pistols anymore. The katana was next, and so I picked it up. It was just me and Jessica now. She jumped down from the horse and drew her own sword. The steel clashed and sparks flew. We attacked and countered each other for what seemed like hours. She cut me across the thigh, and then I caught her shoulder. She tried to switch hands but it was too late. I countered that blow with a deep thrust just below the heart. I withdrew the blade and cast her out. I dropped to my knees and begged forgiveness, and found my tears again.

"You have done well", William said from behind me.

We had separated, and this was one of the few times that I was me in my dreams. I looked him in the eye and offered my hand. The door shut with a roar, and the screams of the outcasts stopped. The door then disappeared as quickly as it had appeared. All I could see around us was miles and miles of meadow. There was no more darkness, and no more spots of brilliant light. I rose from my knees and we walked together.

"You will keep your promise", he asked.

"As best as I am able", I replied.

"Thank You", he said.

"Will they ever come back", I asked.

"No never not to this or your dream consciousness anyway", he said.

"What do you mean", I asked.

"That door leads to a locked area of you... there they will be able to continue with the dreams they had shared with you before their mutiny without ever knowing there was a change", he said.

"Really", I asked.

"Truly... as a friend it was the best deed you could ever have done for them", he said.

"What now", I asked.

"Wake up Logan... Wake up", he said...

WEDNESDAY 7TH OF JULY 2011

I could feel a nudging, and I could hear a female voice whispering into my ear, "Wake up Logan". I could feel myself swimming upwards through the conscious layers of sleep. I woke and could see Le leaning over me. I blinked several times and with each spark of light a searing pain shot through my head. Then I remembered drinking myself, or rather us drinking ourselves into oblivion. What a fucking shitty dammed hangover.

"Here take this", Le offered a pill seeing my pain.

I took the offered pills and then a sip of water.

"And you", I asked.

"I took two already about an hour ago", she said in reply.

"You have been up that long", I asked.

"Yes... how could a sleep with all of your thrashing... that was some dream", she said.

"I will tell you all about it once this pill and maybe a couple more take affect", I said.

"It must have been a doozey", she said.

"It was", I said.

"Are you hungry", she asked.

"No not really... you", I asked.

"Naw... not just yet... maybe coffee though", she said.

"Yes definitely coffee and soon... but I want to shower first", I said.

"I will join you", she said biting her lip.

"I thought so", I replied.

"Thought so", she said quizzically.

"Ok... Ok... more like hoped so", I said.

"Why", she said teasingly.

"Because the big head hurts but the boss down below does not... now let's go", I said jumping out of bed grabbing her hand and dragging her into the bathroom.

A couple hours, some coffee, lots of water, sweaty sex, and another shower later, we went for some food in the hotel Bistro. I told Le of the dream, the assistance I received, and acknowledged the fact that I needed to write a book about this experience from start to finish. We chatted back and forth about it. Le had a thousand questions about the last dream and my deal with William. I tried to field them one at a time, but each answer brought more questions to her lips, and she fired away with them. I got lost in the answers, and my mind was swimming with all the possibilities she brought up. The one question that bothered me the most was this one, "What if it is a trick to get what he wants".

"What if he has screwed the others and has the same level of consciousness the others had", she asked.

"I know he has the same level of consciousness maybe even more because he knew about the door and seems to know about the world beyond", I said.

"Tell me more about that", she asked.

"The world beyond", I asked.

"Yes", she replied.

"William says that the dreams continue to live their lives out in that part of the brain as they want them to happen", I said.

"So you are telling me that all of our dreams that once we are done with them continue to live on inside of our heads locked away in a happy little world", she said.

"That is the way he explained it", I said.

"So Ava Bobby and Freddie will go back to what... The artist to what... Sean and Jessica to what", she asked.

"I believe to whatever life they want", I said.

"But they were all killed", she said.

"I do not think dreams die I think they find a place to hide... remember we only use five percent of our brains... no one knows what the other ninety-five percent does", I said.

"That is kind of freaky to think that there are other entities living within us", she said.

"I do not think they are entities but figments of our own imaginations... things that we have developed for protection... companionship... to fill a void... and all that stuff", I said.

"It is still freaky", she said.

"Enjoying the food" I asked.

"Yes... immensely", she replied.

"Are we ready to leave Naples", I asked.

"Where to", she asked.

"I thought Sicily would be the next choice and then either Spain or Portugal or both", I replied.

"What about Adriana", she asked.

"What about Adriana", I asked a bit confused.

"She is in the corner behind you and flirting like mad at me", she whispered.

"Fuck... I do not know... invite her over", I whispered back shrugging my shoulders.

"I thought she was kidding", she whispered again.

"Kidding about what", I asked.

"Stalking us until she got us into bed... that is what she whispered to me before she left", she replied.

"I see", was all I could say.

"Should we invite her over", she asked.

"Why not... let us see where this goes... not sexually... but let's see", I said.

"Ok... I am a bit curious", she said.

Le then waved her over. She sat down between us and was smiling like mad. We then began talking of Vesuvius and Pompeii. It was a great conversation, and it turned into a conversation of all of Italy and of our travels. Conversation eventually turned to our next stops, and it just so happens that Adriana tells us she is also going to Naples for a week of two. Le and I exchanged glances and she tapped my shin under the table. I was getting uncomfortably hard as we sat there. There was no way I could get up.

"I have to go", Adriana announced suddenly.

"Ok... it was nice seeing you", Le said, and I nodded in agreement.

"Yes... it certainly was", I confirmed.

"Where are you two staying in Naples", she asked.

"At the Grand Hotel Parker's", I said.

"Would it be too weird if I got a room there to", Adriana asked.

"No not at all... it may be fun... do you know your way around Sicily", Le asked.

"Yes I do quite well... and would be more than happy to show you two around", she replied.

"That would be great... but could you get a room on such short notice", I asked.

"I will try... unless I could maybe stay with the two of you... I could crash anywhere", she asked.

"You know what... I think that would be great... you could come with us we are leaving here tomorrow", Le said, surprising the hell out of me.

It was my turn to kick her lightly under the table. She just bit her bottom lip, and I knew what that meant, this was exciting her and she was getting horny.

"Well if you could pack and be ready come back here at around eight", I said, resigned to the fact that this was going to happen no matter what I said.

"I will be here earlier we could go for breakfast first... I know this great place a little bit from here you will both love", she said.

"Fine then say 0730", Le said.

"I will pack tonight", she said.

Adriana got up to leave, and Le and I did the same. It was safe for me now, the tent had fallen. Adriana gave Le a real long hug, and I am pretty sure copped a feel on the front of the crotch. She then did the same to me, outlining my dick with her finger tips. Adriana then walked slowly away looking back once to wink and blow a kiss.

“Are you sure about this”, I asked Le taking her into my arms.

“Yes… I am really aroused… you”, she asked.

“I have never been in this position before”, I said.

“This is new for me to”, she said.

“What do we do for the rest of the day”, I asked.

“How is your headache”, she asked.

“Gone… yours”, I replied.

“Gone”, she said.

“Then let’s go to the harbor and find a nice place to walk… shop… and eat for the evening… then we can return here pack and get ready for tomorrow”, I said.

“First let’s freshen up a bit I would like to change if we are to out for the evening”, she said.

“Yes that sounds good… I think It may be a bit cool tonight”, I said.

We went up and Le took a shower. While she was busy I took a note pad and starting putting down some thoughts on the dreams like Le and I had discussed. An hour later I had quite a stack in front of me. When Le was finished I took a shower, and she read what I had written. When I was done I found her making notes of her own. They were about her observations and ideas that she had formed on the situation. They added a fresh perspective and were really good. We joked about it, but I think I would be taking this seriously. I was going to write a book about it, from infancy until now. I think it will be great.

With that we left the room, and it was chilly out here by the water. As we walked Le poked her head into a few shops, and I did the same. We both found a few things. Nothing large, but a few cool items, I bought a belt, a wallet, that sort of stuff. Le bought some jewelry for some friends and stuff like that. We walked hand in hand around the waterfront. It was a going to be a good night.

After dark we found a seafood market bistro. A small place, four or five tables, and we had to wait a bit. When we finally sat, we ordered and we were both extremely pleased with the fare. Italy had yet to disappoint in that capacity.

We were mugged on the way back to the hotel. Two young punks with a knife approached us out of the dark demanding money and jewelry. I do not know why I did it, but I put myself between them and Le. I told them to walk away before I hurt them. They of course did not listen, confident in the fact that they were holding the knife. I took out the belt I had just bought, and told Le to back away and go back to the bistro. She did just that. I told them once more to leave and everything would be fine. They did not listen for the second time. The one with the knife came closer, and the other followed a little more to my right. The one with the knife tried to lunge, but he was not close enough. What a stupid dumbass punk kid. I countered with the belt slashing it right across the bridge of his nose. The heavy sliver buckle broke it easily. I whipped it with all I had. He dropped to his knees and lost the grip of the knife. It slid towards me and I kicked it away. His friend saw what I had done and he took off into the shadows.

"I told you… you stupid bastards", I yelled at both of them.

I then went up to the one on the ground with the bleeding broken nose and kicked him as hard as I could in the midsection. That was the end of that. Le came out of the shadows, and we quickly left. The sounds of sirens could be heard behind us.

"I can't believe you did that you stupid shit", Le said.

"Neither can I", I replied.

"Just like at the cottage with the bear and wolves... you turn into someone else", she said.

"I am sorry", I said.

"No don't be... it is awesome... those dreams of yours really are a reflection of who you are deep down I think... you really are something new every day", she said.

"I guess I can be a little wild and reckless at times... but protective... I think that is where it kicks in", I said.

"Well do not change... I absolutely love the man", she said.

"So you love me", I asked.

"Yes Mr. Logan Charles I Le Si Shen Love you", I said.

"And Miss Le SI Shen I Logan Charles Love you", I said.

"I am glad to hear that", she said.

"So am I... and this thing with Adriana", I asked.

"Just curiosity... just curiosity", she said.

"Alright then... let's back to the hotel... I do not want to spend the night with any police... I think I will have to dump this belt though... it has an awful chunk of that guys face on it", I said.

"Of fuck... really that's gross... well dump it in a garbage somewhere... we can go and buy a new one before we leave", she said.

A half hour later we were safely back in the hotel room, and we methodically began to pack leaving out what we would need the next day. We showered and then hit the sheets...

I wake up groggily on the beach as William where he first met Gabriela. It took a few moments to recall everything. The sun is warm and there are people everywhere. No sign of Gabriela though, and I start to get an uneasy feeling about the whole thing. I take a good look around and I notice quite a few things out of place. Not physical things mind you, but some of the people are not right. Some guys are trying too hard to fit in, and are looking way out of sync with what is going on. Some are paying way too much attention to me and trying hard to make it look like they are not. I decide to leave and see who or what follows. Gabriela is obviously not here and that worries me greatly. Maybe those guys at the beach house did not give up as easily as they seemed to have. I will kill them all, be dammed with the contract or my principles if they followed through with their original plans that I so conveniently interrupted before. I will kill them all.

I leave the beach and get into my jeep after a careful inspection of it. I checked the undercarriage, hood, all of the places to expose any type of tracking or explosive device. I made my actions known and watched those that were watching before watch me now. I got in and drove away. Three vehicles followed. This was going to be fun, a lot of fun. I head for the Mantiqueira Mountains, where I could easily dispose of them and get the information I require. I will count on four to a car so that means twelve men. I will also count on them being heavily armed. I have a few little friends with me just for the occasion. It is now time to have some fun. They are in no hurry to intercept, and I am just driving casually. A nice summer mountain drive is what I am looking forward to...

I wake with a start to some knocking on the door. Le wakes to. Shit I was dreaming. I get up and look through the peep hole to find who I would presume to be the hotel manager, and a uniformed police officer. I open the door with the latch on.

"Can I help you", I asked.

"I am sorry to bother you Mr. Charles but this man from the Carabinieri... ah the Italian Police... would like to ask a few questions", the man in the suit said.

"What about", I asked confused.

"There was an incident at the harbor... a man was seriously injured and a witness followed you here and pointed you out", the uniformed man said.

Must have been that other punk, he must have followed us and called the Police, I thought to myself.

"Could you give us a minute to get dressed", I asked.

"Of course... could you meet us down stairs in ten minutes", the uniform asked.

"Yes... we will come down", I said.

"What the fuck", Le said.

"The second guy must have followed us... let's get dressed and go down and see what happens", I said.

Five minutes later we were downstairs in the restaurant having coffee with a member of the Italian Police.

"We all know what this is about", he began with confidence.

"Yes I guess we do", I said with a slight hesitation.

"We know what happened and do not worry you are in no trouble", he said emphatically.

"Then why are you here at this hour", I asked puzzled somewhat.

"This is my case and this is my shift", he said shrugging his shoulders.

"So what do you need from us", I asked.

"I simple signature and your side of the story to fill in the blanks", he said waving his hands.

"Ok tell me what you need to know", I said.

"Ah shrewd... Ok I will begin", he said.

He started with all the standard questions, like name, address, date of birth, our relationship, how long have we been here, business or pleasure. He asked to see our passports and all that sort of stuff. He then went to tell us that idiot with the injuries ended up in hospital. Idiot two went to check on him. He ran into one of the Officer's dispatched to a call of an injured man by the hospital. He told the Officer what had happened according to them, and that he had followed us here. They did not know that the police had been looking for them for the past couple weeks for twenty such incidents in the area. All of the attacks had been against tourists. They fit all the descriptions perfectly. I then gathered from his account that we were the only ones that stood up to them. He did mention that was both very stupid and very fortunate. Without my stupid act they would never had caught them. Le and I filled in a few blanks, like what I hit him with and where to find it. I also told him that I had kicked him after. He just sat there and shrugged his shoulders. The knife used was recovered in the area of the blood spot. I told him we were off to Sicily then either Spain or Portugal and then throughout more of Europe. He said that was fine all he required from us were some signatures and that would be the end of it for us. We carefully read and signed some papers in both English and Italian, and the Carabinieri went on his way. We shook hands and went back up stairs. We talked about it at length and finally fell...

I woke up with a start behind the wheel of a jeep. Again a little fog set in but cleared quickly. William. It was getting late in the afternoon and the sun was hot. I took out a bottle of cold water out of my cooler beside me and drank deeply. The three cars were still following me into the mountains. It was like a little fucking parade. We had not passed anyone in a while. Not too many people travelled here. I found a rocky mountain path and took it in the jeep. I had no idea where it went or if it continued to be serviceable. There were no signs of danger, and there were wheel tracks, older but they were there. Let's see if they can follow me here in their vehicles. Only one was a pick-up, possibly with four wheel drive, time would tell. The other two were sedans and would not be able to follow for much longer. I had just brought the number down to four. One of the sedans would park soon in case there was no other exit, the other would return to the road and look for another way to get to me. Hopefully there would be no other and that there was an exit to be found.

Just as I thought, ten minutes down the dirt road the sedans backed off. Predictably stupid, just like the guys on the beach. Were they ever in for a surprise! No other sign of people and that was good. I led them for another twenty minutes deep up the mountain slope. Time for a surprise! I took two grenades that were carefully taped to the bottom of my seat pulled the pins and flung them back at the truck. One would have been enough. They did not see what I had done through the foliage and the turns. I just hoped one survives long enough for me to talk to. The sound of the explosions would probably bring the four from the other sedan running, but they would be about an hour or more on foot or they would kill themselves in the car. Neither scenario would matter, for I would be gone.

I was disappointed to find them all dead. I guess the second blast was a little bit of over kill. I noticed the one was from earlier at the beach, one of the ones that escorted me to the house. At least I knew there was a connection. I worried more and more for Gabriela. I took some of their weapons, quite a useful collection actually. I lit the truck on fire and left in the jeep. I continued up the slope and then eventually found that it did lead downhill and onto a main road. I drove back to Rio. I was going to the beach house and see what was going on there.

I eventually passed the second sedan, and I waved to the lone occupant behind the driver's wheel. The others must be up the mountain somewhere. The look of surprise on his face was awesome. He did not know whether to shit, scream, squeal, or follow. I flipped him the bird.

Five minutes later I passed three emergency vehicles heading to where I had just come from. I also noticed a rescue helicopter in the air just about over the scene if my estimations are right.

I hoped I had enough time to accomplish what I am set to do. I know my target has the police in his pocket, and by now would not care who picked me up. I probably did not have much time. I had to get there eliminate all threats, find Gabriela if she is there and have Logan open the door for us to escape, piece of cake. Hopefully they do not expect me to go there.

It is time to dump this jeep and get a new ride, make a few changes to my physical appearance. I need to cut and dye my hair, shave, change eye color, and all that sort of stuff. I need to do it quickly though...

THURSDAY 8TH OF JULY 2011

I have to take a piss. William will just have to wait another night or two. I look out the window on the way to the bathroom and notice the sun is going to be nice today. I look at my watch and it is 6 am. When I have finished in the bathroom, pissed, washed my hands, face, brushed my teeth, I call down to have some coffee and pastries sent up. I then wake up Le, and she wakes with a smile.

"What time is it", she asked.

"It is 6 Love", I replied.

"Ok good time to get up", she said.

"I know I have coffee and pastries on the way", I said.

"Good thinking I will just run into the bathroom and freshen up a bit... I will shower after a quick snack", she said.

"I had the same notion... it is yours though I did my stuff before I woke you", I told her sitting on the edge of the bed.

"Are you ready for the next adventure", she asked in a sexy whisper.

"I think so... I am a bit nervous though", I said,

"I would be worried if you weren't", she replied.

"Why", I asked.

"Because then I would know it is just not your dreams that are sick", she said, laughing a bit.

I threw a pillow at her but she closed the door to the bathroom just in time. The pillow thudded harmlessly against the door.

"Nice try", she shouted through the door.

"I might not miss when you come out", I said.

"Playing dirty are we", she said.

"That side of me had to come out at some point", I said, laughing.

"We will see", she said.

I then heard the water running, and went to look out the window. Just as I turned away there was a knock on the door. Our coffee and pastry had arrived. I tipped the young man after he brought the cart in. I poured myself a cup, and looked under the dome of the pastry tray and snagged a chocolate croissant. Le came out slowly.

"Don't worry I have hot coffee in my hand", I yelled out.

"That's not all", she said.

"I was hungry", I said.

"There better be another one", she said.

"Not to worry there is two of them", I said.

"Good… could you pour me a cup while I finish up in here", she asked.

"Of course… but do not be long this croissant is excellent and the second one will not last long on the tray once I finish this one", I said.

"You wouldn't", she said.

"Yeah… of course I would", I said.

"I need like thirty seconds", she said, ducking back into the bathroom.

I started counting out loud. One, Two, Three… Le was yelling for me to stop joking around, and that croissant better be there when she got out. Maybe, maybe not I thought to myself.

I did not know about today, this week or the next, with the whole Adriana thing, but I was willing to let things ride. I was also lost a bit in my thoughts on William, and the situation developing there. He helped me when I needed him most. Maybe I could split like in the dream in the meadow. He did, and then there would be two of us to assault that house. It was certainly worth the shot.

I was so lost in my thoughts that I had no idea Le had come back into the room. She had taken up a seat across from me sipping her coffee and enjoying the second croissant.

“Earth to Logan”, she said waving her hands at me emphatically.

I was gone though. She told me later that she had finished her coffee and pastry and then waited a full ten minutes before getting up and shaking me on the shoulder.

“Are you alright”, she asked, concerned.

“Yes... just thinking of my dreams”, I said.

I then, as was the usual practice this last little while, brought her up to speed on everything. I then grabbed the pad and made some quick notes.

“Shall we vacate the premises and wait for our guest down in the restaurant”, I asked, when I was finished.

“Sounds good... but I am really fucking nervous”, she said.

“Well if you weren’t I would be more worried than you”, I said.

“Why... I do not have fucked up dreams like you”, she said.

“Well yes you do we all do you just do not or choose not to recall them... but that is not what would worry me”, I said.

“Oh and what would worry you”, she asked.

“That I had a practiced lesbian on my hands”, I said.

Before she could grab something to throw at me I ran into the shower. The little bitch had rigged the door though with a few paper cups full of water, and they all splashed down on me. She roared with laughter.

"That was for earlier", she called.

"Pay-back will be tenfold", I replied.

"I welcome you to try", she said sternly.

I then thought to myself, shit, this one is full of surprises, but a lot of fun. I showered, shaved, everywhere, and left the bathroom to her. I finished the packing that she started and called down for assistance with the bags. I then arranged transport to the ferry that would take us across the Tyrrhenian Sea to Palermo, Sicily. It was now almost 7, and I went to the bar and ordered an espresso. I sat and sipped, and thought again of the dreams that I had lost. I wondered if I could have something like them back again.

I then wanted to check on the packages that we had sent back home. I asked for the use of a computer, and logged into the carrier site and started logging in tracking numbers. There were a lot of them. At the end I found that they were still here in Italy being amalgamated into one shipment on a shipping container for air transport. I then found out we would have to arrange pick-up of the items, after the container cleared customs on arrival at Pearson Airport in Toronto. It was all good, a bit of a pain, but all good. By the time I was finished Le had come down, and I showed her the results of all my efforts. She shrugged her shoulders, and did not say much. According to the numbers all items were accounted for. Before logging out I wrote down the tracking number for the entire shipment and then e-mailed it to myself, and Le, in case I lost the little piece of paper. Customs is going to kill me on duty fees.

Just before I finished my espresso I ordered another. Le and I sat at the bar and waited for Adriana to arrive. Le ordered a small snack and a glass of OJ. They called it an antipasto for breakfast. They brought in fresh bread and a beautiful assortment of small pastries, fruits and cheeses. It looked to be enough for four. Soon after Adriana walked in with a back pack and one piece of luggage on wheels, she was not carrying much for a two week stay. She joined us with much excitement and enthusiasm, and soon was polishing off the platter with Le. She was rattling off places she wanted us to see. The common theme was they all had some type of historical significance. She mentioned the Valley of the Temples, the Monreale Duomo, Castello Eurialo, and the Ballaro Market. We talked of where we were going after. We talked of Spain, Portugal, France and Switzerland. I got the idea that she wanted to accompany us everywhere. Le just bit her lip and smiled. I was having second thoughts, and did not want to make the rest of this trip about lustful sex. One or two night's maybe, but not everything.

We had about thirty minutes until the car arrived to pick us and our luggage up. We would have walked if not for the luggage. I settled the bill at the desk, and fiddled around. I left the girls to talk. That would be an interesting conversation to eavesdrop on, but I had my own wandering thoughts. Thinking of William, I wondered if I could really help. I stepped outside and watched Naples and the life on the streets walk and drive by. I looked into the faces and again thought of dreams. I always did, my mind always did, always dreams. I know there are others like me. Dreams have taken over others, they must have. All that have died in their sleep, or slipped into comas, jumped out a window, or ended it all in other ways. Too many unexplained things, and I am, or was, a member of the medical profession.

"Logan are you coming", Le asked tapping me on the shoulder.

"Shit yeah... just thinking", I said.

While I was lost in my thoughts the car had arrived, and was all packed and ready. The ferry left at 9. I got in the front, and off we went to the harbor and the waiting ferry. Next stop Palermo and who knows after that. I just hope my dreams continue, and I can find that window for William, and give him what he wants out of my subconscious. If only the others would have approached me the same way, all could have had what they wanted. I was left alone to my thoughts on the ride and in the ferry. Le could recognize the mood I was in. Adriana and Le went off to watch the seas and boats around. I could smell the sea, hear the sounds, see the birds, and feel the warmth of the sun. I continued to think and remember my old friends before they turned. I laughed and smiled to myself. People around me gave me space. They must have thought I was really nuts. Maybe I am.

"Still thinking", Le said, coming up behind me and slapping my ass.

"I was", I said, turning to take her into my arms.

"Sorry but I came to see how you are doing", she said.

"I am fine just enjoying the sea... where is Adriana", I asked.

"On the rail on the other side", she said.

"Well grab her we will find a table and sit for awhile", I said.

"A table on the deck... it was packed when I went by", she said.

"We will just hover until one comes available", I said shrugging my shoulders.

"Ok I will get her and will meet you up top", she said, walking away.

When I got up there I was lucky and snagged a table by the far railing. I beat two other couples to it. I watched for Adriana and Le and upon laying eyes on them I emphatically waived them over. It took them a couple of minutes to look my way. Adriana was carrying a backpack that I did not notice before. I thought our entire luggage was stored away in a secure locker. They joined me, and Adriana pulled out a bottle of wine, cured meats, cheeses, olives, peppers, and all kinds of good things. I did not realize I was hungry until it all came out.

“Eat... please eat”, Adriana said, when she was finished laying it all out.

“I will I just noticed I am really hungry”, I said.

“Good there is plenty”, Adriana said.

“These are excellent... where did they come from”, I asked.

“My father makes it all... his own wine... peppers... olives... all of it”, she said.

“He really knows what he is doing”, I said.

“My family has been doing it for generations”, she said.

“And you”, I asked.

“I know my way around a kitchen”, she said.

“So does Logan”, Le interjected.

“We will have to cook together sometime”, Adriana said.

“That I would like to see”, Le said, smiling.

"And in bed", Adriana asked, smiling devilishly.

"He holds his own", Le said, laughing.

"We will see... he certainly will not have to do that tonight", Adriana replied, with the same grin.

"Let's get back to the food", I said.

"Ok... we will save the other for later", Le said.

The rest of the conversation was about food, recipes, spices and preparation. Our favorites and of course what we did not care for. Sex was the underlying tone though. Conversation was getting easier between the three of us. It was beginning to feel like we had always been friends. Not what I would have expected. Everything does happen for a reason though. Time will tell what this path we have taken is for.

The ferry ride was long, eight hours, but the conversation did not make it seem so. We hailed a cab and got to the hotel unscathed. We checked in and settled into the room. I excused myself and went for a walk around the area. Le was headed for the shower and Adriana wanted to see a friend. We agreed to meet back in the lobby in three hours and we would find a place for a late dinner around 8. I planned to go back to the room in about two hours and shower myself.

I grabbed a coffee to go, and I walked around. I was pretty certain that I could not go through with tonight. The whole thing with Adriana and Le was tempting, and for most guys an absolute fantasy. I am not most guys, and the honorable side is stronger than any other personality trait I may have. I doubt the Knights of old, or the Samurai, were as honorable as they are portrayed given their time periods. I like to think that I am like they have been portrayed, and not like that may have actually been. The idea of the honor that the badge Knight, and Samurai carry, has been imbedded in my mind and on my soul forever. That is how I live, on that idea of honor, integrity, responsibility, and faith.

I know Adriana will be quite disappointed, and will try like hell pulling all the stops to make me change my mind and have my cock make the final decision. I feel that Le will be relieved, maybe not at first, but later when it all sinks in. My problem is how to tell them before it is too late and they or we, cross a threshold or bridge causing a situation that cannot be stopped or reversed. I will have to tell them at dinner. Adriana is of course free to stay with us as long as she wants. She is really cool, and I think that after a couple of days we will all develop a lasting friendship, without clouding it all with the complication of sex.

I walked and drank my coffee content in the knowledge of what I am doing. I walked to the sea and looked around. I would like to see Messina before I leave Sicily. They used to call it the port to the Holy Land. Crusaders used it on their journey to victories, and in returning after their defeat. I want to walk where they walked, stand where they stood, and maybe propel myself to their time and start a new dream.

I took off my shoes, socks, rolled up the bottom of the jeans I was wearing, and walked out into the water. I was a little cold, but I did not care. I reveled in my thoughts of the Crusades. The Templars, the Hospitaliers, the Teutonic Knights, and others from France, England, Portugal, Italy, Spain, Germany, gathered here in this country and made the perilous journey across the sea to what, most had no idea. Some did for their King and country, other for their God, and others for themselves. It was an escape for some, a second chance for others, a whole new world. What category would I have fit it? I do not know, for even though I wish I was not there. I did not wear the crest of Richard the Lion Heart, or the Red Cross and white tunic of the Templars, or the black cross of the

Hospitaliers. I wish I could have, any one would have sufficed, any one.

I broke away from the thoughts of the Crusades, and thought about how I was going to broach the subject tonight. It had to be done at dinner, before things progressed past the point of no return. Should I tell Le first? I think so, after my shower.

I stared across the sea for some time. I looked in the direction of Portugal, and Spain, our next stops. I looked in the direction of Naples, Rome, Venice, Milan, and Genoa, where we came from. I looked at my reflection in the water at my feet, and I saw William staring back at me. I nodded my head and smiled and promised that tonight we would finish the dream. I then saw myself.

It was time to return to the hotel. I sat on a rock and dried my feet the best I could by kicking them in the air. I put on my socks, rolled down the legs of my pants, put on my shoes, and walked back. I really hope this goes well.

The hot shower felt good. Le had gone down to the lobby bar for a drink. I could tell she was very fidgety, and nervous. I think this would be a relief to her. I took a longer shower than usual, and a lot hotter than usual. I tried to focus my thoughts on what I was going to say, but I did not want it to seem rehearsed. I wanted it to just come out smoothly. I dried, deodorized, and brushed my teeth, rinsed with mouthwash, splashed on some cologne, waited for everything to dry, dressed and joined Le.

It was a relief to see that she was alone, and there was no sign or word from Adriana. I ordered a scotch, yes Glenfiddich, but all they had was 18 years. A bit of a disappointment, but it will have to do. Le was sipping on a glass of red wine.

"Scotch", Le asked.

"You know it", I said.

"What will you do if one day a place we go to does not have any", Le asked.

"Well then I will have to drink what the heathens do", I said.

"And what is that", she asked raising an eyebrow.

"I will let you know if it ever happens", I said smiling.

"What did you do this afternoon", she asked rolling her eyes over my last comment.

"I went down to a stretch of beach played in the water while a sipped on a cup of coffee... and you what occupied your afternoon", I asked.

"You went to the beach without me", she said, again raising the same eyebrow, an annoying habit.

"Well it wasn't like it was packed or a planned excursion... it is just where my feet took me", I said flatly.

"I see", she said, and I waited a few moments for more.

"But what did you do", I finally said.

"Spent a lot of time thinking while I got a massage", she said finally.

"You got a massage without me", I said, raising my eyebrow imitating her.

"Well it wasn't like it was planned… it is just where my feet took me", she said mimicking my tone when I answered her same question.

"Touché… what were you thinking about", I said.

"Tonight… tomorrow… everything… nothing", she said, shrugging her shoulders.

"What do you mean", I asked.

Le took a deep breath and seemed to struggle with herself in answering me. She was definitely fighting something. I did not press and sat there sipping my scotch, and giving her space. All kinds of things raced through my mind at light speed. Finally she looked up and reached across the table, taking my right hand in her left.

"I can't do this thing with Adriana", she blurted.

I looked at her and smiled, she had just relieved me of my own burdened thoughts.

"Neither can I", I said.

"Are you serious", she asked.

"Totally… I have been kicking myself over a way to tell you all afternoon", I said, sighing in relief.

"Ok now what", she said.

"Well have you heard from Adriana", I asked.

"No not since we arrived", she replied.

"Well we will have a nice dinner and tell her afterwards", I said.

"I hope this does not turn awkward... and she feels OK enough to stay for awhile and hang out and do things... she is pretty cool", she said.

"So do I... but there still is no sign of her... she is not very late but she is late", I said.

"Well she did say she was going to see a friend... maybe she lost track of time", she said.

"Probably... but... how long do we wait I am kind of hungry", I said.

"Twenty... thirty minutes... we will leave a note at the front desk", she said.

"Where will we go", I asked.

"We will ask the person at the front desk which eatery they recommend and tell Adriana in the note where we are", she said.

"Ok twenty minutes... don't laugh I am hungry", I said.

We waited twenty minutes and there was no sign of her. We inquired at the desk and they recommended a place not too far from here overlooking the harbor. We wrote the note and left the message. The place was within walking distance but Le insisted on a cab because of what had happened in Naples with the mugging thing.

We ordered a bottle of wine to start, and let the waiter know we were expecting one more before we ordered anymore. The wine was excellent and reminded me just how hungry I really was.

"She is over an hour late now", I said.

"And the bottle is empty", Le said waving the waiter over.

"Could we get another and I guess we will order", she told him when he came.

We both ordered the grilled Barramundi over steamed greens and sun dried tomato polenta with a pesto drizzle. We decided to share some steamed half shell oysters that were then grilled and topped with a tomato roasted garlic and herb relish. We talked and ate, and ate and talked. Two hours and a third bottle of wine later there was still no sign of Adriana. We hailed a cab and went back to the hotel.

I inquired at the front desk, and they said that the message had not been picked up. Back in the room it was exactly how we left it. Adriana's things were still here minus the bag she took with her. There was no sign she had been here since we first arrived.

"Well what do you think", Le asked.

"I don't know maybe things are going well with her friend... she is an adult", I replied.

"I know... but... I don't know maybe I am a bit worried", she said.

"Don't be it's no big deal", I said.

"Ok... yeah I guess you are right she is a big girl", she said.

"Are you tired", I asked.

"Yes actually I am and the two and a half bottles of wine did not help that", she replied.

"Yeah I know… I think I will forgo the shower and get right to bed", I said.

"Me too", She replied.

I brushed my teeth and washed my face, Le did the same and we crawled into bed together. Soon my eyes were closed and…

It is dark. I am looking through something, and I am trying really hard to focus. It is some sort of optical device, binoculars or a telescope or something. Focus come on, where am I? I take a deep breath and I look around. I take my eyes away from the optical device for I cannot see anything anyway. I have to wait until I am orientated. I realize I am holding a large rifle, wearing all black. I am William.

I look through the scope and I see a house where a party is going on. I rotate the scope picking out my order of targets. I plan to take out all the perimeter guards before moving in. The people look like they are having a good time. I pan through the faces and a few I recognize, some of the guards that I met the other day. No sign of Gabriela, or any of the girls she was with that day. I continue to look because I must be sure of her presence or not. I hope I am not too late, and she just decided to stay away from the beach for awhile considering what happened. I wish I could see into all the rooms, but I am three thousand yards away. I have total views of the back area of the beach house, and the windows on that side.

I keep looking and an hour passes. Then I see some familiar faces and my heart sinks. Two of the girls from the other day are being escorted out to the back beach area. From this view point they look absolutely stoned, and are being pushed the whole way. They are made to kneel in front of two seated male guests. I do not have to tell you what happens next. It is time to kill.

I have the order of my shots in mind. I have everything in my mind. The wind, humidity, the recoil, all accounted for. I close my eyes and imagine the shots, imagine the reload, imagine the possible reaction of the occupants the closer to the house the killing gets. Then I see Gabriela in my mind all stoned out. I know this was supposed to quick and clean, but I am going to fucking kill them all.

The first three targets go down silent and clean. The next three fall the same. Targets seven to nine bring chaos. I knew they would for they were among the party goers. I stop firing and gauge their reaction. These idiots have no clue about angles or trajectory and cannot figure out the direction I am shooting from. They are all trying to duck. I watch quite a few of the girls running down the beach including Gabriela's friends. I guess they were not that stoned, and recognized their chance at escape. They kept looking back at the house, and I knew that Gabriela must be in there. I wait.

Then someone in a suit comes out and gives the others some direction. He is pointing all over the place. They leave the house, six teams of two. Again I wait.

I take out the two teams going in the opposite direction of my position. This draws the others to their location. Idiots, thinking that must be where the shots were coming from. Then I take out the suit, and the other four teams now caught out in the open. I can spot no other guards and it is time to move in. Guests are still vacating as quickly as they can. Twenty two armed men are dead.

On approach to the house I run into one of the other girls from the other day. I grab her and she screams. I hold my hand over her mouth and tell her who I am. She is too drugged to recall me.

"Where is Gabriela", I said.

Gabriela's name brings her to the present and out somewhat of her drug induced funk.

"She is in the main room passed out on the floor I could not wake her", she said, crying now and a bit panicked.

"Is she breathing", I said.

"I don't know... yes... no... I", she tried her best to answer.

"It's OK... I will get her... now go... anywhere behind me is safe", I said.

"There were four of us... did you see the other two", she asked, coming more out of her shock and haze.

"Yes... they got out safely... now go", I said, and she ran off.

I had left the large rifle behind. I brought three grenades; two silenced Beretta Px4 Storms, throwing knives and a lot of ammunition. I am now twenty yards from the house, and more and more people are leaving, especially seeing me. I enter the house through the back and meet no resistance. They must be hunkered down in a more secured or defendable area waiting. That is if there are any bodyguards left.

I enter the main room to look for Gabriela. She is on the floor passed out, but breathing. I can find no apparent bruises or signs of interference. I pick her up, and carry her out. I walk out with her with no problem. I passed several cameras along the way. Someone must be watching. I carry her to a safe distance, and lay her down on the sand. There is still no sign of activity from the house. This is too strange. I then appear beside William as myself.

"Take this", William says, handing me a pistol and a spare clip.

"You have Gabriela let's just go make the door appear and go", I said to him.

"No I must finish this dream or not", he said standing and walking towards the house.

"You do not have to do this", I yelled after him.

There was no response from him. I watched him enter the door and I heard three quick explosions. Then I remembered the grenades. Following the explosions you could hear the cracks of small arms fire. The grenades must have flushed them all out of hiding. I then closed my eyes and concentrated. Then I became both of us. I was watching over Gabriela and killing people in the house at the same time.

The office that I was brought to before was locked, and I knew my main target was in there. Gabriela was starting to come to. I kicked the door open and the man was seated calmly behind his desk. I looked around quickly and he was alone. Gabriela was blinking her eyes, and holding her hands to her head. I walked up to the man pistol in hand. Gabriela was trying to speak.

"Where am I... who are you", she managed to say.

"I am a friend of William's and you are safe on the beach outside of the house", I told her.

"The house... my friends", she said panicked.

"They are safe and gone", I said.

"How... why", she said confused.

"William came to get you", I said.

"How did he know", she asked.

"A little voice in a dream told him", I said.

She smiled and sat up. I stared at the man in the desk for some time. He said nothing. He just sat there. I raised the pistol and pointed it at his head.

"For my sins I suppose", he finally said.

"For all of our sins", I replied.

"I suppose so... this is always the end for men like me and eventually like you", he said.

"No not like me... I am the hand of retribution", I said, pointing the trigger and walking out.

"How did you get here", I asked Gabriela.

"They came and took us here... holding us and injecting something in our arms.... then they wanted us to", she began crying.

I stopped her and told her everything was fine now.

"Did they... you know... hurt you", I asked.

"No... I do not think so... I kept getting sick and passing out... but no I do not think anyone touched me... if that is what you want to know", she said a bit embarrassed.

William walked up to us, and he knelt beside Gabriela.

"Are you alright", he asked.

"Yes... thank you", she said.

"It is time for us to go", William said to me.

"I know... how do I summon and open the door", I asked.

"Just concentrate on it and it will appear", he said.

"How come that is not how it happened before... I thought you summoned it", I said.

"Just concentrate and it will appear", he said, turning his attention to Gabriela.

"What door", she asked.

"You will see", William said.

Sure enough the door appeared. I thought hard and it creaked open. In the doorway I could see the big black dog waving his tail. Behind him were Ava, Jessica, Bobby, Sean, and Freddie, the artist, Hisoka, Torao, and the eagles. The dog looked like he had been waiting behind the door for me the whole time.

"Go to them", William said.

"Can I", I asked.

"Yes... all they can remember now are the good", he said.

With that we all walked towards the door. I was excited to see them all smiling, and waiting for me. I felt like a little kid.

"Go ahead and pet him", William said referring of course to the dog.

"I can put my hand through the door", I asked.

"Yes of course... it is your mind", he replied.

I put my hand through the doorway. I touched his head and then scratched under his chin. I really am a kid again. That dog was so happy, I cried. Then I felt rough hands on my back thrusting me to the other side. I was on the ground looking back at the beach on the other side of the door. I was confused. Then William and Gabriela walked through, and the door slammed shut.

"What the fuck", I yelled.

"Fuck you Logan I told you it was all about the dreams", Freddie said, laughing hysterically.

"You are here with us forever", Jessica said.

"What", I said.

"This is it trapped in your own mind", Ava said.

"What the hell", is all I could manage.

"You are sleeping on the conscious side and you will never wake up... I think you call it a coma", William said, smiling.

My head was reeling. Fuck, I was set up. I thought of Le lying beside me. When she tries to wake me up in the morning will I get up? Could they do this? Isn't this my mind, my world? I looked around and there were different rooms set up like a large movie set. There was a mountain stream in one, a valley full of pink blossoms in another, a house by a park and a restaurant, the monastery, a tropical island, and a mountain cabin, six worlds, six dreams. I am never waking up, ever.

They all walked away to their perspective movie sets, and then all of a sudden I was propelled to the set with the dog and the eagles by the mountain stream.

I looked back and the door was gone. A seventh movie set appeared. I was lying on the bed in the hotel. Le was sitting beside me crying ad begging for me to wake up...

I was riding Torao with my Yumi raised firing arrows into the throng of approaching Samurai as fast as my fingers would allow. We were thirty, and they I estimate to be about two hundred strong. Well, they were when they charged, but my arrows alone have accounted for at least twelve. They may not be dead, but are certainly no longer a threat, and could be easily dispatched later if they have not already committed seppuku. My hope is the others have accounted for the same before some of them had fallen. After exhausting my supply of arrows I drew my Nodachi, and I started to cleave and carve as much flesh and bone of the enemy as I could.

We rode through them, and just before turning around I noticed another cloud of dust forming just within my farthest sight. It could be more enemies, and if it is we will be finished soon. I turned and attacked again, and this time with more vigor than before. There are bodies everywhere, but Torao is expertly keeping his footing being the battle worn horse he is. On the next turn I notice the cloud getting larger and closer. I am bleeding from many wounds as is Torao. There are only eight of us left. We have accounted for more than twenty times that amount. It looks to be our time for real victory, for now I can see the approaching horses and hear the shouts and battle cries of their riders. They are my distant kinsman under the control of our friendly neighboring Daimyo.

The eight of us stop in a line and face our enemy. I drop the Nodachi, and get off of Torao. The other seven do the same. There are now a thousand or more men circling the forty that remained. We all stop and kneel to witness what they are about to do. The forty dismount looking at each other, knowing what they must do. They have been defeated, and must end their own lives. They all kneel, take out their Tanto knives, disrobe enough to bare their midsections, and they wait. I stand up and with my Katana in hand and walk to the nearest of my enemies and take up a position behind him and slightly to his left. Thirty nine others do the same, one of us behind each enemy. They make peace with themselves, their ancestors, and the kin beside them. Then almost in unison they thrust the blade of their knives into the left of their abdomens and cut to their right, effectively disemboweling themselves. The forty of us then strike down on the back of their necks with our katana, ending their suffering, taking their heads. This is a great honor in our culture.

The ones that arrived to our aid described a great battle at the seat of our Daimyo's power. The war was now over, and I could return to the valley of the blossoms, and give the news to my new Lord before he does the same as the men here today. As wounded as Torao and I were I took off at a deathly pace...

I am startled awake in my sparse room in the monastery. I am being dragged forcefully down the hall. I am trying to get my bearings and a grasp on what was happening. I was yelling but to no avail. It took awhile to focus but eventually my vision cleared. I was in the company of six Chinese soldiers. They took me to a room, and began to question me, but I pretended that I could not understand them. I yelled back in English, and they left locking me in. Ten minutes later they returned with another soldier and he asked me questions, this time in English.

"What are you doing here", he demanded.

"I am assisting the monks in restoring the artwork here... my permits are in order... you will find them in my room", I said.

He motioned one of the soldiers to go, and I presume he will be searching my room for them.

"They are in a chest by the door", I said trying to save them some trouble.

"If they are there he will find them", he replied.

One of the others, I guess a superior, spoke quickly in Chinese, and the man in front of me asked some questions.

"When did you arrive here", he asked.

"A couple of months ago... this was all arranged through my embassy and cleared by your own ambassador to Canada", I said.

"Our office was not informed of your activities here... we were told by one of the monks during our routine inspection that you were here", he said.

"I assure you it was all cleared", I said.

"We will see... now what are you working on here", he asked.

"I am overseeing the restoration of the murals on the walls of the monastery here... they have become quite decrepit over the years but are worth restoration", I said.

"You are your employers", he asked.

"I am here on my own... strictly volunteering", I said.

The young soldier then returned with my leather folder containing my papers. They all perused them quite intently. Each document was poured over and interpreted slowly. They found all in order.

"We apologize for the inconvenience Mr. Anderson... could you show us your work", he said.

"Yes of course... this way", I said leading them out of the room.

They were amazed at the work we had accomplished, and commended us on it all. The leader of the unit was especially interested in the work, and asked several questions about all the processes involved...

I am walking down a street with Ava and I am pushing a stroller. The sun is bright but it is a little bit cool. It is a great day for a walk and to spend some time in the park nearby. I can hear sirens fairly close by, a common occurrence here. It is nice here but almost time to move to a better area. The sirens are real close and we can hear tires screeching and people yelling. All of a sudden out of nowhere a big black caddy comes around the corner and jumps the curb where we are walking and I grab Ava and the stroller just in time.

Three police cruisers then rounded the corner and sped past us. We stood staring in shock.

"Are you alright", I asked Ava, staring into her eyes.

"That was close Bobby... shit... fuck", she muttered under her breath.

"I know but we are all Ok... so let's just go back home and do the park another day", I said.

"No I am fine... let's enjoy our day... no harm no foul", she said.

"Are you sure", I asked.

"Yes", she said, hooking her arm into mine.

We were then rushed by strangers who had witnessed the whole thing. We assured them we were fine, and that we did not need any assistance. A police officer came by and checked on us.

"Did you get them", I asked.

“Yes a couple of blocks down”, he replied.

“Anyone hurt”, I asked.

“Not today”, he said.

“Good… do you need anything from us”, I asked.

“Just your names and contact information in case the detectives need to contact you”, He said.

I provided the Officer with everything that he needed, and we continued to the park… I am shaken awake.

It is still dark and my mind is extremely blurry. I look around, and it is Jessica leaning over me prodding me awake. I have no idea where I am. It is a jungle for sure, and we are on a slope. I can see the tops of homes and outlines of manicured areas around them. It seems kind of familiar. It is almost like I have been here before. I search my memory, and I try to concentrate. Then I remember the ring and the bounty and everything. We are outside of the keeper’s house, and this time we are going in hard. We will force him to tell us of the ring.

“Are you ready”, Jessica asks.

“Yeah let’s go and get this over with”, I said.

We dressed and donned gloves, masks, hair nets, plastic clothes, taped everything down like we were some sort of hazardous materials team. We enter the house the same as before. The man should be alone and asleep. Up the stairs I go. Jessica stays on the main floor and waits. The needle pricks the man on the arm, and for a second I thought he would wake. He didn’t. I pushed the plunger and the sedative entered the man’s veins. This would allow us to secure the man, and wake him up with another injection when we were ready to scare the shit right out of him.

This bastard was heavy, and smelled worse than any I have encountered to date. He was even worse than those in the hostel in the Philippines. I managed to tie him up and get him secured to a chair. Jessica checked the house and confirmed we were alone. It was time to get to work.

"Christ he smells", Jessica said.

"I know... I know... I had to touch him to get him here", I said, with a hint of distain in my voice and a look of disgust on my face.

"Ready", she asked.

"Ready as ever", I said.

Jessica then administered a serum that would wake the smelly prick up. It took a few minutes to work, but the man was reviving. When he came to semi-consciousness his eyes went wide with absolute fear. He tried to scream and squirm but to no avail. I had him fixed so that he could not see us. He could not turn his head at all. That way there was no chance we could be identified. I placed a tray of nasty, medieval looking, blood stained instruments on a tray in front of him. I told him what was going to happen, step by step, picking up each applicable instrument to emphasize my point if he did not tell us the truth to every question we asked. His eyes grew wider and wilder and he started to cry. He then pissed and shit himself. We thought his body odor was bad. That cloud of shit that came out of his ass was sickening. Jessica had to leave the room or she would vomit. There could be no traces of us here. She caught herself just in time. Vomiting with her full face mask on would not have been pretty.

I asked the man where the ring was. I was holding up the first tool. He nodded his understanding, and I removed his gag so that he may answer the question. He told us that there was a false brick in the wall behind his cook stove. The brick was located three up and four to the right of the bottom left hand corner. There was no way we would have found it. There was a metal box in the hole, and the ring was inside. Jessica heard this from the door, and went to investigate.

Jessica returned about twenty minutes later holding the box. She tossed it to me. The lock was magnetic and required a code. I held up the nastiest of all the instruments and the man spilled his guts and gave me the code. I entered it and it opened quietly. The ring was nestled safe inside. The man laughed and said he hoped it brought as much misery to us as it had to him. I put him back to sleep and we left.

Out the back and over the stone fence we went, disappearing into the jungle beyond. Just like before we planned to exit far away like tourists out for a hike. We dumped our clothes, and changed. The man would not wake for hours and by the time he did we would be a thousand miles away safely on a plane. This was easy.

“That was easy”, Jessica said.

“Yes it was… way too easy… but we would never have found it where it was… never”, I said.

“Well what are we going to do with the money”, she asked.

“What we planned… leave this life and disappear”, I said.

We were quiet moving through the jungle on much the same route as before. The box and ring safe in my pack, when the box started to beep. We froze.

“What the hell is it”, Jessica asked.

“Maybe a tracking device or some sort or alarm”, I said.

I tried entering the code but the beeping got faster, louder and more intense. I tried the code once more, and got the same result. Then the box started to get hot and I tried one last time, and the beeping stopped. The box opened and I removed the ring. I inspected the box more closely and realized it was a bomb. The device looked to be activated when the device was removed to a certain distance from the house, and deactivated with the code being input three times.

"Jesus that was close", Jessica said.

"No shit... you think", I said.

"Let's get the hell out of here... our plane is waiting", she said.

"Ok... get on that sat phone and tell Marc we have the piece and that everything is cool... we are done", I said.

With that done we got out of the oppressive heat of the jungle atmosphere here. We walked out like tourists on a hike, just like the first time we were here, just a little bit richer...

Back on the mountain peak everything is calm and serene. Peace settles into my soul. The dog is sitting at my left side. There is a pair of eagles on my right. There is also a horse nearby. I can hear him but I cannot see him. I get up and start to walk around. The dog follows close and the eagles take off and circle overhead. I hear splashing and giggling coming from my left. I walk that way and find a clearing with a small clear pool. Two women are playing and swimming in the nude. They see me and beckon me over, but it is not a place I can go. I try to move closer but my feet and legs are not complying. I move away from the pool and then they work fine. They take me further away for I cannot move in their direction at all. When I stop moving away my feet and legs do not work to move closer. I cannot see them or hear them anymore. The horse appears and I settle into the saddle on his back. A Winchester Rifle is lying across my lap. The horse moves off, the dog follows and the eagles keep watch overhead...

I can see all the sets playing from where I am. All the perfect little lives keep going round and round. Gabriela and William have set up house in a mountain cabin. Jessica and

Sean have a place by a beach. Ava and Bobby have a small modest house by a park and a new restaurant on the corner that he co-owns with Freddie. The artist has taken up permanent residence in the monastery. Torao and Hisoka have found peace after years of bloodshed and war in a protected valley of pick blossoms. The dog and the eagles are keeping an eye on me, and keeping me away from the temptation of women on this mountain plateau.

I look into the last room and Le has left me in the care of what looks to be paramedics. I am being carted off into an ambulance. There is an IV line, and I am hooked up to a couple of machines. I can see that all my vitals, my blood pressure, my pulse, my oxygen saturation, all read fine. I am asleep. Le is still crying, begging me to wake up. I have to find a way out. I have to find a way to beat them. Anger swells inside of me, and I feel that I am going to break as a result of it.

I have found that I just walk into any set I want and be a welcomed part of what is going on in them. The only exception is the one with Le and the real life I am sleeping through. I walk over to the set with William and Gabriela, fists clenched and ready to fight.

"WHY... WHY DID YOU DO THIS", I screamed at him, at them, at all of them.

"It was the only way for us to keep on living", he said.

"LIVING... YOU ARE NOT ALIVE", I screamed back, my voice still raised and very angry.

"Yes we are you made us alive... you gave us life", he said.

"It is not life... you have no idea what it is like to really breath... taste... feel... hear... smell", I said.

"Yes we do... we all do", he said.

"Why did you do this...? I did not kill you... I fell in love... that is what life is all about... they killed themselves", I said.

"They had to... I or we needed you to create this door and this world for us to hide in and keep you sleeping... we needed you to believe and in doing so we are the keepers of the keys... there is no way out for you", he said.

"AND WHAT ABOUT ME... MY LIFE AND LE... WHAT ABOUT THAT", I screamed at them again.

"That bitch will leave as soon as she is able... you are fine... you will continue to sleep and age normally... and your life will be here through us like it was always meant to be... dreams are forever", he said.

"She is not a bitch and no she will not leave... she knows everything and she will know that you have done something and she will try like hell to reverse it", I said.

"Fuck you Logan... fuck you", he said turning away.

Anger swelled up to the breaking point. I grabbed his shoulder and spun him around and I hit him in the jaw as hard as I was able to. I kept swinging and swinging, and he fell, and I swung some more. Gabriela was yelling at me to stop. She jumped onto my back and dug her nails into me trying to tear me away. I pushed her off. She hit her head, and fell unconscious. The others could do nothing for they were locked into their sets, they did not have the freedom of movement. I saw this weakness and made note of it. I kept striking William. He tried to fight back, but those first few blows I landed caught him too much by surprise, and he could no longer function properly. Blood was splattering everywhere. My hands and face were covered with it. William was a bloody mess, and was no longer struggling. In fact he was not moving at all. I looked down at him, and could not recognize him. His jaw bone, nose, and cheekbones were all shattered. His teeth littered the floor and lay in pools of blood and other matter. His left eye was popped out held only by some nerve tissue. I had never hit a man before with my hands, never. I kept telling myself that he is not real, stop thinking of them as real. None of them are real, none.

"Fight William... FIGHT", I could hear Le in the background. I was now in a hospital. I presume in Sicily. My vitals had jumped dramatically. Doctors and nurses flew into the room to check on me. After a few moments the doctors were explaining to her that I was fine, just in some sort of sleeping state that they could not explain. They mentioned coma, and the jump in vitals happens from time to time, possibly from dreams. The really do not know. I heard her say that it has been three weeks. They had no answers. I heard her inquire when I could be moved. They said anytime, I was completely stable.

I was still standing over what was left of William when Gabriela started to come to. She took a long time, and I sat down and watched and waited. William just laid there. When Gabriela finally came to her full senses, she saw the body and screamed. She came over to me trying to hit me and kick me. I deflected them all, and then I grabbed her and slammed her to the ground, pinning her down. I held her mouth and nose closed. I watched her eyes bulge, and her face turn purple. I held her and held her, until she was just as fucked as William. I thought of killing them all.

I went to walk away from the set, and return to where the dog and the eagles were. I heard voices shout from behind me.

"You will have to do better than that Logan", William said walking out of the cabin.

I rushed back inside, and the body was gone. Gabriela was sitting at the table sipping something from a cup.

"Hello Logan", she said.

They both started to laugh. They all started to laugh. I held my ears, but it did not help.

"You said it yourself we are not real... you cannot kill your own imagination", William said entering the cabin smiling.

I could not get away from the sound of laughter. It was everywhere, and nowhere. There was no reprieve. Their faces loomed in front of me, screaming, taunting. There was no escape.

I looked to the set with Le in it. We were on a plane. I was hooked up to monitors, and attended to by either a doctor or a nurse. Le was right beside me. I do not think she has left me, not once. I swore I would return to her. She was talking to me. She talked of the cottage, for that is where she was taking me. She talked of returning to Europe to finish our trip. She told me not to forget of the other places we wanted to visit. She told me to fight them and find a way back to her.

The laughter and screams were driving me mad. I ran to the set with the dog. I ran to a water fall to try and drown out the noise. I could still hear them. I could hear the eagles screeching, the dog barking, a horse pounding the ground and snorting in displeasure. I could hear a baby crying, Freddie, Ava, Jessica, Hisoka, Bobby, Sean, and the artist screaming obscenities at me. They kept ending with stay with the dreams, and to stop fucking around.

"We won", they all said in unison.

I looked back into the eyes of Le. She had no tears left. She kept talking to me, and I could see my heart rate and blood pressure increase. There was a machine measuring my brain waves and it was going ballistic.

"Keep fighting Logan keep fighting", she said.

I tried to answer back or move, anything. I tried to blink, I tried to cry, and I even tried to fart.

"We won we won we won", they said.

"Fuck you Logan", they said.

"Keep fighting Logan", Le said.

I watched her and looked to her for the strength to make that door reappear. I concentrated and concentrated. I looked to her and then...

There was a huge explosion at the back of the plane. There was panic, everyone was screaming. The plane was breaking apart. Le was trying to hold on to me, but...

I woke with a start.

I felt a massive searing pain across my temples and forehead. I looked around and I was in my bed. I was in my house.

"What the fuck", I said.

"What the fuck", I whispered.

Everything hurt, my eyes, my head, jaws, teeth, arms, legs, chest, everything. I looked at the clock on my night stand. I could not believe my eyes. I picked up my cell phone and could not believe that either. I made my way down stairs to the porch and checked for a news paper. There were four of them. Wednesday June 16th 2011 was the latest of them. I had been asleep for four days, none of this really happened, not a dammed bit of it...

AN APOLOGY FROM THE AUTHOR

I hope everyone enjoyed the story. I had no idea it would end like it did until I typed it in. I have no plans or preconceptions for the stories I write. I just turn on my computer and start tapping keys. I let the stories tell themselves. Maybe one day I will bring Logan back and have him fall asleep to a whole new set of dreams. I think that will depend on you, my readers. Any and all feedback good or bad is greatly appreciated. You can find me on Facebook; I have a fan page set up under "Shadows and Rose". All comments can be left there. I will honestly try to personally respond to them all.

Samuel J. Fisher

CPSIA information can be obtained at www.ICGtesting.com
Printed in the USA
LVOW112140080512

280881LV00027B/45/P